Heart of the West

Heart of the West

O. Henry

MINT EDITIONS

Heart of the West was first published in 1904.

This edition published by Mint Editions 2020.

ISBN 9781513269979 | E-ISBN 9781513274973

Published by Mint Editions®

 MINT
EDITIONS

minteditionbooks.com

Publishing Director: Jennifer Newens
Design & Production: Rachel Lopez Metzger
Project Manager: Micaela Clark
Typesetting: Westchester Publishing Services

Contents

I

Hearts and Crosses

B aldy Woods reached for the bottle, and got it. Whenever Baldy went for anything he usually—but this is not Baldy's story. He poured out a third drink that was larger by a finger than the first and second. Baldy was in consultation; and the consultee is worthy of his hire.

"I'd be king if I was you," said Baldy, so positively that his holster creaked and his spurs rattled.

Webb Yeager pushed back his flat-brimmed Stetson, and made further disorder in his straw-coloured hair. The tonsorial recourse being without avail, he followed the liquid example of the more resourceful Baldy.

"If a man marries a queen, it oughtn't to make him a two-spot," declared Webb, epitomising his grievances.

"Sure not," said Baldy, sympathetic, still thirsty, and genuinely solicitous concerning the relative value of the cards. "By rights you're a king. If I was you, I'd call for a new deal. The cards have been stacked on you—I'll tell you what you are, Webb Yeager."

"What?" asked Webb, with a hopeful look in his pale-blue eyes.

"You're a prince-consort."

"Go easy," said Webb. "I never blackguarded you none."

"It's a title," explained Baldy, "up among the picture-cards; but it don't take no tricks. I'll tell you, Webb. It's a brand they've got for certain animals in Europe. Say that you or me or one of them Dutch dukes marries in a royal family. Well, by and by our wife gets to be queen. Are we king? Not in a million years. At the coronation ceremonies we march between little casino and the Ninth Grand Custodian of the Royal Hall Bedchamber. The only use we are is to appear in photographs, and accept the responsibility for the heir-apparent. That ain't any square deal. Yes, sir, Webb, you're a prince-consort; and if I was you, I'd start a interregnum or a habeus corpus or somethin'; and I'd be king if I had to turn from the bottom of the deck."

Baldy emptied his glass to the ratification of his Warwick pose.

"Baldy," said Webb, solemnly, "me and you punched cows in the same outfit for years. We been runnin' on the same range, and ridin' the same trails since we was boys. I wouldn't talk about my family affairs to nobody but you. You was line-rider on the Nopalito Ranch when I married Santa McAllister. I was foreman then; but what am I now? I don't amount to a knot in a stake rope."

"When old McAllister was the cattle king of West Texas," continued Baldy with Satanic sweetness, "you was some tallow. You had as much to say on the ranch as he did."

"I did," admitted Webb, "up to the time he found out I was tryin' to get my rope over Santa's head. Then he kept me out on the range as far from the ranch-house as he could. When the old man died they commenced to call Santa the 'cattle queen.' I'm boss of the cattle—that's all. She 'tends to all the business; she handles all the money; I can't sell even a beef-steer to a party of campers, myself. Santa's the 'queen'; and I'm Mr. Nobody."

"I'd be king if I was you," repeated Baldy Woods, the royalist. "When a man marries a queen he ought to grade up with her—on the hoof—dressed—dried—corned—any old way from the chaparral to the packing-house. Lots of folks thinks it's funny, Webb, that you don't have the say-so on the Nopalito. I ain't reflectin' none on Miz Yeager—she's the finest little lady between the Rio Grande and next Christmas—but a man ought to be boss of his own camp."

The smooth, brown face of Yeager lengthened to a mask of wounded melancholy. With that expression, and his rumpled yellow hair and guileless blue eyes, he might have been likened to a schoolboy whose leadership had been usurped by a youngster of superior strength. But his active and sinewy seventy-two inches, and his girded revolvers forbade the comparison.

"What was that you called me, Baldy?" he asked. "What kind of a concert was it?"

"A 'consort,'" corrected Baldy—"a 'prince-consort.' It's a kind of short-card pseudonym. You come in sort of between Jack-high and a four-card flush."

Webb Yeager sighed, and gathered the strap of his Winchester scabbard from the floor.

"I'm ridin' back to the ranch to-day," he said half-heartedly. "I've got to start a bunch of beeves for San Antone in the morning."

"I'm your company as far as Dry Lake," announced Baldy. "I've got a round-up camp on the San Marcos cuttin' out two-year-olds."

The two *companeros* mounted their ponies and trotted away from the little railroad settlement, where they had foregathered in the thirsty morning.

At Dry Lake, where their routes diverged, they reined up for a parting cigarette. For miles they had ridden in silence save for the soft drum of the ponies' hoofs on the matted mesquite grass, and the rattle of the chaparral against their wooden stirrups. But in Texas discourse is seldom continuous. You may fill in a mile, a meal, and a murder between your paragraphs without detriment to your thesis. So, without apology, Webb offered an addendum to the conversation that had begun ten miles away.

"You remember, yourself, Baldy, that there was a time when Santa wasn't quite so independent. You remember the days when old McAllister was keepin' us apart, and how she used to send me the sign that she wanted to see me? Old man Mac promised to make me look like a colander if I ever come in gun-shot of the ranch. You remember the sign she used to send, Baldy—the heart with a cross inside of it?"

"Me?" cried Baldy, with intoxicated archness. "You old sugar-stealing coyote! Don't I remember! Why, you dad-blamed old long-horned turtle-dove, the boys in camp was all cognoscious about them hiroglyphs. The 'gizzard-and-crossbones' we used to call it. We used to see 'em on truck that was sent out from the ranch. They was marked in charcoal on the sacks of flour and in lead-pencil on the newspapers. I see one of 'em once chalked on the back of a new cook that old man McAllister sent out from the ranch—danged if I didn't."

"Santa's father," explained Webb gently, "got her to promise that she wouldn't write to me or send me any word. That heart-and-cross sign was her scheme. Whenever she wanted to see me in particular she managed to put that mark on somethin' at the ranch that she knew I'd see. And I never laid eyes on it but what I burnt the wind for the ranch the same night. I used to see her in that coma mott back of the little horse-corral."

"We knowed it," chanted Baldy; "but we never let on. We was all for you. We knowed why you always kept that fast paint in camp. And when we see that gizzard-and-crossbones figured out on the truck from the ranch we knowed old Pinto was goin' to eat up miles that night instead of grass. You remember Scurry—that educated horse-wrangler we had—the college fellow that tangle-foot drove to the range? Whenever Scurry saw that come-meet-your-honey brand on anything from the ranch, he'd wave his hand like that, and say, 'Our friend Lee Andrews will again swim the Hell's point to-night.'"

"The last time Santa sent me the sign," said Webb, "was once when she was sick. I noticed it as soon as I hit camp, and I galloped Pinto forty mile that night. She wasn't at the coma mott. I went to the house; and old McAllister met me at the door. 'Did you come here to get killed?' says he; 'I'll disoblige you for once. I just started a Mexican to bring you. Santa wants you. Go in that room and see her. And then come out here and see me.'

"Santa was lyin' in bed pretty sick. But she gives out a kind of a smile, and her hand and mine lock horns, and I sets down by the bed—mud and spurs and chaps and all. 'I've heard you ridin' across the grass for hours, Webb,' she says. 'I was sure you'd come. You saw the sign?' she whispers. 'The minute I hit camp,' says I. ''Twas marked on the bag of potatoes and onions.' 'They're always together,' says she, soft like—'always together in life.' 'They go well together,' I says, 'in a stew.' 'I mean hearts and crosses,' says Santa. 'Our sign—to love and to suffer—that's what they mean.'

"And there was old Doc Musgrove amusin' himself with whisky and a palm-leaf fan. And by and by Santa goes to sleep; and Doc feels her forehead; and he says to me: 'You're not such a bad febrifuge. But you'd better slide out now; for the diagnosis don't call for you in regular doses. The little lady'll be all right when she wakes up.'

"I seen old McAllister outside. 'She's asleep,' says I. 'And now you can start in with your colander-work. Take your time; for I left my gun on my saddle-horn.'

"Old Mac laughs, and he says to me: 'Pumpin' lead into the best ranch-boss in West Texas don't seem to me good business policy. I don't know where I could get as good a one. It's the son-in-law idea, Webb, that makes me admire for to use you as a target. You ain't my idea for a member of the family. But I can use you on the Nopalito if you'll keep outside of a radius with the ranch-house in the middle of it. You go upstairs and lay down on a cot, and when you get some sleep we'll talk it over.'"

Baldy Woods pulled down his hat, and uncurled his leg from his saddle-horn. Webb shortened his rein, and his pony danced, anxious to be off. The two men shook hands with Western ceremony.

"*Adios*, Baldy," said Webb, "I'm glad I seen you and had this talk."

With a pounding rush that sounded like the rise of a covey of quail, the riders sped away toward different points of the compass. A hundred yards on his route Baldy reined in on the top of a bare knoll, and emitted a yell. He swayed on his horse; had he been on foot, the earth would have risen and conquered him; but in the saddle he was a master of equilibrium, and laughed at whisky, and despised the centre of gravity.

Webb turned in his saddle at the signal.

"If I was you," came Baldy's strident and perverting tones, "I'd be king!"

At eight o'clock on the following morning Bud Turner rolled from his saddle in front of the Nopalito ranch-house, and stumbled with whizzing rowels toward the gallery. Bud was in charge of the bunch of beef-cattle that was to strike the trail that morning for San Antonio. Mrs. Yeager was on the gallery watering a cluster of hyacinths growing in a red earthenware jar.

"King" McAllister had bequeathed to his daughter many of his strong characteristics—his resolution, his gay courage, his contumacious self-reliance, his pride as a reigning monarch of hoofs and horns. *Allegro* and *fortissimo* had been McAllister's temp and tone. In Santa they survived, transposed to the feminine key. Substantially, she preserved the image of the mother who had been summoned to wander in other and less finite green pastures long before the waxing herds of kine had conferred royalty upon the house. She had her mother's slim, strong figure and grave, soft prettiness that relieved in her the severity of the imperious McAllister eye and the McAllister air of royal independence.

Webb stood on one end of the gallery giving orders to two or three sub-bosses of various camps and outfits who had ridden in for instructions.

"Morning," said Bud briefly. "Where do you want them beeves to go in town—to Barber's, as usual?"

Now, to answer that had been the prerogative of the queen. All the reins of business—buying, selling, and banking—had been held by her capable fingers. The handling of cattle had been entrusted fully to her husband. In the days of "King" McAllister, Santa had been his secretary and helper; and she had continued her work with wisdom and profit. But before she could reply, the prince-consort spake up with calm decision:

"You drive that bunch to Zimmerman and Nesbit's pens. I spoke to Zimmerman about it some time ago."

Bud turned on his high boot-heels.

"Wait!" called Santa quickly. She looked at her husband with surprise in her steady gray eyes.

"Why, what do you mean, Webb?" she asked, with a small wrinkle gathering between her brows. "I never deal with Zimmerman and Nesbit. Barber has handled every head of stock from this ranch in that market for five years. I'm not going to take the business out of his hands." She faced Bud Turner. "Deliver those cattle to Barber," she concluded positively.

Bud gazed impartially at the water-jar hanging on the gallery, stood on his other leg, and chewed a mesquite-leaf.

"I want this bunch of beeves to go to Zimmerman and Nesbit," said Webb, with a frosty light in his blue eyes.

"Nonsense," said Santa impatiently. "You'd better start on, Bud, so as to noon at the Little Elm water-hole. Tell Barber we'll have another lot of culls ready in about a month."

Bud allowed a hesitating eye to steal upward and meet Webb's. Webb saw apology in his look, and fancied he saw commiseration.

"You deliver them cattle," he said grimly, "to—"

"Barber," finished Santa sharply. "Let that settle it. Is there anything else you are waiting for, Bud?"

"No, m'm," said Bud. But before going he lingered while a cow's tail could have switched thrice; for man is man's ally; and even the Philistines must have blushed when they took Samson in the way they did.

"You hear your boss!" cried Webb sardonically. He took off his hat, and bowed until it touched the floor before his wife.

"Webb," said Santa rebukingly, "you're acting mighty foolish to-day."

"Court fool, your Majesty," said Webb, in his slow tones, which had changed their quality. "What else can you expect? Let me tell you. I was a man before I married a cattle-queen. What am I now? The laughing-stock of the camps. I'll be a man again."

Santa looked at him closely.

"Don't be unreasonable, Webb," she said calmly. "You haven't been slighted in any way. Do I ever interfere in your management of the cattle? I know the business side of the ranch much better than you do. I learned it from Dad. Be sensible."

"Kingdoms and queendoms," said Webb, "don't suit me unless I am in the pictures, too. I punch the cattle and you wear the crown. All right.

I'd rather be High Lord Chancellor of a cow-camp than the eight-spot in a queen-high flush. It's your ranch; and Barber gets the beeves."

Webb's horse was tied to the rack. He walked into the house and brought out his roll of blankets that he never took with him except on long rides, and his "slicker," and his longest stake-rope of plaited rawhide. These he began to tie deliberately upon his saddle. Santa, a little pale, followed him.

Webb swung up into the saddle. His serious, smooth face was without expression except for a stubborn light that smouldered in his eyes.

"There's a herd of cows and calves," said he, "near the Hondo waterhole on the Frio that ought to be moved away from timber. Lobos have killed three of the calves. I forgot to leave orders. You'd better tell Simms to attend to it."

Santa laid a hand on the horse's bridle, and looked her husband in the eye.

"Are you going to leave me, Webb?" she asked quietly.

"I am going to be a man again," he answered.

"I wish you success in a praiseworthy attempt," she said, with a sudden coldness. She turned and walked directly into the house.

Webb Yeager rode to the southeast as straight as the topography of West Texas permitted. And when he reached the horizon he might have ridden on into blue space as far as knowledge of him on the Nopalito went. And the days, with Sundays at their head, formed into hebdomadal squads; and the weeks, captained by the full moon, closed ranks into menstrual companies crying "Tempus fugit" on their banners; and the months marched on toward the vast camp-ground of the years; but Webb Yeager came no more to the dominions of his queen.

One day a being named Bartholomew, a sheep-man—and therefore of little account—from the lower Rio Grande country, rode in sight of the Nopalito ranch-house, and felt hunger assail him. *Ex consuetudine* he was soon seated at the mid-day dining table of that hospitable kingdom. Talk like water gushed from him: he might have been smitten with Aaron's rod—that is your gentle shepherd when an audience is vouchsafed him whose ears are not overgrown with wool.

"Missis Yeager," he babbled, "I see a man the other day on the Rancho Seco down in Hidalgo County by your name—Webb Yeager was his. He'd just been engaged as manager. He was a tall, light-haired man, not saying much. Perhaps he was some kin of yours, do you think?"

"A husband," said Santa cordially. "The Seco has done well. Mr. Yeager is one of the best stockmen in the West."

The dropping out of a prince-consort rarely disorganises a monarchy. Queen Santa had appointed as *mayordomo* of the ranch a trusty subject, named Ramsay, who had been one of her father's faithful vassals. And there was scarcely a ripple on the Nopalito ranch save when the gulf-breeze created undulations in the grass of its wide acres.

For several years the Nopalito had been making experiments with an English breed of cattle that looked down with aristocratic contempt upon the Texas long-horns. The experiments were found satisfactory; and a pasture had been set aside for the blue-bloods. The fame of them had gone forth into the chaparral and pear as far as men ride in saddles. Other ranches woke up, rubbed their eyes, and looked with new dissatisfaction upon the long-horns.

As a consequence, one day a sunburned, capable, silk-kerchiefed nonchalant youth, garnished with revolvers, and attended by three Mexican *vaqueros*, alighted at the Nopalito ranch and presented the following business-like epistle to the queen thereof:

Mrs. Yeager—The Nopalito Ranch:

Dear Madam

I am instructed by the owners of the Rancho Seco to purchase 100 head of two and three-year-old cows of the Sussex breed owned by you. If you can fill the order please deliver the cattle to the bearer; and a check will be forwarded to you at once.

Respectfully,
Webster Yeager,
Manager the Rancho Seco

Business is business, even—very scantily did it escape being written "especially"—in a kingdom.

That night the 100 head of cattle were driven up from the pasture and penned in a corral near the ranch-house for delivery in the morning.

When night closed down and the house was still, did Santa Yeager throw herself down, clasping that formal note to her bosom, weeping, and calling out a name that pride (either in one or the other) had kept from her lips many a day? Or did she file the letter, in her business way, retaining her royal balance and strength?

Wonder, if you will; but royalty is sacred; and there is a veil. But this much you shall learn:

At midnight Santa slipped softly out of the ranch-house, clothed in something dark and plain. She paused for a moment under the live-oak trees. The prairies were somewhat dim, and the moonlight was pale orange, diluted with particles of an impalpable, flying mist. But the mock-bird whistled on every bough of vantage; leagues of flowers scented the air; and a kindergarten of little shadowy rabbits leaped and played in an open space near by. Santa turned her face to the southeast and threw three kisses thitherward; for there was none to see.

Then she sped silently to the blacksmith-shop, fifty yards away; and what she did there can only be surmised. But the forge glowed red; and there was a faint hammering such as Cupid might make when he sharpens his arrow-points.

Later she came forth with a queer-shaped, handled thing in one hand, and a portable furnace, such as are seen in branding-camps, in the other. To the corral where the Sussex cattle were penned she sped with these things swiftly in the moonlight.

She opened the gate and slipped inside the corral. The Sussex cattle were mostly a dark red. But among this bunch was one that was milky white—notable among the others.

And now Santa shook from her shoulder something that we had not seen before—a rope lasso. She freed the loop of it, coiling the length in her left hand, and plunged into the thick of the cattle.

The white cow was her object. She swung the lasso, which caught one horn and slipped off. The next throw encircled the forefeet and the animal fell heavily. Santa made for it like a panther; but it scrambled up and dashed against her, knocking her over like a blade of grass.

Again she made her cast, while the aroused cattle milled around the four sides of the corral in a plunging mass. This throw was fair; the white cow came to earth again; and before it could rise Santa had made the lasso fast around a post of the corral with a swift and simple knot, and had leaped upon the cow again with the rawhide hobbles.

In one minute the feet of the animal were tied (no record-breaking deed) and Santa leaned against the corral for the same space of time, panting and lax.

And then she ran swiftly to her furnace at the gate and brought the branding-iron, queerly shaped and white-hot.

The bellow of the outraged white cow, as the iron was applied, should have stirred the slumbering auricular nerves and consciences of the near-by subjects of the Nopalito, but it did not. And it was amid the deepest nocturnal silence that Santa ran like a lapwing back to the ranch-house and there fell upon a cot and sobbed—sobbed as though queens had hearts as simple ranchmen's wives have, and as though she would gladly make kings of prince-consorts, should they ride back again from over the hills and far away.

In the morning the capable, revolvered youth and his *vaqueros* set forth, driving the bunch of Sussex cattle across the prairies to the Rancho Seco. Ninety miles it was; a six days' journey, grazing and watering the animals on the way.

The beasts arrived at Rancho Seco one evening at dusk; and were received and counted by the foreman of the ranch.

The next morning at eight o'clock a horseman loped out of the brush to the Nopalito ranch-house. He dismounted stiffly, and strode, with whizzing spurs, to the house. His horse gave a great sigh and swayed foam-streaked, with down-drooping head and closed eyes.

But waste not your pity upon Belshazzar, the flea-bitten sorrel. To-day, in Nopalito horse-pasture he survives, pampered, beloved, unridden, cherished record-holder of long-distance rides.

The horseman stumbled into the house. Two arms fell around his neck, and someone cried out in the voice of woman and queen alike: "Webb—oh, Webb!"

"I was a skunk," said Webb Yeager.

"Hush," said Santa, "did you see it?"

"I saw it," said Webb.

What they meant God knows; and you shall know, if you rightly read the primer of events.

"Be the cattle-queen," said Webb; "and overlook it if you can. I was a mangy, sheep-stealing coyote."

"Hush!" said Santa again, laying her fingers upon his mouth. "There's no queen here. Do you know who I am? I am Santa Yeager, First Lady of the Bedchamber. Come here."

She dragged him from the gallery into the room to the right. There stood a cradle with an infant in it—a red, ribald, unintelligible, babbling, beautiful infant, sputtering at life in an unseemly manner.

"There's no queen on this ranch," said Santa again. "Look at the king. He's got your eyes, Webb. Down on your knees and look at his Highness."

But jingling rowels sounded on the gallery, and Bud Turner stumbled there again with the same query that he had brought, lacking a few days, a year ago.

"'Morning. Them beeves is just turned out on the trail. Shall I drive 'em to Barber's, or—"

He saw Webb and stopped, open-mouthed.

"Ba-ba-ba-ba-ba-ba!" shrieked the king in his cradle, beating the air with his fists.

"You hear your boss, Bud," said Webb Yeager, with a broad grin—just as he had said a year ago.

And that is all, except that when old man Quinn, owner of the Rancho Seco, went out to look over the herd of Sussex cattle that he had bought from the Nopalito ranch, he asked his new manager:

"What's the Nopalito ranch brand, Wilson?"

"X Bar Y," said Wilson.

"I thought so," said Quinn. "But look at that white heifer there; she's got another brand—a heart with a cross inside of it. What brand is that?"

II

The Ransom of Mack

Me and old Mack Lonsbury, we got out of that Little Hide-and-Seek gold mine affair with about $40,000 apiece. I say "old" Mack; but he wasn't old. Forty-one, I should say; but he always seemed old.

"Andy," he says to me, "I'm tired of hustling. You and me have been working hard together for three years. Say we knock off for a while, and spend some of this idle money we've coaxed our way."

"The proposition hits me just right," says I. "Let's be nabobs for a while and see how it feels. What'll we do—take in the Niagara Falls, or buck at faro?"

"For a good many years," says Mack, "I've thought that if I ever had extravagant money I'd rent a two-room cabin somewhere, hire a Chinaman to cook, and sit in my stocking feet and read Buckle's History of Civilisation."

"That sounds self-indulgent and gratifying without vulgar ostentation," says I; "and I don't see how money could be better invested. Give me a cuckoo clock and a Sep Winner's Self-Instructor for the Banjo, and I'll join you."

A week afterwards me and Mack hits this small town of Pina, about thirty miles out from Denver, and finds an elegant two-room house that just suits us. We deposited half-a-peck of money in the Pina bank and shook hands with every one of the 340 citizens in the town. We brought along the Chinaman and the cuckoo clock and Buckle and the Instructor with us from Denver; and they made the cabin seem like home at once.

Never believe it when they tell you riches don't bring happiness. If you could have seen old Mack sitting in his rocking-chair with his blue-yarn sock feet up in the window and absorbing in that Buckle stuff through his specs you'd have seen a picture of content that would have made Rockefeller jealous. And I was learning to pick out "Old Zip Coon" on the banjo, and the cuckoo was on time with his remarks, and Ah Sing was messing up the atmosphere with the handsomest smell of ham and eggs that ever laid the honeysuckle in the shade. When it got too dark to make out Buckle's nonsense and the notes in the Instructor, me and Mack would light our pipes and talk about science and pearl diving and sciatica and Egypt and spelling and fish and trade-winds and leather and gratitude and eagles, and a lot of subjects that we'd never had time to explain our sentiments about before.

One evening Mack spoke up and asked me if I was much apprised in the habits and policies of women folks.

"Why, yes," says I, in a tone of voice; "I know 'em from Alfred to Omaha. The feminine nature and similitude," says I, "is as plain to my sight as the Rocky Mountains is to a blue-eyed burro. I'm onto all their little side-steps and punctual discrepancies."

"I tell you, Andy," says Mack, with a kind of sigh, "I never had the least amount of intersection with their predispositions. Maybe I might have had a proneness in respect to their vicinity, but I never took the time. I made my own living since I was fourteen; and I never seemed to get my ratiocinations equipped with the sentiments usually depicted toward the sect. I sometimes wish I had," says old Mack.

"They're an adverse study," says I, "and adapted to points of view. Although they vary in rationale, I have found 'em quite often obviously differing from each other in divergences of contrast."

"It seems to me," goes on Mack, "that a man had better take 'em in and secure his inspirations of the sect when he's young and so preordained. I let my chance go by; and I guess I'm too old now to go hopping into the curriculum."

"Oh, I don't know," I tells him. "Maybe you better credit yourself with a barrel of money and a lot of emancipation from a quantity of uncontent. Still, I don't regret my knowledge of 'em," I says. "It takes a man who understands the symptoms and by-plays of women-folks to take care of himself in this world."

We stayed on in Pina because we liked the place. Some folks might enjoy their money with noise and rapture and locomotion; but me and Mack we had had plenty of turmoils and hotel towels. The people were friendly; Ah Sing got the swing of the grub we liked; Mack and Buckle were as thick as two body-snatchers, and I was hitting out a cordial resemblance to "Buffalo Gals, Can't You Come Out To-night," on the banjo.

One day I got a telegram from Speight, the man that was working on a mine I had an interest in out in New Mexico. I had to go out there; and I was gone two months. I was anxious to get back to Pina and enjoy life once more.

When I struck the cabin I nearly fainted. Mack was standing in the door; and if angels ever wept, I saw no reason why they should be smiling then.

That man was a spectacle. Yes; he was worse; he was a spyglass; he was the great telescope in the Lick Observatory. He had on a coat and shiny shoes and a white vest and a high silk hat; and a geranium as big as an order of spinach was spiked onto his front. And he was smirking and warping his face like an infernal storekeeper or a kid with colic.

"Hello, Andy," says Mack, out of his face. "Glad to see you back. Things have happened since you went away."

"I know it," says I, "and a sacrilegious sight it is. God never made you that way, Mack Lonsbury. Why do you scarify His works with this presumptuous kind of ribaldry?"

"Why, Andy," says he, "they've elected me justice of the peace since you left."

I looked at Mack close. He was restless and inspired. A justice of the peace ought to be disconsolate and assuaged.

Just then a young woman passed on the sidewalk; and I saw Mack kind of half snicker and blush, and then he raised up his hat and smiled and bowed, and she smiled and bowed, and went on by.

"No hope for you," says I, "if you've got the Mary-Jane infirmity at your age. I thought it wasn't going to take on you. And patent leather shoes! All this in two little short months!"

"I'm going to marry the young lady who just passed to-night," says Mack, in a kind of flutter.

"I forgot something at the post-office," says I, and walked away quick.

I overtook that young woman a hundred yards away. I raised my hat and told her my name. She was about nineteen; and young for her age. She blushed, and then looked at me cool, like I was the snow scene from the "Two Orphans."

"I understand you are to be married to-night," I said.

"Correct," says she. "You got any objections?"

"Listen, sissy," I begins.

"My name is Miss Rebosa Redd," says she in a pained way.

"I know it," says I. "Now, Rebosa, I'm old enough to have owed money to your father. And that old, specious, dressed-up, garbled, sea-sick ptomaine prancing about avidiously like an irremediable turkey gobbler with patent leather shoes on is my best friend. Why did you go and get him invested in this marriage business?"

"Why, he was the only chance there was," answers Miss Rebosa.

"Nay," says I, giving a sickening look of admiration at her complexion and style of features; "with your beauty you might pick any kind of a man. Listen, Rebosa. Old Mack ain't the man you want. He was twenty-two when you was *nee* Reed, as the papers say. This bursting into bloom won't last with him. He's all ventilated with oldness and rectitude and decay. Old Mack's down with a case of Indian summer. He overlooked his bet when he was young; and now he's suing Nature for the interest on the promissory note he took from Cupid instead of the cash. Rebosa, are you bent on having this marriage occur?"

"Why, sure I am," says she, oscillating the pansies on her hat, "and so is somebody else, I reckon."

"What time is it to take place?" I asks.

"At six o'clock," says she.

I made up my mind right away what to do. I'd save old Mack if I could. To have a good, seasoned, ineligible man like that turn chicken for a girl that hadn't quit eating slate pencils and buttoning in the back was more than I could look on with easiness.

"Rebosa," says I, earnest, drawing upon my display of knowledge concerning the feminine intuitions of reason—"ain't there a young man in Pina—a nice young man that you think a heap of?"

"Yep," says Rebosa, nodding her pansies—"Sure there is! What do you think! Gracious!"

"Does he like you?" I asks. "How does he stand in the matter?"

"Crazy," says Rebosa. "Ma has to wet down the front steps to keep him from sitting there all the time. But I guess that'll be all over after to-night," she winds up with a sigh.

"Rebosa," says I, "you don't really experience any of this adoration called love for old Mack, do you?"

"Lord! no," says the girl, shaking her head. "I think he's as dry as a lava bed. The idea!"

"Who is this young man that you like, Rebosa?" I inquires.

"It's Eddie Bayles," says she. "He clerks in Crosby's grocery. But he don't make but thirty-five a month. Ella Noakes was wild about him once."

"Old Mack tells me," I says, "that he's going to marry you at six o'clock this evening."

"That's the time," says she. "It's to be at our house."

"Rebosa," says I, "listen to me. If Eddie Bayles had a thousand dollars cash—a thousand dollars, mind you, would buy him a store of his own—if you and Eddie had that much to excuse matrimony on, would you consent to marry him this evening at five o'clock?"

The girl looks at me a minute; and I can see these inaudible cogitations going on inside of her, as women will.

"A thousand dollars?" says she. "Of course I would."

"Come on," says I. "We'll go and see Eddie."

We went up to Crosby's store and called Eddie outside. He looked to be estimable and freckled; and he had chills and fever when I made my proposition.

"At five o'clock?" says he, "for a thousand dollars? Please don't wake me up! Well, you *are* the rich uncle retired from the spice business in India! I'll buy out old Crosby and run the store myself."

We went inside and got old man Crosby apart and explained it. I wrote my check for a thousand dollars and handed it to him. If Eddie and Rebosa married each other at five he was to turn the money over to them.

And then I gave 'em my blessing, and went to wander in the wildwood for a season. I sat on a log and made cogitations on life and old age and the zodiac and the ways of women and all the disorder that goes with a lifetime. I passed myself congratulations that I had probably saved my old friend Mack from his attack of Indian summer. I knew when he got well of it and shed his infatuation and his patent leather shoes, he would feel grateful. "To keep old Mack disinvolved," thinks I, "from relapses like this, is worth more than a thousand dollars." And most of all I was glad that I'd made a study of women, and wasn't to be deceived any by their means of conceit and evolution.

It must have been half-past five when I got back home. I stepped in; and there sat old Mack on the back of his neck in his old clothes with his blue socks on the window and the History of Civilisation propped up on his knees.

"This don't look like getting ready for a wedding at six," I says, to seem innocent.

"Oh," says Mack, reaching for his tobacco, "that was postponed back to five o'clock. They sent me over a note saying the hour had been changed. It's all over now. What made you stay away so long, Andy?"

"You heard about the wedding?" I asks.

"I operated it," says he. "I told you I was justice of the peace. The preacher is off East to visit his folks, and I'm the only one in town that can perform the dispensations of marriage. I promised Eddie and

Rebosa a month ago I'd marry 'em. He's a busy lad; and he'll have a grocery of his own some day."

"He will," says I.

"There was lots of women at the wedding," says Mack, smoking up. "But I didn't seem to get any ideas from 'em. I wish I was informed in the structure of their attainments like you said you was."

"That was two months ago," says I, reaching up for the banjo.

III

Telemachus, Friend

Returning from a hunting trip, I waited at the little town of Los Pinos, in New Mexico, for the south-bound train, which was one hour late. I sat on the porch of the Summit House and discussed the functions of life with Telemachus Hicks, the hotel proprietor.

Perceiving that personalities were not out of order, I asked him what species of beast had long ago twisted and mutilated his left ear. Being a hunter, I was concerned in the evils that may befall one in the pursuit of game.

"That ear," says Hicks, "is the relic of true friendship."

"An accident?" I persisted.

"No friendship is an accident," said Telemachus; and I was silent.

"The only perfect case of true friendship I ever knew," went on my host, "was a cordial intent between a Connecticut man and a monkey. The monkey climbed palms in Barranquilla and threw down cocoanuts to the man. The man sawed them in two and made dippers, which he sold for two *reales* each and bought rum. The monkey drank the milk of the nuts. Through each being satisfied with his own share of the graft, they lived like brothers.

"But in the case of human beings, friendship is a transitory art, subject to discontinuance without further notice.

"I had a friend once, of the entitlement of Paisley Fish, that I imagined was sealed to me for an endless space of time. Side by side for seven years we had mined, ranched, sold patent churns, herded sheep, took photographs and other things, built wire fences, and picked prunes. Thinks I, neither homocide nor flattery nor riches nor sophistry nor drink can make trouble between me and Paisley Fish. We was friends an amount you could hardly guess at. We was friends in business, and we let our amicable qualities lap over and season our hours of recreation and folly. We certainly had days of Damon and nights of Pythias.

"One summer me and Paisley gallops down into these San Andres mountains for the purpose of a month's surcease and levity, dressed in the natural store habiliments of man. We hit this town of Los Pinos, which certainly was a roof-garden spot of the world, and flowing with condensed milk and honey. It had a street or two, and air, and hens, and a eating-house; and that was enough for us.

"We strikes the town after supper-time, and we concludes to sample whatever efficacy there is in this eating-house down by the railroad tracks. By the time we had set down and pried up our plates with a knife from the red oil-cloth, along intrudes Widow Jessup with the hot biscuit and the fried liver.

"Now, there was a woman that would have tempted an anchovy to forget his vows. She was not so small as she was large; and a kind of welcome air seemed to mitigate her vicinity. The pink of her face was the *in hoc signo* of a culinary temper and a warm disposition, and her smile would have brought out the dogwood blossoms in December.

"Widow Jessup talks to us a lot of garrulousness about the climate and history and Tennyson and prunes and the scarcity of mutton, and finally wants to know where we came from.

"'Spring Valley,' says I.

"'Big Spring Valley,' chips in Paisley, out of a lot of potatoes and knuckle-bone of ham in his mouth.

"That was the first sign I noticed that the old *fidus Diogenes* business between me and Paisley Fish was ended forever. He knew how I hated a talkative person, and yet he stampedes into the conversation with his amendments and addendums of syntax. On the map it was Big Spring Valley; but I had heard Paisley himself call it Spring Valley a thousand times.

"Without saying any more, we went out after supper and set on the railroad track. We had been pardners too long not to know what was going on in each other's mind.

"'I reckon you understand,' says Paisley, 'that I've made up my mind to accrue that widow woman as part and parcel in and to my hereditaments forever, both domestic, sociable, legal, and otherwise, until death us do part.'

"'Why, yes,' says I, 'I read it between the lines, though you only spoke one. And I suppose you are aware,' says I, 'that I have a movement on foot that leads up to the widow's changing her name to Hicks, and leaves you writing to the society column to inquire whether the best man wears a japonica or seamless socks at the wedding!'

"'There'll be some hiatuses in your program,' says Paisley, chewing up a piece of a railroad tie. 'I'd give in to you,' says he, 'in 'most any respect if it was secular affairs, but this is not so. The smiles of woman,' goes on Paisley, 'is the whirlpool of Squills and Chalybeates, into which vortex the good ship Friendship is often drawn and dismembered. I'd assault a bear that was annoying you,' says Paisley, 'or I'd endorse your note, or rub the place between your shoulder-blades with opodeldoc the same as ever; but there my sense of etiquette ceases. In this fracas with Mrs. Jessup we play it alone. I've notified you fair.'

"And then I collaborates with myself, and offers the following resolutions and by-laws:

"'Friendship between man and man,' says I, 'is an ancient historical virtue enacted in the days when men had to protect each other against lizards with eighty-foot tails and flying turtles. And they've kept up the habit to this day, and stand by each other till the bellboy comes up and tells them the animals are not really there. I've often heard,' I says, 'about ladies stepping in and breaking up a friendship between men. Why should that be? I'll tell you, Paisley, the first sight and hot biscuit of Mrs. Jessup appears to have inserted a oscillation into each of our bosoms. Let the best man of us have her. I'll play you a square game, and won't do any underhanded work. I'll do all of my courting of her in your presence, so you will have an equal opportunity. With that arrangement I don't see why our steamboat of friendship should fall overboard in the medicinal whirlpools you speak of, whichever of us wins out.'

"'Good old hoss!' says Paisley, shaking my hand. 'And I'll do the same,' says he. 'We'll court the lady synonymously, and without any of the prudery and bloodshed usual to such occasions. And we'll be friends still, win or lose.'

"At one side of Mrs. Jessup's eating-house was a bench under some trees where she used to sit in the breeze after the south-bound had been fed and gone. And there me and Paisley used to congregate after supper and make partial payments on our respects to the lady of our choice. And we was so honorable and circuitous in our calls that if one of us got there first we waited for the other before beginning any gallivantery.

"The first evening that Mrs. Jessup knew about our arrangement I got to the bench before Paisley did. Supper was just over, and Mrs. Jessup was out there with a fresh pink dress on, and almost cool enough to handle.

"I sat down by her and made a few specifications about the moral surface of nature as set forth by the landscape and the contiguous perspective. That evening was surely a case in point. The moon was attending to business in the section of sky where it belonged, and the trees was making shadows on the ground according to science and nature, and there was a kind of conspicuous hullabaloo going on in the bushes between the bullbats and the orioles and the jack-rabbits and other feathered insects of the forest. And the wind out of the mountains was singing like a Jew's-harp in the pile of old tomato-cans by the railroad track.

"I felt a kind of sensation in my left side—something like dough rising in a crock by the fire. Mrs. Jessup had moved up closer.

"'Oh, Mr. Hicks,' says she, 'when one is alone in the world, don't they feel it more aggravated on a beautiful night like this?'

"I rose up off the bench at once.

"'Excuse me, ma'am,' says I, 'but I'll have to wait till Paisley comes before I can give a audible hearing to leading questions like that.'

"And then I explained to her how we was friends cinctured by years of embarrassment and travel and complicity, and how we had agreed to take no advantage of each other in any of the more mushy walks of life, such as might be fomented by sentiment and proximity. Mrs. Jessup appears to think serious about the matter for a minute, and then she breaks into a species of laughter that makes the wildwood resound.

"In a few minutes Paisley drops around, with oil of bergamot on his hair, and sits on the other side of Mrs. Jessup, and inaugurates a sad tale of adventure in which him and Pieface Lumley has a skinning-match of dead cows in '95 for a silver-mounted saddle in the Santa Rita valley during the nine months' drought.

"Now, from the start of that courtship I had Paisley Fish hobbled and tied to a post. Each one of us had a different system of reaching out for the easy places in the female heart. Paisley's scheme was to petrify 'em with wonderful relations of events that he had either come across personally or in large print. I think he must have got his idea of subjugation from one of Shakespeare's shows I see once called 'Othello.' There is a coloured man in it who acquires a duke's daughter by disbursing to her a mixture of the talk turned out by Rider Haggard, Lew Dockstader, and Dr. Parkhurst. But that style of courting don't work well off the stage.

"Now, I give you my own recipe for inveigling a woman into that state of affairs when she can be referred to as '*nee* Jones.' Learn how to pick up her hand and hold it, and she's yours. It ain't so easy. Some men grab at it so much like they was going to set a dislocation of the shoulder that you can smell the arnica and hear 'em tearing off bandages. Some take it up like a hot horseshoe, and hold it off at arm's length like a druggist pouring tincture of asafoetida in a bottle. And most of 'em catch hold of it and drag it right out before the lady's eyes like a boy finding a baseball in the grass, without giving her a chance to forget that the hand is growing on the end of her arm. Them ways are all wrong.

"I'll tell you the right way. Did you ever see a man sneak out in the back yard and pick up a rock to throw at a tomcat that was sitting on a fence looking at him? He pretends he hasn't got a thing in his hand, and that the cat don't see him, and that he don't see the cat. That's the idea. Never drag her hand out where she'll have to take notice of it. Don't let her know that you think she knows you have the least idea she is aware you are holding her hand. That was my rule of tactics; and as far as Paisley's serenade about hostilities and misadventure went, he might as well have been reading to her a time-table of the Sunday trains that stop at Ocean Grove, New Jersey.

"One night when I beat Paisley to the bench by one pipeful, my friendship gets subsidised for a minute, and I asks Mrs. Jessup if she didn't think a 'H' was easier to write than a 'J.' In a second her head was mashing the oleander flower in my button-hole, and I leaned over and—but I didn't.

"'If you don't mind,' says I, standing up, 'we'll wait for Paisley to come before finishing this. I've never done anything dishonourable yet to our friendship, and this won't be quite fair.'

"'Mr. Hicks,' says Mrs. Jessup, looking at me peculiar in the dark, 'if it wasn't for but one thing, I'd ask you to hike yourself down the gulch and never disresume your visits to my house.'

"'And what is that, ma'am?' I asks.

"'You are too good a friend not to make a good husband,' says she.

"In five minutes Paisley was on his side of Mrs. Jessup.

"'In Silver City, in the summer of '98,' he begins, 'I see Jim Batholomew chew off a Chinaman's ear in the Blue Light Saloon on account of a crossbarred muslin shirt that—what was that noise?'

"I had resumed matters again with Mrs. Jessup right where we had left off.

"'Mrs. Jessup,' says I, 'has promised to make it Hicks. And this is another of the same sort.'

"Paisley winds his feet round a leg of the bench and kind of groans.

"'Lem,' says he, 'we been friends for seven years. Would you mind not kissing Mrs. Jessup quite so loud? I'd do the same for you.'

"'All right,' says I. 'The other kind will do as well.'

"'This Chinaman,' goes on Paisley, 'was the one that shot a man named Mullins in the spring of '97, and that was—'

"Paisley interrupted himself again.

"'Lem,' says he, 'if you was a true friend you wouldn't hug Mrs. Jessup quite so hard. I felt the bench shake all over just then. You know you told me you would give me an even chance as long as there was any.'

"'Mr. Man,' says Mrs. Jessup, turning around to Paisley, 'if you was to drop in to the celebration of mine and Mr. Hicks's silver wedding, twenty-five years from now, do you think you could get it into that Hubbard squash you call your head that you are *nix cum rous* in this business? I've put up with you a long time because you was Mr. Hicks's friend; but it seems to me it's time for you to wear the willow and trot off down the hill.'

"'Mrs. Jessup,' says I, without losing my grasp on the situation as fiance, 'Mr. Paisley is my friend, and I offered him a square deal and a equal opportunity as long as there was a chance.'

"'A chance!' says she. 'Well, he may think he has a chance; but I hope he won't think he's got a cinch, after what he's been next to all the evening.'

"Well, a month afterwards me and Mrs. Jessup was married in the Los Pinos Methodist Church; and the whole town closed up to see the performance.

"When we lined up in front and the preacher was beginning to sing out his rituals and observances, I looks around and misses Paisley. I calls time on the preacher. 'Paisley ain't here,' says I. 'We've got to wait for Paisley. A friend once, a friend always—that's Telemachus Hicks,' says I. Mrs. Jessup's eyes snapped some; but the preacher holds up the incantations according to instructions.

"In a few minutes Paisley gallops up the aisle, putting on a cuff as he comes. He explains that the only dry-goods store in town was closed for the wedding, and he couldn't get the kind of a boiled shirt that his taste called for until he had broke open the back window of the store and helped himself. Then he ranges up on the other side of the bride, and the wedding goes on. I always imagined that Paisley calculated as a last chance that the preacher might marry him to the widow by mistake.

"After the proceedings was over we had tea and jerked antelope and canned apricots, and then the populace hiked itself away. Last of all Paisley shook me by the hand and told me I'd acted square and on the level with him and he was proud to call me a friend.

"The preacher had a small house on the side of the street that he'd fixed up to rent; and he allowed me and Mrs. Hicks to occupy it till the ten-forty train the next morning, when we was going on a bridal tour to El Paso. His wife had decorated it all up with hollyhocks and poison ivy, and it looked real festal and bowery.

"About ten o'clock that night I sets down in the front door and pulls off my boots a while in the cool breeze, while Mrs. Hicks was fixing around in the room. Right soon the light went out inside; and I sat there a while reverberating over old times and scenes. And then I heard Mrs. Hicks call out, 'Ain't you coming in soon, Lem?'

"'Well, well!' says I, kind of rousing up. 'Durn me if I wasn't waiting for old Paisley to—'

"But when I got that far," concluded Telemachus Hicks, "I thought somebody had shot this left ear of mine off with a forty-five. But it turned out to be only a lick from a broomhandle in the hands of Mrs. Hicks."

IV

The Handbook of Hymen

'T is the opinion of myself, Sanderson Pratt, who sets this down, that the educational system of the United States should be in the hands of the weather bureau. I can give you good reasons for it; and you can't tell me why our college professors shouldn't be transferred to the meteorological department. They have been learned to read; and they could very easily glance at the morning papers and then wire in to the main office what kind of weather to expect. But there's the other side of the proposition. I am going on to tell you how the weather furnished me and Idaho Green with an elegant education.

We was up in the Bitter Root Mountains over the Montana line prospecting for gold. A chin-whiskered man in Walla-Walla, carrying a line of hope as excess baggage, had grubstaked us; and there we was in the foothills pecking away, with enough grub on hand to last an army through a peace conference.

Along one day comes a mail-rider over the mountains from Carlos, and stops to eat three cans of greengages, and leave us a newspaper of modern date. This paper prints a system of premonitions of the weather, and the card it dealt Bitter Root Mountains from the bottom of the deck was "warmer and fair, with light westerly breezes."

That evening it began to snow, with the wind strong in the east. Me and Idaho moved camp into an old empty cabin higher up the mountain, thinking it was only a November flurry. But after falling three foot on a level it went to work in earnest; and we knew we was snowed in. We got in plenty of firewood before it got deep, and we had grub enough for two months, so we let the elements rage and cut up all they thought proper.

If you want to instigate the art of manslaughter just shut two men up in a eighteen by twenty-foot cabin for a month. Human nature won't stand it.

When the first snowflakes fell me and Idaho Green laughed at each other's jokes and praised the stuff we turned out of a skillet and called bread. At the end of three weeks Idaho makes this kind of a edict to me. Says he:

"I never exactly heard sour milk dropping out of a balloon on the bottom of a tin pan, but I have an idea it would be music of the spears compared to this attenuated stream of asphyxiated thought that emanates out of your organs of conversation. The kind of half-masticated noises that you emit every day puts me in mind of a cow's cud, only she's lady enough to keep hers to herself, and you ain't."

"Mr. Green," says I, "you having been a friend of mine once, I have some hesitations in confessing to you that if I had my choice for society between you and a common yellow, three-legged cur pup, one of the inmates of this here cabin would be wagging a tail just at present."

This way we goes on for two or three days, and then we quits speaking to one another. We divides up the cooking implements, and Idaho cooks his grub on one side of the fireplace, and me on the other. The snow is up to the windows, and we have to keep a fire all day.

You see me and Idaho never had any education beyond reading and doing "if John had three apples and James five" on a slate. We never felt any special need for a university degree, though we had acquired a species of intrinsic intelligence in knocking around the world that we could use in emergencies. But, snowbound in that cabin in the Bitter Roots, we felt for the first time that if we had studied Homer or Greek and fractions and the higher branches of information, we'd have had some resources in the line of meditation and private thought. I've seen them Eastern college fellows working in camps all through the West, and I never noticed but what education was less of a drawback to 'em than you would think. Why, once over on Snake River, when Andrew McWilliams' saddle horse got the botts, he sent a buckboard ten miles for one of these strangers that claimed to be a botanist. But that horse died.

One morning Idaho was poking around with a stick on top of a little shelf that was too high to reach. Two books fell down to the floor. I started toward 'em, but caught Idaho's eye. He speaks for the first time in a week.

"Don't burn your fingers," says he. "In spite of the fact that you're only fit to be the companion of a sleeping mud-turtle, I'll give you a square deal. And that's more than your parents did when they turned you loose in the world with the sociability of a rattle-snake and the bedside manner of a frozen turnip. I'll play you a game of seven-up, the winner to pick up his choice of the book, the loser to take the other."

We played; and Idaho won. He picked up his book; and I took mine. Then each of us got on his side of the house and went to reading.

I never was as glad to see a ten-ounce nugget as I was that book. And Idaho took at his like a kid looks at a stick of candy.

Mine was a little book about five by six inches called "Herkimer's Handbook of Indispensable Information." I may be wrong, but I think that was the greatest book that ever was written. I've got it to-day; and I can stump you or any man fifty times in five minutes with the information in it. Talk about Solomon or the New York *Tribune*! Herkimer had cases on both of 'em. That man must have put in fifty years and travelled a million miles to find out all that stuff. There was the population of all cities in it, and the way to tell a girl's age, and the number of teeth a camel has. It told you the longest tunnel in the world, the number of the stars, how long it takes for chicken pox to break out, what a lady's neck ought to measure, the veto powers of Governors, the dates of the Roman aqueducts, how many pounds of rice going without three beers a day would buy, the average annual temperature of Augusta, Maine, the quantity of seed required to plant an acre of carrots in drills, antidotes for poisons, the number of hairs on a blond lady's head, how to preserve eggs, the height of all the mountains in the world, and the dates of all wars and battles, and how to restore drowned persons, and sunstroke, and the number of tacks in a pound, and how to make dynamite and flowers and beds, and what to do before the doctor comes—and a hundred times as many things besides. If there was anything Herkimer didn't know I didn't miss it out of the book.

I sat and read that book for four hours. All the wonders of education was compressed in it. I forgot the snow, and I forgot that me and old Idaho was on the outs. He was sitting still on a stool reading away with a kind of partly soft and partly mysterious look shining through his tan-bark whiskers.

"Idaho," says I, "what kind of a book is yours?"

Idaho must have forgot, too, for he answered moderate, without any slander or malignity.

"Why," says he, "this here seems to be a volume by Homer K. M."

"Homer K. M. what?" I asks.

"Why, just Homer K. M.," says he.

"You're a liar," says I, a little riled that Idaho should try to put me up a tree. "No man is going 'round signing books with his initials. If it's Homer K. M. Spoopendyke, or Homer K. M. McSweeney, or

Homer K. M. Jones, why don't you say so like a man instead of biting off the end of it like a calf chewing off the tail of a shirt on a clothesline?"

"I put it to you straight, Sandy," says Idaho, quiet. "It's a poem book," says he, "by Homer K. M. I couldn't get colour out of it at first, but there's a vein if you follow it up. I wouldn't have missed this book for a pair of red blankets."

"You're welcome to it," says I. "What I want is a disinterested statement of facts for the mind to work on, and that's what I seem to find in the book I've drawn."

"What you've got," says Idaho, "is statistics, the lowest grade of information that exists. They'll poison your mind. Give me old K. M.'s system of surmises. He seems to be a kind of a wine agent. His regular toast is 'nothing doing,' and he seems to have a grouch, but he keeps it so well lubricated with booze that his worst kicks sound like an invitation to split a quart. But it's poetry," says Idaho, "and I have sensations of scorn for that truck of yours that tries to convey sense in feet and inches. When it comes to explaining the instinct of philosophy through the art of nature, old K. M. has got your man beat by drills, rows, paragraphs, chest measurement, and average annual rainfall."

So that's the way me and Idaho had it. Day and night all the excitement we got was studying our books. That snowstorm sure fixed us with a fine lot of attainments apiece. By the time the snow melted, if you had stepped up to me suddenly and said: "Sanderson Pratt, what would it cost per square foot to lay a roof with twenty by twenty-eight tin at nine dollars and fifty cents per box?" I'd have told you as quick as light could travel the length of a spade handle at the rate of one hundred and ninety-two thousand miles per second. How many can do it? You wake up 'most any man you know in the middle of the night, and ask him quick to tell you the number of bones in the human skeleton exclusive of the teeth, or what percentage of the vote of the Nebraska Legislature overrules a veto. Will he tell you? Try him and see.

About what benefit Idaho got out of his poetry book I didn't exactly know. Idaho boosted the wine-agent every time he opened his mouth; but I wasn't so sure.

This Homer K. M., from what leaked out of his libretto through Idaho, seemed to me to be a kind of a dog who looked at life like it was a tin can tied to his tail. After running himself half to death, he sits down, hangs his tongue out, and looks at the can and says:

"Oh, well, since we can't shake the growler, let's get it filled at the corner, and all have a drink on me."

Besides that, it seems he was a Persian; and I never hear of Persia producing anything worth mentioning unless it was Turkish rugs and Maltese cats.

That spring me and Idaho struck pay ore. It was a habit of ours to sell out quick and keep moving. We unloaded our grubstaker for eight thousand dollars apiece; and then we drifted down to this little town of Rosa, on the Salmon river, to rest up, and get some human grub, and have our whiskers harvested.

Rosa was no mining-camp. It laid in the valley, and was as free of uproar and pestilence as one of them rural towns in the country. There was a three-mile trolley line champing its bit in the environs; and me and Idaho spent a week riding on one of the cars, dropping off at nights at the Sunset View Hotel. Being now well read as well as travelled, we was soon *pro re nata* with the best society in Rosa, and was invited out to the most dressed-up and high-toned entertainments. It was at a piano recital and quail-eating contest in the city hall, for the benefit of the fire company, that me and Idaho first met Mrs. De Ormond Sampson, the queen of Rosa society.

Mrs. Sampson was a widow, and owned the only two-story house in town. It was painted yellow, and whichever way you looked from you could see it as plain as egg on the chin of an O'Grady on a Friday. Twenty-two men in Rosa besides me and Idaho was trying to stake a claim on that yellow house.

There was a dance after the song books and quail bones had been raked out of the Hall. Twenty-three of the bunch galloped over to Mrs. Sampson and asked for a dance. I side-stepped the two-step, and asked permission to escort her home. That's where I made a hit.

On the way home says she:

"Ain't the stars lovely and bright to-night, Mr. Pratt?"

"For the chance they've got," says I, "they're humping themselves in a mighty creditable way. That big one you see is sixty-six million miles distant. It took thirty-six years for its light to reach us. With an eighteen-foot telescope you can see forty-three millions of 'em, including them of the thirteenth magnitude, which, if one was to go out now, you would keep on seeing it for twenty-seven hundred years."

"My!" says Mrs. Sampson. "I never knew that before. How warm it is! I'm as damp as I can be from dancing so much."

"That's easy to account for," says I, "when you happen to know that you've got two million sweat-glands working all at once. If every one of your perspiratory ducts, which are a quarter of an inch long, was placed end to end, they would reach a distance of seven miles."

"Lawsy!" says Mrs. Sampson. "It sounds like an irrigation ditch you was describing, Mr. Pratt. How do you get all this knowledge of information?"

"From observation, Mrs. Sampson," I tells her. "I keep my eyes open when I go about the world."

"Mr. Pratt," says she, "I always did admire a man of education. There are so few scholars among the sap-headed plug-uglies of this town that it is a real pleasure to converse with a gentleman of culture. I'd be gratified to have you call at my house whenever you feel so inclined."

And that was the way I got the goodwill of the lady in the yellow house. Every Tuesday and Friday evening I used to go there and tell her about the wonders of the universe as discovered, tabulated, and compiled from nature by Herkimer. Idaho and the other gay Lutherans of the town got every minute of the rest of the week that they could.

I never imagined that Idaho was trying to work on Mrs. Sampson with old K. M.'s rules of courtship till one afternoon when I was on my way over to take her a basket of wild hog-plums. I met the lady coming down the lane that led to her house. Her eyes was snapping, and her hat made a dangerous dip over one eye.

"Mr. Pratt," she opens up, "this Mr. Green is a friend of yours, I believe."

"For nine years," says I.

"Cut him out," says she. "He's no gentleman!"

"Why ma'am," says I, "he's a plain incumbent of the mountains, with asperities and the usual failings of a spendthrift and a liar, but I never on the most momentous occasion had the heart to deny that he was a gentleman. It may be that in haberdashery and the sense of arrogance and display Idaho offends the eye, but inside, ma'am, I've found him impervious to the lower grades of crime and obesity. After nine years of Idaho's society, Mrs. Sampson," I winds up, "I should hate to impute him, and I should hate to see him imputed."

"It's right plausible of you, Mr. Pratt," says Mrs. Sampson, "to take up the curmudgeons in your friend's behalf; but it don't alter the fact that he has made proposals to me sufficiently obnoxious to ruffle the ignominy of any lady."

"Why, now, now, now!" says I. "Old Idaho do that! I could believe it of myself, sooner. I never knew but one thing to deride in him; and a blizzard was responsible for that. Once while we was snow-bound in the mountains he became a prey to a kind of spurious and uneven poetry, which may have corrupted his demeanour."

"It has," says Mrs. Sampson. "Ever since I knew him he has been reciting to me a lot of irreligious rhymes by some person he calls Ruby Ott, and who is no better than she should be, if you judge by her poetry."

"Then Idaho has struck a new book," says I, "for the one he had was by a man who writes under the *nom de plume* of K. M."

"He'd better have stuck to it," says Mrs. Sampson, "whatever it was. And to-day he caps the vortex. I get a bunch of flowers from him, and on 'em is pinned a note. Now, Mr. Pratt, you know a lady when you see her; and you know how I stand in Rosa society. Do you think for a moment that I'd skip out to the woods with a man along with a jug of wine and a loaf of bread, and go singing and cavorting up and down under the trees with him? I take a little claret with my meals, but I'm not in the habit of packing a jug of it into the brush and raising Cain in any such style as that. And of course he'd bring his book of verses along, too. He said so. Let him go on his scandalous picnics alone! Or let him take his Ruby Ott with him. I reckon she wouldn't kick unless it was on account of there being too much bread along. And what do you think of your gentleman friend now, Mr. Pratt?"

"Well, 'm," says I, "it may be that Idaho's invitation was a kind of poetry, and meant no harm. May be it belonged to the class of rhymes they call figurative. They offend law and order, but they get sent through the mails on the grounds that they mean something that they don't say. I'd be glad on Idaho's account if you'd overlook it," says I, "and let us extricate our minds from the low regions of poetry to the higher planes of fact and fancy. On a beautiful afternoon like this, Mrs. Sampson," I goes on, "we should let our thoughts dwell accordingly. Though it is warm here, we should remember that at the equator the line of perpetual frost is at an altitude of fifteen thousand feet. Between the latitudes of forty degrees and forty-nine degrees it is from four thousand to nine thousand feet."

"Oh, Mr. Pratt," says Mrs. Sampson, "it's such a comfort to hear you say them beautiful facts after getting such a jar from that minx of a Ruby's poetry!"

"Let us sit on this log at the roadside," says I, "and forget the inhumanity and ribaldry of the poets. It is in the glorious columns of ascertained facts and legalised measures that beauty is to be found. In this very log we sit upon, Mrs. Sampson," says I, "is statistics more wonderful than any poem. The rings show it was sixty years old. At the depth of two thousand feet it would become coal in three thousand years. The deepest coal mine in the world is at Killingworth, near Newcastle. A box four feet long, three feet wide, and two feet eight inches deep will hold one ton of coal. If an artery is cut, compress it above the wound. A man's leg contains thirty bones. The Tower of London was burned in 1841."

"Go on, Mr. Pratt," says Mrs. Sampson. "Them ideas is so original and soothing. I think statistics are just as lovely as they can be."

But it wasn't till two weeks later that I got all that was coming to me out of Herkimer.

One night I was waked up by folks hollering "Fire!" all around. I jumped up and dressed and went out of the hotel to enjoy the scene. When I see it was Mrs. Sampson's house, I gave forth a kind of yell, and I was there in two minutes.

The whole lower story of the yellow house was in flames, and every masculine, feminine, and canine in Rosa was there, screeching and barking and getting in the way of the firemen. I saw Idaho trying to get away from six firemen who were holding him. They was telling him the whole place was on fire down-stairs, and no man could go in it and come out alive.

"Where's Mrs. Sampson?" I asks.

"She hasn't been seen," says one of the firemen. "She sleeps up-stairs. We've tried to get in, but we can't, and our company hasn't got any ladders yet."

I runs around to the light of the big blaze, and pulls the Handbook out of my inside pocket. I kind of laughed when I felt it in my hands—I reckon I was some daffy with the sensation of excitement.

"Herky, old boy," I says to it, as I flipped over the pages, "you ain't ever lied to me yet, and you ain't ever throwed me down at a scratch yet. Tell me what, old boy, tell me what!" says I.

I turned to "What to do in Case of Accidents," on page 117. I run my finger down the page, and struck it. Good old Herkimer, he never overlooked anything! It said:

Suffocation from Inhaling Smoke or Gas.—There is nothing better than flaxseed. Place a few seed in the outer corner of the eye.

I shoved the Handbook back in my pocket, and grabbed a boy that was running by.

"Here," says I, giving him some money, "run to the drug store and bring a dollar's worth of flaxseed. Hurry, and you'll get another one for yourself. Now," I sings out to the crowd, "we'll have Mrs. Sampson!" And I throws away my coat and hat.

Four of the firemen and citizens grabs hold of me. It's sure death, they say, to go in the house, for the floors was beginning to fall through.

"How in blazes," I sings out, kind of laughing yet, but not feeling like it, "do you expect me to put flaxseed in a eye without the eye?"

I jabbed each elbow in a fireman's face, kicked the bark off of one citizen's shin, and tripped the other one with a side hold. And then I busted into the house. If I die first I'll write you a letter and tell you if it's any worse down there than the inside of that yellow house was; but don't believe it yet. I was a heap more cooked than the hurry-up orders of broiled chicken that you get in restaurants. The fire and smoke had me down on the floor twice, and was about to shame Herkimer, but the firemen helped me with their little stream of water, and I got to Mrs. Sampson's room. She'd lost conscientiousness from the smoke, so I wrapped her in the bed clothes and got her on my shoulder. Well, the floors wasn't as bad as they said, or I never could have done it—not by no means.

I carried her out fifty yards from the house and laid her on the grass. Then, of course, every one of them other twenty-two plaintiff's to the lady's hand crowded around with tin dippers of water ready to save her. And up runs the boy with the flaxseed.

I unwrapped the covers from Mrs. Sampson's head. She opened her eyes and says:

"Is that you, Mr. Pratt?"

"S-s-sh," says I. "Don't talk till you've had the remedy."

I runs my arm around her neck and raises her head, gentle, and breaks the bag of flaxseed with the other hand; and as easy as I could I bends over and slips three or four of the seeds in the outer corner of her eye.

Up gallops the village doc by this time, and snorts around, and grabs at Mrs. Sampson's pulse, and wants to know what I mean by any such sandblasted nonsense.

"Well, old Jalap and Jerusalem oakseed," says I, "I'm no regular practitioner, but I'll show you my authority, anyway."

They fetched my coat, and I gets out the Handbook.

"Look on page 117," says I, "at the remedy for suffocation by smoke or gas. Flaxseed in the outer corner of the eye, it says. I don't know whether it works as a smoke consumer or whether it hikes the compound gastro-hippopotamus nerve into action, but Herkimer says it, and he was called to the case first. If you want to make it a consultation, there's no objection."

Old doc takes the book and looks at it by means of his specs and a fireman's lantern.

"Well, Mr. Pratt," says he, "you evidently got on the wrong line in reading your diagnosis. The recipe for suffocation says: 'Get the patient into fresh air as quickly as possible, and place in a reclining position.' The flaxseed remedy is for 'Dust and Cinders in the Eye,' on the line above. But, after all—"

"See here," interrupts Mrs. Sampson, "I reckon I've got something to say in this consultation. That flaxseed done me more good than anything I ever tried." And then she raises up her head and lays it back on my arm again, and says: "Put some in the other eye, Sandy dear."

And so if you was to stop off at Rosa to-morrow, or any other day, you'd see a fine new yellow house with Mrs. Pratt, that was Mrs. Sampson, embellishing and adorning it. And if you was to step inside you'd see on the marble-top centre table in the parlour "Herkimer's Handbook of Indispensable Information," all rebound in red morocco, and ready to be consulted on any subject pertaining to human happiness and wisdom.

O. HENRY

V

The Pimienta Pancakes

While we were rounding up a bunch of the Triangle-O cattle in the Frio bottoms a projecting branch of a dead mesquite caught my wooden stirrup and gave my ankle a wrench that laid me up in camp for a week.

On the third day of my compulsory idleness I crawled out near the grub wagon, and reclined helpless under the conversational fire of Judson Odom, the camp cook. Jud was a monologist by nature, whom Destiny, with customary blundering, had set in a profession wherein he was bereaved, for the greater portion of his time, of an audience.

Therefore, I was manna in the desert of Jud's obmutescence.

Betimes I was stirred by invalid longings for something to eat that did not come under the caption of "grub." I had visions of the maternal pantry "deep as first love, and wild with all regret," and then I asked:

"Jud, can you make pancakes?"

Jud laid down his six-shooter, with which he was preparing to pound an antelope steak, and stood over me in what I felt to be a menacing attitude. He further endorsed my impression that his pose was resentful by fixing upon me with his light blue eyes a look of cold suspicion.

"Say, you," he said, with candid, though not excessive, choler, "did you mean that straight, or was you trying to throw the gaff into me? Some of the boys been telling you about me and that pancake racket?"

"No, Jud," I said, sincerely, "I meant it. It seems to me I'd swap my pony and saddle for a stack of buttered brown pancakes with some first crop, open kettle, New Orleans sweetening. Was there a story about pancakes?"

Jud was mollified at once when he saw that I had not been dealing in allusions. He brought some mysterious bags and tin boxes from the grub wagon and set them in the shade of the hackberry where I lay reclined. I watched him as he began to arrange them leisurely and untie their many strings.

"No, not a story," said Jud, as he worked, "but just the logical disclosures in the case of me and that pink-eyed snoozer from Mired Mule Canada and Miss Willella Learight. I don't mind telling you.

"I was punching then for old Bill Toomey, on the San Miguel. One day I gets all ensnared up in aspirations for to eat some canned grub that hasn't ever mooed or baaed or grunted or been in peck measures. So, I gets on my bronc and pushes the wind for Uncle Emsley Telfair's store at the Pimienta Crossing on the Nueces.

"About three in the afternoon I throwed my bridle rein over a mesquite limb and walked the last twenty yards into Uncle Emsley's store. I got up on the counter and told Uncle Emsley that the signs pointed to the devastation of the fruit crop of the world. In a minute I had a bag of crackers and a long-handled spoon, with an open can each of apricots and pineapples and cherries and greengages beside of me with Uncle Emsley busy chopping away with the hatchet at the yellow clings. I was feeling like Adam before the apple stampede, and was digging my spurs into the side of the counter and working with my twenty-four-inch spoon when I happened to look out of the window into the yard of Uncle Emsley's house, which was next to the store.

"There was a girl standing there—an imported girl with fixings on—philandering with a croquet maul and amusing herself by watching my style of encouraging the fruit canning industry.

"I slid off the counter and delivered up my shovel to Uncle Emsley.

"'That's my niece,' says he; 'Miss Willella Learight, down from Palestine on a visit. Do you want that I should make you acquainted?'

"'The Holy Land,' I says to myself, my thoughts milling some as I tried to run 'em into the corral. 'Why not? There was sure angels in Pales—Why, yes, Uncle Emsley,' I says out loud, 'I'd be awful edified to meet Miss Learight.'

"So Uncle Emsley took me out in the yard and gave us each other's entitlements.

"I never was shy about women. I never could understand why some men who can break a mustang before breakfast and shave in the dark, get all left-handed and full of perspiration and excuses when they see a bold of calico draped around what belongs to it. Inside of eight minutes me and Miss Willella was aggravating the croquet balls around as amiable as second cousins. She gave me a dig about the quantity of canned fruit I had eaten, and I got back at her, flat-footed, about how a certain lady named Eve started the fruit trouble in the first free-grass pasture—'Over in Palestine, wasn't it?' says I, as easy and pat as roping a one-year-old.

"That was how I acquired cordiality for the proximities of Miss Willella Learight; and the disposition grew larger as time passed. She was stopping at Pimienta Crossing for her health, which was very good, and for the climate, which was forty per cent. hotter than Palestine. I rode over to see her once every week for a while; and then I figured it out that if I doubled the number of trips I would see her twice as often.

"One week I slipped in a third trip; and that's where the pancakes and the pink-eyed snoozer busted into the game.

"That evening, while I set on the counter with a peach and two damsons in my mouth, I asked Uncle Emsley how Miss Willella was.

"'Why,' says Uncle Emsley, 'she's gone riding with Jackson Bird, the sheep man from over at Mired Mule Canada.'

"I swallowed the peach seed and the two damson seeds. I guess somebody held the counter by the bridle while I got off; and then I walked out straight ahead till I butted against the mesquite where my roan was tied.

"'She's gone riding,' I whisper in my bronc's ear, 'with Birdstone Jack, the hired mule from Sheep Man's Canada. Did you get that, old Leather-and-Gallops?'

"That bronc of mine wept, in his way. He'd been raised a cow pony and he didn't care for snoozers.

"I went back and said to Uncle Emsley: 'Did you say a sheep man?'

"'I said a sheep man,' says Uncle Emsley again. 'You must have heard tell of Jackson Bird. He's got eight sections of grazing and four thousand head of the finest Merinos south of the Arctic Circle.'

"I went out and sat on the ground in the shade of the store and leaned against a prickly pear. I sifted sand into my boots with unthinking hands while I soliloquised a quantity about this bird with the Jackson plumage to his name.

"I never had believed in harming sheep men. I see one, one day, reading a Latin grammar on hossback, and I never touched him! They never irritated me like they do most cowmen. You wouldn't go to work now, and impair and disfigure snoozers, would you, that eat on tables and wear little shoes and speak to you on subjects? I had always let 'em pass, just as you would a jack-rabbit; with a polite word and a guess about the weather, but no stopping to swap canteens. I never thought it was worth while to be hostile with a snoozer. And because I'd been lenient, and let 'em live, here was one going around riding with Miss Willella Learight!

"An hour by sun they come loping back, and stopped at Uncle Emsley's gate. The sheep person helped her off; and they stood throwing each other sentences all sprightful and sagacious for a while. And then this feathered Jackson flies up in his saddle and raises his little stewpot of a hat, and trots off in the direction of his mutton ranch. By this time I had turned the sand out of my boots and unpinned myself from the prickly pear; and by the time he gets half a mile out of Pimienta, I singlefoots up beside him on my bronc.

"I said that snoozer was pink-eyed, but he wasn't. His seeing arrangement was grey enough, but his eye-lashes was pink and his hair was sandy, and that gave you the idea. Sheep man?—he wasn't more than a lamb man, anyhow—a little thing with his neck involved in a yellow silk handkerchief, and shoes tied up in bowknots.

"'Afternoon!' says I to him. 'You now ride with a equestrian who is commonly called Dead-Moral-Certainty Judson, on account of the way I shoot. When I want a stranger to know me I always introduce myself before the draw, for I never did like to shake hands with ghosts.'

"'Ah,' says he, just like that—'Ah, I'm glad to know you, Mr. Judson. I'm Jackson Bird, from over at Mired Mule Ranch.'

"Just then one of my eyes saw a roadrunner skipping down the hill with a young tarantula in his bill, and the other eye noticed a rabbit-hawk sitting on a dead limb in a water-elm. I popped over one after the other with my forty-five, just to show him. 'Two out of three,' says I. 'Birds just naturally seem to draw my fire wherever I go.'

"'Nice shooting,' says the sheep man, without a flutter. 'But don't you sometimes ever miss the third shot? Elegant fine rain that was last week for the young grass, Mr. Judson?' says he.

"'Willie,' says I, riding over close to his palfrey, 'your infatuated parents may have denounced you by the name of Jackson, but you sure moulted into a twittering Willie—let us slough off this here analysis of rain and the elements, and get down to talk that is outside the vocabulary of parrots. That is a bad habit you have got of riding with young ladies over at Pimienta. I've known birds,' says I, 'to be served on toast for less than that. Miss Willella,' says I, 'don't ever want any nest made out of sheep's wool by a tomtit of the Jacksonian branch of ornithology. Now, are you going to quit, or do you wish for to gallop up against this Dead-Moral-Certainty attachment to my name, which is good for two hyphens and at least one set of funeral obsequies?'

"Jackson Bird flushed up some, and then he laughed.

"'Why, Mr. Judson,' says he, 'you've got the wrong idea. I've called on Miss Learight a few times; but not for the purpose you imagine. My object is purely a gastronomical one.'

"I reached for my gun.

"'Any coyote,' says I, 'that would boast of dishonourable—'

"'Wait a minute,' says this Bird, 'till I explain. What would I do with a wife? If you ever saw that ranch of mine! I do my own cooking and mending. Eating—that's all the pleasure I get out of sheep raising. Mr. Judson, did you ever taste the pancakes that Miss Learight makes?'

"'Me? No,' I told him. 'I never was advised that she was up to any culinary manoeuvres.'

"'They're golden sunshine,' says he, 'honey-browned by the ambrosial fires of Epicurus. I'd give two years of my life to get the recipe for making them pancakes. That's what I went to see Miss Learight for,' says Jackson Bird, 'but I haven't been able to get it from her. It's an old recipe that's been in the family for seventy-five years. They hand it down from one generation to another, but they don't give it away to outsiders. If I could get that recipe, so I could make them pancakes for myself on my ranch, I'd be a happy man,' says Bird.

"'Are you sure,' I says to him, 'that it ain't the hand that mixes the pancakes that you're after?'

"'Sure,' says Jackson. 'Miss Learight is a mighty nice girl, but I can assure you my intentions go no further than the gastro—' but he seen my hand going down to my holster and he changed his similitude— 'than the desire to procure a copy of the pancake recipe,' he finishes.

"'You ain't such a bad little man,' says I, trying to be fair. 'I was thinking some of making orphans of your sheep, but I'll let you fly away this time. But you stick to pancakes,' says I, 'as close as the middle one of a stack; and don't go and mistake sentiments for syrup, or there'll be singing at your ranch, and you won't hear it.'

"'To convince you that I am sincere,' says the sheep man, 'I'll ask you to help me. Miss Learight and you being closer friends, maybe she would do for you what she wouldn't for me. If you will get me a copy of that pancake recipe, I give you my word that I'll never call upon her again.'

"'That's fair,' I says, and I shook hands with Jackson Bird. 'I'll get it for you if I can, and glad to oblige.' And he turned off down the big pear flat on the Piedra, in the direction of Mired Mule; and I steered northwest for old Bill Toomey's ranch.

"It was five days afterward when I got another chance to ride over to Pimienta. Miss Willella and me passed a gratifying evening at Uncle Emsley's. She sang some, and exasperated the piano quite a lot with quotations from the operas. I gave imitations of a rattlesnake, and told her about Snaky McFee's new way of skinning cows, and described the trip I made to Saint Louis once. We was getting along in one another's estimations fine. Thinks I, if Jackson Bird can now be persuaded to migrate, I win. I recollect his promise about the pancake receipt, and I thinks I will persuade it from Miss Willella and give it to him; and then if I catches Birdie off of Mired Mule again, I'll make him hop the twig.

"So, along about ten o'clock, I put on a wheedling smile and says to Miss Willella: 'Now, if there's anything I do like better than the sight of a red steer on green grass it's the taste of a nice hot pancake smothered in sugar-house molasses.'

"Miss Willella gives a little jump on the piano stool, and looked at me curious.

"'Yes,' says she, 'they're real nice. What did you say was the name of that street in Saint Louis, Mr. Odom, where you lost your hat?'

"'Pancake Avenue,' says I, with a wink, to show her that I was on about the family receipt, and couldn't be side-corralled off of the subject. 'Come, now, Miss Willella,' I says; 'let's hear how you make 'em. Pancakes is just whirling in my head like wagon wheels. Start her off, now—pound of flour, eight dozen eggs, and so on. How does the catalogue of constituents run?'

"'Excuse me for a moment, please,' says Miss Willella, and she gives me a quick kind of sideways look, and slides off the stool. She ambled out into the other room, and directly Uncle Emsley comes in in his shirt sleeves, with a pitcher of water. He turns around to get a glass on the table, and I see a forty-five in his hip pocket. 'Great post-holes!' thinks I, 'but here's a family thinks a heap of cooking receipts, protecting it with firearms. I've known outfits that wouldn't do that much by a family feud.'

"'Drink this here down,' says Uncle Emsley, handing me the glass of water. 'You've rid too far to-day, Jud, and got yourself over-excited. Try to think about something else now.'

"'Do you know how to make them pancakes, Uncle Emsley?' I asked.

"'Well, I'm not as apprised in the anatomy of them as some,' says Uncle Emsley, 'but I reckon you take a sifter of plaster of Paris and a little dough and saleratus and corn meal, and mix 'em with eggs and buttermilk as usual. Is old Bill going to ship beeves to Kansas City again this spring, Jud?'

"That was all the pancake specifications I could get that night. I didn't wonder that Jackson Bird found it uphill work. So I dropped the subject and talked with Uncle Emsley for a while about hollow-horn and cyclones. And then Miss Willella came and said 'Good-night,' and I hit the breeze for the ranch.

"About a week afterward I met Jackson Bird riding out of Pimienta as I rode in, and we stopped on the road for a few frivolous remarks.

"'Got the bill of particulars for them flapjacks yet?' I asked him.

"'Well, no,' says Jackson. 'I don't seem to have any success in getting hold of it. Did you try?'

"'I did,' says I, 'and 'twas like trying to dig a prairie dog out of his hole with a peanut hull. That pancake receipt must be a jookalorum, the way they hold on to it.'

"'I'm most ready to give it up,' says Jackson, so discouraged in his pronunciations that I felt sorry for him; 'but I did want to know how to make them pancakes to eat on my lonely ranch,' says he. 'I lie awake at nights thinking how good they are.'

"'You keep on trying for it,' I tells him, 'and I'll do the same. One of us is bound to get a rope over its horns before long. Well, so-long, Jacksy.'

"You see, by this time we were on the peacefullest of terms. When I saw that he wasn't after Miss Willella, I had more endurable contemplations of that sandy-haired snoozer. In order to help out the ambitions of his appetite I kept on trying to get that receipt from Miss Willella. But every time I would say 'pancakes' she would get sort of remote and fidgety about the eye, and try to change the subject. If I held her to it she would slide out and round up Uncle Emsley with his pitcher of water and hip-pocket howitzer.

"One day I galloped over to the store with a fine bunch of blue verbenas that I cut out of a herd of wild flowers over on Poisoned Dog Prairie. Uncle Emsley looked at 'em with one eye shut and says:

"'Haven't ye heard the news?'

"'Cattle up?' I asks.

"'Willella and Jackson Bird was married in Palestine yesterday,' says he. 'Just got a letter this morning.'

"I dropped them flowers in a cracker-barrel, and let the news trickle in my ears and down toward my upper left-hand shirt pocket until it got to my feet.

"'Would you mind saying that over again once more, Uncle Emsley?' says I. 'Maybe my hearing has got wrong, and you only said that prime heifers was 4.80 on the hoof, or something like that.'

"'Married yesterday,' says Uncle Emsley, 'and gone to Waco and Niagara Falls on a wedding tour. Why, didn't you see none of the signs all along? Jackson Bird has been courting Willella ever since that day he took her out riding.'

"'Then,' says I, in a kind of yell, 'what was all this zizzaparoola he gives me about pancakes? Tell me *that*.'

"When I said 'pancakes' Uncle Emsley sort of dodged and stepped back.

"'Somebody's been dealing me pancakes from the bottom of the deck,' I says, 'and I'll find out. I believe you know. Talk up,' says I, 'or we'll mix a panful of batter right here.'

"I slid over the counter after Uncle Emsley. He grabbed at his gun, but it was in a drawer, and he missed it two inches. I got him by the front of his shirt and shoved him in a corner.

"'Talk pancakes,' says I, 'or be made into one. Does Miss Willella make 'em?'

"'She never made one in her life and I never saw one,' says Uncle Emsley, soothing. 'Calm down now, Jud—calm down. You've got excited, and that wound in your head is contaminating your sense of intelligence. Try not to think about pancakes.'

"'Uncle Emsley,' says I, 'I'm not wounded in the head except so far as my natural cognitive instincts run to runts. Jackson Bird told me he was calling on Miss Willella for the purpose of finding out her system of producing pancakes, and he asked me to help him get the bill of lading of the ingredients. I done so, with the results as you see. Have I been sodded down with Johnson grass by a pink-eyed snoozer, or what?'

"'Slack up your grip in my dress shirt,' says Uncle Emsley, 'and I'll tell you. Yes, it looks like Jackson Bird has gone and humbugged you some. The day after he went riding with Willella he came back and told me and her to watch out for you whenever you got to talking about pancakes. He said you was in camp once where they was cooking flapjacks, and one of the fellows cut you over the head with a frying pan. Jackson said that whenever you got overhot or excited that wound hurt you and made you kind of crazy, and you went raving about pancakes. He told us to just get you worked off of the subject and soothed down, and you wouldn't be dangerous. So, me and Willella done the best by you we knew how. Well, well,' says Uncle Emsley, 'that Jackson Bird is sure a seldom kind of a snoozer.'"

During the progress of Jud's story he had been slowly but deftly combining certain portions of the contents of his sacks and cans. Toward the close of it he set before me the finished product—a pair of red-hot, rich-hued pancakes on a tin plate. From some secret hoarding he also brought a lump of excellent butter and a bottle of golden syrup.

"How long ago did these things happen?" I asked him.

"Three years," said Jud. "They're living on the Mired Mule Ranch now. But I haven't seen either of 'em since. They say Jackson Bird was fixing his ranch up fine with rocking chairs and window curtains all the time he was putting me up the pancake tree. Oh, I got over it after a while. But the boys kept the racket up."

"Did you make these cakes by the famous recipe?" I asked.

"Didn't I tell you there wasn't no receipt?" said Jud. "The boys hollered pancakes till they got pancake hungry, and I cut this recipe out of a newspaper. How does the truck taste?"

"They're delicious," I answered. "Why don't you have some, too, Jud?"

I was sure I heard a sigh.

"Me?" said Jud. "I don't ever eat 'em."

VI

Seats of the Haughty

Golden by day and silver by night, a new trail now leads to us across the Indian Ocean. Dusky kings and princes have found our Bombay of the West; and few be their trails that do not lead down to Broadway on their journey for to admire and for to see.

If chance should ever lead you near a hotel that transiently shelters some one of these splendid touring grandees, I counsel you to seek Lucullus Polk among the republican tuft-hunters that besiege its entrances. He will be there. You will know him by his red, alert, Wellington-nosed face, by his manner of nervous caution mingled with determination, by his assumed promoter's or broker's air of busy impatience, and by his bright-red necktie, gallantly redressing the wrongs of his maltreated blue serge suit, like a battle standard still waving above a lost cause. I found him profitable; and so may you. When you do look for him, look among the light-horse troop of Bedouins that besiege the picket-line of the travelling potentate's guards and secretaries—among the wild-eyed genii of Arabian Afternoons that gather to make astounding and egregrious demands upon the prince's coffers.

I first saw Mr. Polk coming down the steps of the hotel at which sojourned His Highness the Gaekwar of Baroda, most enlightened of the Mahratta princes, who, of late, ate bread and salt in our Metropolis of the Occident.

Lucullus moved rapidly, as though propelled by some potent moral force that imminently threatened to become physical. Behind him closely followed the impetus—a hotel detective, if ever white Alpine hat, hawk's nose, implacable watch chain, and loud refinement of manner spoke the truth. A brace of uniformed porters at his heels preserved the smooth decorum of the hotel, repudiating by their air of disengagement any suspicion that they formed a reserve squad of ejectment.

Safe on the sidewalk, Lucullus Polk turned and shook a freckled fist at the caravansary. And, to my joy, he began to breathe deep invective in strange words:

"Rides in howdays, does he?" he cried loudly and sneeringly. "Rides on elephants in howdahs and calls himself a prince! Kings—yah! Comes over here and talks horse till you would think he was a president; and then goes home and rides in a private dining-room strapped onto an elephant. Well, well, well!"

The ejecting committee quietly retired. The scorner of princes turned to me and snapped his fingers.

"What do you think of that?" he shouted derisively. "The Gaekwar of Baroda rides in an elephant in a howdah! And there's old Bikram Shamsher Jang scorching up and down the pig-paths of Khatmandu on a motor-cycle. Wouldn't that maharajah you? And the Shah of Persia, that ought to have been Muley-on-the-spot for at least three, he's got the palanquin habit. And that funny-hat prince from Korea—wouldn't you think he could afford to amble around on a milk-white palfrey once in a dynasty or two? Nothing doing! His idea of a Balaklava charge is to tuck his skirts under him and do his mile in six days over the hog-wallows of Seoul in a bull-cart. That's the kind of visiting potentates that come to this country now. It's a hard deal, friend."

I murmured a few words of sympathy. But it was uncomprehending, for I did not know his grievance against the rulers who flash, meteor-like, now and then upon our shores.

"The last one I sold," continued the displeased one, "was to that three-horse-tailed Turkish pasha that came over a year ago. Five hundred dollars he paid for it, easy. I says to his executioner or secretary—he was a kind of a Jew or a Chinaman—'His Turkey Gibbets is fond of horses, then?'

"'Him?' says the secretary. 'Well, no. He's got a big, fat wife in the harem named Bad Dora that he don't like. I believe he intends to saddle her up and ride her up and down the board-walk in the Bulbul Gardens a few times every day. You haven't got a pair of extra-long spurs you could throw in on the deal, have you?' Yes, sir; there's mighty few real rough-riders among the royal sports these days."

As soon as Lucullus Polk got cool enough I picked him up, and with no greater effort than you would employ in persuading a drowning man to clutch a straw, I inveigled him into accompanying me to a cool corner in a dim cafe.

And it came to pass that man-servants set before us brewage; and Lucullus Polk spake unto me, relating the wherefores of his beleaguering the antechambers of the princes of the earth.

"Did you ever hear of the S.A. & A.P. Railroad in Texas? Well, that don't stand for Samaritan Actor's Aid Philanthropy. I was down that way managing a summer bunch of the gum and syntax-chewers that play the Idlewild Parks in the Western hamlets. Of course, we went to pieces when the soubrette ran away with a prominent barber of Beeville. I don't know what became of the rest of the company. I believe there were some salaries due; and the last I saw of the troupe was when I told them that forty-three cents was all the treasury contained. I say I never saw any of them after that; but I heard them for about twenty minutes. I didn't have time to look back. But after dark I came out of the woods and struck the S.A. & A.P. agent for means of transportation. He at once extended to me the courtesies of the entire railroad, kindly warning me, however, not to get aboard any of the rolling stock.

"About ten the next morning I steps off the ties into a village that calls itself Atascosa City. I bought a thirty-cent breakfast and a ten-cent cigar, and stood on the Main Street jingling the three pennies in my pocket—dead broke. A man in Texas with only three cents in his pocket is no better off than a man that has no money and owes two cents.

"One of luck's favourite tricks is to soak a man for his last dollar so quick that he don't have time to look it. There I was in a swell St. Louis tailor-made, blue-and-green plaid suit, and an eighteen-carat sulphate-of-copper scarf-pin, with no hope in sight except the two great Texas industries, the cotton fields and grading new railroads. I never picked cotton, and I never cottoned to a pick, so the outlook had ultramarine edges.

"All of a sudden, while I was standing on the edge of the wooden sidewalk, down out of the sky falls two fine gold watches in the middle of the street. One hits a chunk of mud and sticks. The other falls hard and flies open, making a fine drizzle of little springs and screws and wheels. I looks up for a balloon or an airship; but not seeing any, I steps off the sidewalk to investigate.

"But I hear a couple of yells and see two men running up the street in leather overalls and high-heeled boots and cartwheel hats. One man is six or eight feet high, with open-plumbed joints and a heartbroken cast of countenance. He picks up the watch that has stuck in the mud. The other man, who is little, with pink hair and white eyes, goes for the empty case, and says, 'I win.' Then the elevated pessimist goes down under his leather leg-holsters and hands a handful of twenty-dollar gold pieces to his albino friend. I don't know how much money it was; it looked as big as an earthquake-relief fund to me.

"'I'll have this here case filled up with works,' says Shorty, 'and throw you again for five hundred.'

"'I'm your company,' says the high man. 'I'll meet you at the Smoked Dog Saloon an hour from now.'

"The little man hustles away with a kind of Swiss movement toward a jewelry store. The heartbroken person stoops over and takes a telescopic view of my haberdashery.

"'Them's a mighty slick outfit of habiliments you have got on, Mr. Man,' says he. 'I'll bet a hoss you never acquired the right, title, and interest in and to them clothes in Atascosa City.'

"'Why, no,' says I, being ready enough to exchange personalities with this moneyed monument of melancholy. 'I had this suit tailored from a special line of coatericks, vestures, and pantings in St. Louis. Would you mind putting me sane,' says I, 'on this watch-throwing contest? I've been used to seeing time-pieces treated with more politeness and esteem—except women's watches, of course, which by nature they abuse by cracking walnuts with 'em and having 'em taken showing in tintype pictures.'

"'Me and George,' he explains, 'are up from the ranch, having a spell of fun. Up to last month we owned four sections of watered grazing down on the San Miguel. But along comes one of these oil prospectors and begins to bore. He strikes a gusher that flows out twenty thousand—or maybe it was twenty million—barrels of oil a day. And me and George gets one hundred and fifty thousand dollars—seventy-five thousand dollars apiece—for the land. So now and then we saddles up and hits the breeze for Atascosa City for a few days of excitement and damage. Here's a little bunch of the *dinero* that I drawed out of the bank this morning,' says he, and shows a roll of twenties and fifties as big around as a sleeping-car pillow. The yellowbacks glowed like a sunset on the gable end of John D.'s barn. My knees got weak, and I sat down on the edge of the board sidewalk.

"'You must have knocked around a right smart,' goes on this oil Grease-us. 'I shouldn't be surprised if you have saw towns more livelier than what Atascosa City is. Sometimes it seems to me that there ought to be some more ways of having a good time than there is here, 'specially when you've got plenty of money and don't mind spending it.'

"Then this Mother Cary's chick of the desert sits down by me and we hold a conversationfest. It seems that he was money-poor. He'd lived in ranch camps all his life; and he confessed to me that his supreme idea of luxury was to ride into camp, tired out from a round-up, eat a peck of Mexican beans, hobble his brains with a pint of raw whisky, and go to sleep with his boots for a pillow. When this barge-load of unexpected money came to him and his pink but perky partner, George, and they hied themselves to this clump of outhouses called Atascosa City, you know what happened to them. They had money to buy anything they wanted; but they didn't know what to want. Their ideas of spendthriftiness were limited to three—whisky, saddles, and gold watches. If there was anything else in the world to throw away fortunes on, they had never heard about it. So, when they wanted to have a hot time, they'd ride into town and get a city directory and stand in front of the principal saloon and call up the population alphabetically for free drinks. Then they would order three or four new California saddles from the storekeeper, and play crack-loo on the sidewalk with twenty-dollar gold pieces. Betting who could throw his gold watch the farthest was an inspiration of George's; but even that was getting to be monotonous.

"Was I on to the opportunity? Listen.

"In thirty minutes I had dashed off a word picture of metropolitan joys that made life in Atascosa City look as dull as a trip to Coney Island with your own wife. In ten minutes more we shook hands on an agreement that I was to act as his guide, interpreter and friend in and to the aforesaid wassail and amenity. And Solomon Mills, which was his name, was to pay all expenses for a month. At the end of that time, if I had made good as director-general of the rowdy life, he was to pay me one thousand dollars. And then, to clinch the bargain, we called the roll of Atascosa City and put all of its citizens except the ladies and minors under the table, except one man named Horace Westervelt St. Clair. Just for that we bought a couple of hatfuls of cheap silver watches and egged him out of town with 'em. We wound up by dragging the harness-maker out of bed and setting him to work on three new saddles; and then we went to sleep across the railroad track at the depot, just to annoy the S.A. & A.P. Think of having seventy-five thousand dollars and trying to avoid the disgrace of dying rich in a town like that!

"The next day George, who was married or something, started back to the ranch. Me and Solly, as I now called him, prepared to shake off our moth balls and wing our way against the arc-lights of the joyous and tuneful East.

"'No way-stops,' says I to Solly, 'except long enough to get you barbered and haberdashed. This is no Texas feet shampetter,' says I, 'where you eat chili-concarne-con-huevos and then holler "Whoopee!" across the plaza. We're now going against the real high life. We're going to mingle with the set that carries a Spitz, wears spats, and hits the ground in high spots.'

"Solly puts six thousand dollars in century bills in one pocket of his brown ducks, and bills of lading for ten thousand dollars on Eastern banks in another. Then I resume diplomatic relations with the S.A. & A.P., and we hike in a northwesterly direction on our circuitous route to the spice gardens of the Yankee Orient.

"We stopped in San Antonio long enough for Solly to buy some clothes, and eight rounds of drinks for the guests and employees of the Menger Hotel, and order four Mexican saddles with silver trimmings and white Angora *suaderos* to be shipped down to the ranch. From there we made a big jump to St. Louis. We got there in time for dinner; and I put our thumb-prints on the register of the most expensive hotel in the city.

"'Now,' says I to Solly, with a wink at myself, 'here's the first dinner-station we've struck where we can get a real good plate of beans.' And while he was up in his room trying to draw water out of the gas-pipe, I got one finger in the buttonhole of the head waiter's Tuxedo, drew him apart, inserted a two-dollar bill, and closed him up again.

"'Frankoyse,' says I, 'I have a pal here for dinner that's been subsisting for years on cereals and short stogies. You see the chef and order a dinner for us such as you serve to Dave Francis and the general passenger agent of the Iron Mountain when they eat here. We've got more than Bernhardt's tent full of money; and we want the nose-bags crammed with all the Chief Deveries *de cuisine*. Object is no expense. Now, show us.'

"At six o'clock me and Solly sat down to dinner. Spread! There's nothing been seen like it since the Cambon snack. It was all served at once. The chef called it *dinnay a la poker*. It's a famous thing among the gormands of the West. The dinner comes in threes of a kind. There was guinea-fowls, guinea-pigs, and Guinness's stout; roast veal, mock turtle soup, and chicken pate; shad-roe, caviar, and tapioca; canvas-back duck, canvas-back ham, and cotton-tail rabbit; Philadelphia capon, fried snails, and sloe-gin—and so on, in threes. The idea was that you eat nearly all you can of them, and then the waiter takes away the discard and gives you pears to fill on.

"I was sure Solly would be tickled to death with these hands, after the bobtail flushes he'd been eating on the ranch; and I was a little anxious that he should, for I didn't remember his having honoured my efforts with a smile since we left Atascosa City.

"We were in the main dining-room, and there was a fine-dressed crowd there, all talking loud and enjoyable about the two St. Louis topics, the water supply and the colour line. They mix the two subjects so fast that strangers often think they are discussing water-colours; and that has given the old town something of a rep as an art centre. And over in the corner was a fine brass band playing; and now, thinks I, Solly will become conscious of the spiritual oats of life nourishing and exhilarating his system. But *nong, mong frang*.

"He gazed across the table at me. There was four square yards of it, looking like the path of a cyclone that has wandered through a stock-yard, a poultry-farm, a vegetable-garden, and an Irish linen mill. Solly gets up and comes around to me.

"'Luke,' says he, 'I'm pretty hungry after our ride. I thought you said they had some beans here. I'm going out and get something I can eat. You can stay and monkey with this artificial layout of grub if you want to.'

"'Wait a minute,' says I.

"I called the waiter, and slapped 'S. Mills' on the back of the check for thirteen dollars and fifty cents.

"'What do you mean,' says I, 'by serving gentlemen with a lot of truck only suitable for deck-hands on a Mississippi steamboat? We're going out to get something decent to eat.'

"I walked up the street with the unhappy plainsman. He saw a saddle-shop open, and some of the sadness faded from his eyes. We went in, and he ordered and paid for two more saddles—one with a solid silver horn and nails and ornaments and a six-inch border of rhinestones and imitation rubies around the flaps. The other one had to have a gold-mounted horn, quadruple-plated stirrups, and the leather inlaid with silver beadwork wherever it would stand it. Eleven hundred dollars the two cost him.

"Then he goes out and heads toward the river, following his nose. In a little side street, where there was no street and no sidewalks and no houses, he finds what he is looking for. We go into a shanty and sit on high stools among stevedores and boatmen, and eat beans with tin spoons. Yes, sir, beans—beans boiled with salt pork.

"'I kind of thought we'd strike some over this way,' says Solly.

"'Delightful,' says I, 'That stylish hotel grub may appeal to some; but for me, give me the husky *table d'goat*.'

"When we had succumbed to the beans I leads him out of the tarpaulin-steam under a lamp post and pulls out a daily paper with the amusement column folded out.

"'But now, what ho for a merry round of pleasure,' says I. 'Here's one of Hall Caine's shows, and a stock-yard company in "Hamlet," and skating at the Hollowhorn Rink, and Sarah Bernhardt, and the Shapely Syrens Burlesque Company. I should think, now, that the Shapely—'

"But what does this healthy, wealthy, and wise man do but reach his arms up to the second-story windows and gape noisily.

"'Reckon I'll be going to bed,' says he; 'it's about my time. St. Louis is a kind of quiet place, ain't it?'

"'Oh, yes,' says I; 'ever since the railroads ran in here the town's been practically ruined. And the building-and-loan associations and the fair have about killed it. Guess we might as well go to bed. Wait till you see Chicago, though. Shall we get tickets for the Big Breeze to-morrow?'

"'Mought as well,' says Solly. 'I reckon all these towns are about alike.'

"Well, maybe the wise cicerone and personal conductor didn't fall hard in Chicago! Loolooville-on-the-Lake is supposed to have one or two things in it calculated to keep the rural visitor awake after the curfew rings. But not for the grass-fed man of the pampas! I tried him with theatres, rides in automobiles, sails on the lake, champagne suppers, and all those little inventions that hold the simple life in check; but in vain. Solly grew sadder day by day. And I got fearful about my salary, and knew I must play my trump card. So I mentioned New York to him, and informed him that these Western towns were no more than gateways to the great walled city of the whirling dervishes.

"After I bought the tickets I missed Solly. I knew his habits by then; so in a couple of hours I found him in a saddle-shop. They had some new ideas there in the way of trees and girths that had strayed down from the Canadian mounted police; and Solly was so interested that he almost looked reconciled to live. He invested about nine hundred dollars in there.

"At the depot I telegraphed a cigar-store man I knew in New York to meet me at the Twenty-third Street ferry with a list of all the saddle-stores in the city. I wanted to know where to look for Solly when he got lost.

"Now I'll tell you what happened in New York. I says to myself: 'Friend Heherezade, you want to get busy and make Bagdad look pretty to the sad sultan of the sour countenance, or it'll be the bowstring for yours.' But I never had any doubt I could do it.

"I began with him like you'd feed a starving man. I showed him the horse-cars on Broadway and the Staten Island ferry-boats. And then I piled up the sensations on him, but always keeping a lot of warmer ones up my sleeve.

"At the end of the third day he looked like a composite picture of five thousand orphans too late to catch a picnic steamboat, and I was wilting down a collar every two hours wondering how I could please him and whether I was going to get my thou. He went to sleep looking at the Brooklyn Bridge; he disregarded the sky-scrapers above the third story; it took three ushers to wake him up at the liveliest vaudeville in town.

"Once I thought I had him. I nailed a pair of cuffs on him one morning before he was awake; and I dragged him that evening to the palm-cage of one of the biggest hotels in the city—to see the Johnnies and the Alice-sit-by-the-hours. They were out in numerous quantities, with the fat of the land showing in their clothes. While we were looking them over, Solly divested himself of a fearful, rusty kind of laugh—like moving a folding bed with one roller broken. It was his first in two weeks, and it gave me hope.

"'Right you are,' says I. 'They're a funny lot of post-cards, aren't they?'

"'Oh, I wasn't thinking of them dudes and culls on the hoof,' says he. 'I was thinking of the time me and George put sheep-dip in Horsehead Johnson's whisky. I wish I was back in Atascosa City,' says he.

"I felt a cold chill run down my back. 'Me to play and mate in one move,' says I to myself.

"I made Solly promise to stay in the cafe for half an hour and I hiked out in a cab to Lolabelle Delatour's flat on Forty-third Street. I knew her well. She was a chorus-girl in a Broadway musical comedy.

"'Jane,' says I when I found her, 'I've got a friend from Texas here. He's all right, but—well, he carries weight. I'd like to give him a little whirl after the show this evening—bubbles, you know, and a buzz out to a casino for the whitebait and pickled walnuts. Is it a go?'

"'Can he sing?' asks Lolabelle.

"'You know,' says I, 'that I wouldn't take him away from home unless his notes were good. He's got pots of money—bean-pots full of it.'

"'Bring him around after the second act,' says Lolabelle, 'and I'll examine his credentials and securities.'

"So about ten o'clock that evening I led Solly to Miss Delatour's dressing-room, and her maid let us in. In ten minutes in comes Lolabelle, fresh from the stage, looking stunning in the costume she wears when she steps from the ranks of the lady grenadiers and says to the king, 'Welcome to our May-day revels.' And you can bet it wasn't the way she spoke the lines that got her the part.

"As soon as Solly saw her he got up and walked straight out through the stage entrance into the street. I followed him. Lolabelle wasn't paying my salary. I wondered whether anybody was.

"'Luke,' says Solly, outside, 'that was an awful mistake. We must have got into the lady's private room. I hope I'm gentleman enough to do anything possible in the way of apologies. Do you reckon she'd ever forgive us?'

"'She may forget it,' says I. 'Of course it was a mistake. Let's go find some beans.'

"That's the way it went. But pretty soon afterward Solly failed to show up at dinner-time for several days. I cornered him. He confessed that he had found a restaurant on Third Avenue where they cooked beans in Texas style. I made him take me there. The minute I set foot inside the door I threw up my hands.

"There was a young woman at the desk, and Solly introduced me to her. And then we sat down and had beans.

"Yes, sir, sitting at the desk was the kind of a young woman that can catch any man in the world as easy as lifting a finger. There's a way of doing it. She knew. I saw her working it. She was healthy-looking and plain dressed. She had her hair drawn back from her forehead and face— no curls or frizzes; that's the way she looked. Now I'll tell you the way they work the game; it's simple. When she wants a man, she manages it so that every time he looks at her he finds her looking at him. That's all.

"The next evening Solly was to go to Coney Island with me at seven. At eight o'clock he hadn't showed up. I went out and found a cab. I felt sure there was something wrong.

"'Drive to the Back Home Restaurant on Third Avenue,' says I. 'And if I don't find what I want there, take in these saddle-shops.' I handed him the list.

"'Boss,' says the cabby, 'I et a steak in that restaurant once. If you're real hungry, I advise you to try the saddle-shops first.'

"'I'm a detective,' says I, 'and I don't eat. Hurry up!'

"As soon as I got to the restaurant I felt in the lines of my palms that I should beware of a tall, red, damfool man, and I was going to lose a sum of money.

"Solly wasn't there. Neither was the smooth-haired lady.

"I waited; and in an hour they came in a cab and got out, hand in hand. I asked Solly to step around the corner for a few words. He was grinning clear across his face; but I had not administered the grin.

"'She's the greatest that ever sniffed the breeze,' says he.

"'Congrats,' says I. 'I'd like to have my thousand now, if you please.'

"'Well, Luke,' says he, 'I don't know that I've had such a skyhoodlin' fine time under your tutelage and dispensation. But I'll do the best I can for you—I'll do the best I can,' he repeats. 'Me and Miss Skinner was married an hour ago. We're leaving for Texas in the morning.'

"'Great!' says I. 'Consider yourself covered with rice and Congress gaiters. But don't let's tie so many satin bows on our business relations that we lose sight of 'em. How about my honorarium?'

"'Missis Mills,' says he, 'has taken possession of my money and papers except six bits. I told her what I'd agreed to give you; but she says it's an irreligious and illegal contract, and she won't pay a cent of it. But I ain't going to see you treated unfair,' says he. 'I've got eighty-seven saddles on the ranch what I've bought on this trip; and when I get back I'm going to pick out the best six in the lot and send 'em to you.'"

"And did he?" I asked, when Lucullus ceased talking.

"He did. And they are fit for kings to ride on. The six he sent me must have cost him three thousand dollars. But where is the market for 'em? Who would buy one except one of these rajahs and princes of Asia and Africa? I've got 'em all on the list. I know every tan royal dub and smoked princerino from Mindanao to the Caspian Sea."

"It's a long time between customers," I ventured.

"They're coming faster," said Polk. "Nowadays, when one of the murdering mutts gets civilised enough to abolish suttee and quit using his whiskers for a napkin, he calls himself the Roosevelt of the East, and comes over to investigate our Chautauquas and cocktails. I'll place 'em all yet. Now look here."

From an inside pocket he drew a tightly folded newspaper with much-worn edges, and indicated a paragraph.

"Read that," said the saddler to royalty. The paragraph ran thus:

His Highness Seyyid Feysal bin Turkee, Imam of Muskat, is one of the most progressive and enlightened rulers of the Old World. His stables contain more than a thousand horses of the purest Persian breeds. It is said that this powerful prince contemplates a visit to the United States at an early date.

"There!" said Mr. Polk triumphantly. "My best saddle is as good as sold—the one with turquoises set in the rim of the cantle. Have you three dollars that you could loan me for a short time?"

It happened that I had; and I did.

If this should meet the eye of the Imam of Muskat, may it quicken his whim to visit the land of the free! Otherwise I fear that I shall be longer than a short time separated from my dollars three.

VII

HYGEIA AT THE SOLITO

If you are knowing in the chronicles of the ring you will recall to mind an event in the early 'nineties when, for a minute and sundry odd seconds, a champion and a "would-be" faced each other on the alien side of an international river. So brief a conflict had rarely imposed upon the fair promise of true sport. The reporters made what they could of it, but, divested of padding, the action was sadly fugacious. The champion merely smote his victim, turned his back upon him, remarking, "I know what I done to dat stiff," and extended an arm like a ship's mast for his glove to be removed.

Which accounts for a trainload of extremely disgusted gentlemen in an uproar of fancy vests and neck-wear being spilled from their pullmans in San Antonio in the early morning following the fight. Which also partly accounts for the unhappy predicament in which "Cricket" McGuire found himself as he tumbled from his car and sat upon the depot platform, torn by a spasm of that hollow, racking cough so familiar to San Antonian ears. At that time, in the uncertain light of dawn, that way passed Curtis Raidler, the Nueces County cattleman—may his shadow never measure under six foot two.

The cattleman, out this early to catch the south-bound for his ranch station, stopped at the side of the distressed patron of sport, and spoke in the kindly drawl of his ilk and region, "Got it pretty bad, bud?"

"Cricket" McGuire, ex-feather-weight prizefighter, tout, jockey, follower of the "ponies," all-round sport, and manipulator of the gum balls and walnut shells, looked up pugnaciously at the imputation cast by "bud."

"G'wan," he rasped, "telegraph pole. I didn't ring for yer."

Another paroxysm wrung him, and he leaned limply against a convenient baggage truck. Raidler waited patiently, glancing around at the white hats, short overcoats, and big cigars thronging the platform. "You're from the No'th, ain't you, bud?" he asked when the other was partially recovered. "Come down to see the fight?"

"Fight!" snapped McGuire. "Puss-in-the-corner! 'Twas a hypodermic injection. Handed him just one like a squirt of dope, and he's asleep, and no tanbark needed in front of his residence. Fight!" He rattled a bit, coughed, and went on, hardly addressing the cattleman, but rather for the relief of voicing his troubles. "No more dead sure t'ings for me. But Rus Sage himself would have snatched at it. Five to one dat de boy from Cork wouldn't stay t'ree rounds is what I invested in. Put my last cent on, and could already smell the sawdust in dat all-night joint of Jimmy Delaney's on T'irty-seventh Street I was goin' to buy. And den—say, telegraph pole, what a gazaboo a guy is to put his whole roll on one turn of the gaboozlum!"

"You're plenty right," said the big cattleman; "more 'specially when you lose. Son, you get up and light out for a hotel. You got a mighty bad cough. Had it long?"

"Lungs," said McGuire comprehensively. "I got it. The croaker says I'll come to time for six months longer—maybe a year if I hold my gait. I wanted to settle down and take care of myself. Dat's why I speculated on dat five to one perhaps. I had a t'ousand iron dollars saved up. If I winned I was goin' to buy Delaney's cafe. Who'd a t'ought dat stiff would take a nap in de foist round—say?"

"It's a hard deal," commented Raidler, looking down at the diminutive form of McGuire crumpled against the truck. "But you go to a hotel and rest. There's the Menger and the Maverick, and—"

"And the Fi'th Av'noo, and the Waldorf-Astoria," mimicked McGuire. "Told you I went broke. I'm on de bum proper. I've got one dime left. Maybe a trip to Europe or a sail in me private yacht would fix me up—pa-per!"

He flung his dime at a newsboy, got his *Express*, propped his back against the truck, and was at once rapt in the account of his Waterloo, as expanded by the ingenious press.

Curtis Raidler interrogated an enormous gold watch, and laid his hand on McGuire's shoulder.

"Come on, bud," he said. "We got three minutes to catch the train."

Sarcasm seemed to be McGuire's vein.

"You ain't seen me cash in any chips or call a turn since I told you I was broke, a minute ago, have you? Friend, chase yourself away."

"You're going down to my ranch," said the cattleman, "and stay till you get well. Six months'll fix you good as new." He lifted McGuire with one hand, and half-dragged him in the direction of the train.

"What about the money?" said McGuire, struggling weakly to escape.

"Money for what?" asked Raidler, puzzled. They eyed each other, not understanding, for they touched only as at the gear of bevelled cog-wheels—at right angles, and moving upon different axes.

Passengers on the south-bound saw them seated together, and wondered at the conflux of two such antipodes. McGuire was five feet one, with a countenance belonging to either Yokohama or Dublin. Bright-beady of eye, bony of cheek and jaw, scarred, toughened, broken and reknit, indestructible, grisly, gladiatorial as a hornet, he was a type neither new nor unfamiliar. Raidler was the product of a different soil. Six feet two in height, miles broad, and no deeper than a crystal brook, he represented the union of the West and South. Few accurate pictures of his kind have been made, for art galleries are so small and the mutoscope is as yet unknown in Texas. After all, the only possible medium of portrayal of Raidler's kind would be the fresco—something high and simple and cool and unframed.

They were rolling southward on the International. The timber was huddling into little, dense green motts at rare distances before the inundation of the downright, vert prairies. This was the land of the ranches; the domain of the kings of the kine.

McGuire sat, collapsed into his corner of the seat, receiving with acid suspicion the conversation of the cattleman. What was the "game" of this big "geezer" who was carrying him off? Altruism would have been McGuire's last guess. "He ain't no farmer," thought the captive, "and he ain't no con man, for sure. W'at's his lay? You trail in, Cricket, and see how many cards he draws. You're up against it, anyhow. You got a nickel and gallopin' consumption, and you better lay low. Lay low and see w'at's his game."

At Rincon, a hundred miles from San Antonio, they left the train for a buckboard which was waiting there for Raidler. In this they travelled the thirty miles between the station and their destination. If anything could, this drive should have stirred the acrimonious McGuire to a sense of his ransom. They sped upon velvety wheels across an exhilarant savanna. The pair of Spanish ponies struck a nimble, tireless trot, which gait they occasionally relieved by a wild, untrammelled gallop. The air was wine and seltzer, perfumed, as they absorbed it, with the delicate redolence of prairie flowers. The road perished, and the buckboard swam the uncharted billows of the grass itself, steered by the practised hand of Raidler, to whom each tiny distant mott of trees was a signboard, each convolution of the low hills a voucher of course and distance. But

McGuire reclined upon his spine, seeing nothing but a desert, and receiving the cattleman's advances with sullen distrust. "W'at's he up to?" was the burden of his thoughts; "w'at kind of a gold brick has the big guy got to sell?" McGuire was only applying the measure of the streets he had walked to a range bounded by the horizon and the fourth dimension.

A week before, while riding the prairies, Raidler had come upon a sick and weakling calf deserted and bawling. Without dismounting he had reached and slung the distressed bossy across his saddle, and dropped it at the ranch for the boys to attend to. It was impossible for McGuire to know or comprehend that, in the eyes of the cattleman, his case and that of the calf were identical in interest and demand upon his assistance. A creature was ill and helpless; he had the power to render aid—these were the only postulates required for the cattleman to act. They formed his system of logic and the most of his creed. McGuire was the seventh invalid whom Raidler had picked up thus casually in San Antonio, where so many thousand go for the ozone that is said to linger about its contracted streets. Five of them had been guests of Solito Ranch until they had been able to leave, cured or better, and exhausting the vocabulary of tearful gratitude. One came too late, but rested very comfortably, at last, under a ratama tree in the garden.

So, then, it was no surprise to the ranchhold when the buckboard spun to the door, and Raidler took up his debile *protege* like a handful of rags and set him down upon the gallery.

McGuire looked upon things strange to him. The ranch-house was the best in the country. It was built of brick hauled one hundred miles by wagon, but it was of but one story, and its four rooms were completely encircled by a mud floor "gallery." The miscellaneous setting of horses, dogs, saddles, wagons, guns, and cow-punchers' paraphernalia oppressed the metropolitan eyes of the wrecked sportsman.

"Well, here we are at home," said Raidler, cheeringly.

"It's a h—l of a looking place," said McGuire promptly, as he rolled upon the gallery floor in a fit of coughing.

"We'll try to make it comfortable for you, buddy," said the cattleman gently. "It ain't fine inside; but it's the outdoors, anyway, that'll do you the most good. This'll be your room, in here. Anything we got, you ask for it."

He led McGuire into the east room. The floor was bare and clean. White curtains waved in the gulf breeze through the open windows.

A big willow rocker, two straight chairs, a long table covered with newspapers, pipes, tobacco, spurs, and cartridges stood in the centre. Some well-mounted heads of deer and one of an enormous black javeli projected from the walls. A wide, cool cot-bed stood in a corner. Nueces County people regarded this guest chamber as fit for a prince. McGuire showed his eyeteeth at it. He took out his nickel and spun it up to the ceiling.

"T'ought I was lyin' about the money, did ye? Well, you can frisk me if you wanter. Dat's the last simoleon in the treasury. Who's goin' to pay?"

The cattleman's clear grey eyes looked steadily from under his grizzly brows into the huckleberry optics of his guest. After a little he said simply, and not ungraciously, "I'll be much obliged to you, son, if you won't mention money any more. Once was quite a plenty. Folks I ask to my ranch don't have to pay anything, and they very scarcely ever offers it. Supper'll be ready in half an hour. There's water in the pitcher, and some, cooler, to drink, in that red jar hanging on the gallery."

"Where's the bell?" asked McGuire, looking about.

"Bell for what?"

"Bell to ring for things. I can't—see here," he exploded in a sudden, weak fury, "I never asked you to bring me here. I never held you up for a cent. I never gave you a hard-luck story till you asked me. Here I am fifty miles from a bellboy or a cocktail. I'm sick. I can't hustle. Gee! but I'm up against it!" McGuire fell upon the cot and sobbed shiveringly.

Raidler went to the door and called. A slender, bright-complexioned Mexican youth about twenty came quickly. Raidler spoke to him in Spanish.

"Ylario, it is in my mind that I promised you the position of *vaquero* on the San Carlos range at the fall *rodeo*."

"*Si, senor*, such was your goodness."

"Listen. This *senorito* is my friend. He is very sick. Place yourself at his side. Attend to his wants at all times. Have much patience and care with him. And when he is well, or—and when he is well, instead of *vaquero* I will make you *mayordomo* of the Rancho de las Piedras. *Esta bueno?*"

"*Si, si—mil gracias, senor.*" Ylario tried to kneel upon the floor in his gratitude, but the cattleman kicked at him benevolently, growling, "None of your opery-house antics, now."

Ten minutes later Ylario came from McGuire's room and stood before Raidler.

"The little *senor*," he announced, "presents his compliments" (Raidler credited Ylario with the preliminary) "and desires some pounded ice, one hot bath, one gin feez-z, that the windows be all closed, toast, one shave, one Newyorkheral', cigarettes, and to send one telegram."

Raidler took a quart bottle of whisky from his medicine cabinet. "Here, take him this," he said.

Thus was instituted the reign of terror at the Solito Ranch. For a few weeks McGuire blustered and boasted and swaggered before the cow-punchers who rode in for miles around to see this latest importation of Raidler's. He was an absolutely new experience to them. He explained to them all the intricate points of sparring and the tricks of training and defence. He opened to their minds' view all the indecorous life of a tagger after professional sports. His jargon of slang was a continuous joy and surprise to them. His gestures, his strange poses, his frank ribaldry of tongue and principle fascinated them. He was like a being from a new world.

Strange to say, this new world he had entered did not exist to him. He was an utter egoist of bricks and mortar. He had dropped out, he felt, into open space for a time, and all it contained was an audience for his reminiscences. Neither the limitless freedom of the prairie days nor the grand hush of the close-drawn, spangled nights touched him. All the hues of Aurora could not win him from the pink pages of a sporting journal. "Get something for nothing," was his mission in life; "Thirty-seventh" Street was his goal.

Nearly two months after his arrival he began to complain that he felt worse. It was then that he became the ranch's incubus, its harpy, its Old Man of the Sea. He shut himself in his room like some venomous kobold or flibbertigibbet, whining, complaining, cursing, accusing. The keynote of his plaint was that he had been inveigled into a gehenna against his will; that he was dying of neglect and lack of comforts. With all his dire protestations of increasing illness, to the eye of others he remained unchanged. His currant-like eyes were as bright and diabolic as ever; his voice was as rasping; his callous face, with the skin drawn tense as a drum-head, had no flesh to lose. A flush on his prominent cheek bones each afternoon hinted that a clinical thermometer might have revealed a symptom, and percussion might have established the fact that McGuire was breathing with only one lung, but his appearance remained the same.

In constant attendance upon him was Ylario, whom the coming reward of the *mayordomo*ship must have greatly stimulated, for McGuire chained him to a bitter existence. The air—the man's only chance for life—he commanded to be kept out by closed windows and drawn curtains. The room was always blue and foul with cigarette smoke; whosoever entered it must sit, suffocating, and listen to the imp's interminable gasconade concerning his scandalous career.

The oddest thing of all was the relation existing between McGuire and his benefactor. The attitude of the invalid toward the cattleman was something like that of a peevish, perverse child toward an indulgent parent. When Raidler would leave the ranch McGuire would fall into a fit of malevolent, silent sullenness. When he returned, he would be met by a string of violent and stinging reproaches. Raidler's attitude toward his charge was quite inexplicable in its way. The cattleman seemed actually to assume and feel the character assigned to him by McGuire's intemperate accusations—the character of tyrant and guilty oppressor. He seemed to have adopted the responsibility of the fellow's condition, and he always met his tirades with a pacific, patient, and even remorseful kindness that never altered.

One day Raidler said to him, "Try more air, son. You can have the buckboard and a driver every day if you'll go. Try a week or two in one of the cow camps. I'll fix you up plumb comfortable. The ground, and the air next to it—them's the things to cure you. I knowed a man from Philadelphy, sicker than you are, got lost on the Guadalupe, and slept on the bare grass in sheep camps for two weeks. Well, sir, it started him getting well, which he done. Close to the ground—that's where the medicine in the air stays. Try a little hossback riding now. There's a gentle pony—"

"What've I done to yer?" screamed McGuire. "Did I ever doublecross yer? Did I ask you to bring me here? Drive me out to your camps if you wanter; or stick a knife in me and save trouble. Ride! I can't lift my feet. I couldn't sidestep a jab from a five-year-old kid. That's what your d—d ranch has done for me. There's nothing to eat, nothing to see, and nobody to talk to but a lot of Reubens who don't know a punching bag from a lobster salad."

"It's a lonesome place, for certain," apologised Raidler abashedly. "We got plenty, but it's rough enough. Anything you think of you want, the boys'll ride up and fetch it down for you."

It was Chad Murchison, a cow-puncher from the Circle Bar outfit, who first suggested that McGuire's illness was fraudulent. Chad had brought a basket of grapes for him thirty miles, and four out of his way,

O. HENRY

tied to his saddle-horn. After remaining in the smoke-tainted room for a while, he emerged and bluntly confided his suspicions to Raidler.

"His arm," said Chad, "is harder'n a diamond. He interduced me to what he called a shore-perplexus punch, and 'twas like being kicked twice by a mustang. He's playin' it low down on you, Curt. He ain't no sicker'n I am. I hate to say it, but the runt's workin' you for range and shelter."

The cattleman's ingenuous mind refused to entertain Chad's view of the case, and when, later, he came to apply the test, doubt entered not into his motives.

One day, about noon, two men drove up to the ranch, alighted, hitched, and came in to dinner; standing and general invitations being the custom of the country. One of them was a great San Antonio doctor, whose costly services had been engaged by a wealthy cowman who had been laid low by an accidental bullet. He was now being driven back to the station to take the train back to town. After dinner Raidler took him aside, pushed a twenty-dollar bill against his hand, and said:

"Doc, there's a young chap in that room I guess has got a bad case of consumption. I'd like for you to look him over and see just how bad he is, and if we can do anything for him."

"How much was that dinner I just ate, Mr. Raidler?" said the doctor bluffly, looking over his spectacles. Raidler returned the money to his pocket. The doctor immediately entered McGuire's room, and the cattleman seated himself upon a heap of saddles on the gallery, ready to reproach himself in the event the verdict should be unfavourable.

In ten minutes the doctor came briskly out. "Your man," he said promptly, "is as sound as a new dollar. His lungs are better than mine. Respiration, temperature, and pulse normal. Chest expansion four inches. Not a sign of weakness anywhere. Of course I didn't examine for the bacillus, but it isn't there. You can put my name to the diagnosis. Even cigarettes and a vilely close room haven't hurt him. Coughs, does he? Well, you tell him it isn't necessary. You asked if there is anything we could do for him. Well, I advise you to set him digging post-holes or breaking mustangs. There's our team ready. Good-day, sir." And like a puff of wholesome, blustery wind the doctor was off.

Raidler reached out and plucked a leaf from a mesquite bush by the railing, and began chewing it thoughtfully.

The branding season was at hand, and the next morning Ross Hargis, foreman of the outfit, was mustering his force of some twenty-five men at the ranch, ready to start for the San Carlos range, where the work was to begin. By six o'clock the horses were all saddled, the grub wagon ready, and the cow-punchers were swinging themselves upon their mounts, when Raidler bade them wait. A boy was bringing up an extra pony, bridled and saddled, to the gate. Raidler walked to McGuire's room and threw open the door. McGuire was lying on his cot, not yet dressed, smoking.

"Get up," said the cattleman, and his voice was clear and brassy, like a bugle.

"How's that?" asked McGuire, a little startled.

"Get up and dress. I can stand a rattlesnake, but I hate a liar. Do I have to tell you again?" He caught McGuire by the neck and stood him on the floor.

"Say, friend," cried McGuire wildly, "are you bug-house? I'm sick—see? I'll croak if I got to hustle. What've I done to yer?"—he began his chronic whine—"I never asked yer to—"

"Put on your clothes," called Raidler in a rising tone.

Swearing, stumbling, shivering, keeping his amazed, shining eyes upon the now menacing form of the aroused cattleman, McGuire managed to tumble into his clothes. Then Raidler took him by the collar and shoved him out and across the yard to the extra pony hitched at the gate. The cow-punchers lolled in their saddles, open-mouthed.

"Take this man," said Raidler to Ross Hargis, "and put him to work. Make him work hard, sleep hard, and eat hard. You boys know I done what I could for him, and he was welcome. Yesterday the best doctor in San Antone examined him, and says he's got the lungs of a burro and the constitution of a steer. You know what to do with him, Ross."

Ross Hargis only smiled grimly.

"Aw," said McGuire, looking intently at Raidler, with a peculiar expression upon his face, "the croaker said I was all right, did he? Said I was fakin', did he? You put him onto me. You t'ought I wasn't sick. You said I was a liar. Say, friend, I talked rough, I know, but I didn't mean most of it. If you felt like I did—aw! I forgot—I ain't sick, the croaker says. Well, friend, now I'll go work for yer. Here's where you play even."

He sprang into the saddle easily as a bird, got the quirt from the horn, and gave his pony a slash with it. "Cricket," who once brought in Good Boy by a neck at Hawthorne—and a 10 to 1 shot—had his foot in the stirrups again.

McGuire led the cavalcade as they dashed away for San Carlos, and the cow-punchers gave a yell of applause as they closed in behind his dust.

But in less than a mile he had lagged to the rear, and was last man when they struck the patch of high chaparral below the horse pens. Behind a clump of this he drew rein, and held a handkerchief to his mouth. He took it away drenched with bright, arterial blood, and threw it carefully into a clump of prickly pear. Then he slashed with his quirt again, gasped "G'wan" to his astonished pony, and galloped after the gang.

That night Raidler received a message from his old home in Alabama. There had been a death in the family; an estate was to divide, and they called for him to come. Daylight found him in the buckboard, skimming the prairies for the station. It was two months before he returned. When he arrived at the ranch house he found it well-nigh deserted save for Ylario, who acted as a kind of steward during his absence. Little by little the youth made him acquainted with the work done while he was away. The branding camp, he was informed, was still doing business. On account of many severe storms the cattle had been badly scattered, and the branding had been accomplished but slowly. The camp was now in the valley of the Guadalupe, twenty miles away.

"By the way," said Raidler, suddenly remembering, "that fellow I sent along with them—McGuire—is he working yet?"

"I do not know," said Ylario. "Mans from the camp come verree few times to the ranch. So plentee work with the leetle calves. They no say. Oh, I think that fellow McGuire he dead much time ago."

"Dead!" said Raidler. "What you talking about?"

"Verree sick fellow, McGuire," replied Ylario, with a shrug of his shoulder. "I theenk he no live one, two month when he go away."

"Shucks!" said Raidler. "He humbugged you, too, did he? The doctor examined him and said he was sound as a mesquite knot."

"That doctor," said Ylario, smiling, "he tell you so? That doctor no see McGuire."

"Talk up," ordered Raidler. "What the devil do you mean?"

"McGuire," continued the boy tranquilly, "he getting drink water outside when that doctor come in room. That doctor take me and pound me all over here with his fingers"—putting his hand to his chest—"I not know for what. He put his ear here and here and here, and listen—I not know for what. He put little glass stick in my mouth. He feel my arm here. He make me count like whisper—so—twenty, *treinta*, *cuarenta*. Who knows," concluded Ylario, with a deprecating spread of his hands, "for what that doctor do those verree droll and such-like things?"

"What horses are up?" asked Raidler shortly.

"Paisano is grazing out behind the little corral, *senor*."

"Saddle him for me at once."

Within a very few minutes the cattleman was mounted and away. Paisano, well named after that ungainly but swift-running bird, struck into his long lope that ate up the ground like a strip of macaroni. In two hours and a quarter Raidler, from a gentle swell, saw the branding camp by a water hole in the Guadalupe. Sick with expectancy of the news he feared, he rode up, dismounted, and dropped Paisano's reins. So gentle was his heart that at that moment he would have pleaded guilty to the murder of McGuire.

The only being in the camp was the cook, who was just arranging the hunks of barbecued beef, and distributing the tin coffee cups for supper. Raidler evaded a direct question concerning the one subject in his mind.

"Everything all right in camp, Pete?" he managed to inquire.

"So, so," said Pete, conservatively. "Grub give out twice. Wind scattered the cattle, and we've had to rake the brush for forty mile. I need a new coffee-pot. And the mosquitos is some more hellish than common."

"The boys—all well?"

Pete was no optimist. Besides, inquiries concerning the health of cow-punchers were not only superfluous, but bordered on flaccidity. It was not like the boss to make them.

"What's left of 'em don't miss no calls to grub," the cook conceded.

"What's left of 'em?" repeated Raidler in a husky voice. Mechanically he began to look around for McGuire's grave. He had in his mind a white slab such as he had seen in the Alabama church-yard. But immediately he knew that was foolish.

"Sure," said Pete; "what's left. Cow camps change in two months. Some's gone."

Raidler nerved himself.

"That—chap—I sent along—McGuire—did—he—"

"Say," interrupted Pete, rising with a chunk of corn bread in each hand, "that was a dirty shame, sending that poor, sick kid to a cow camp. A doctor that couldn't tell he was graveyard meat ought to be skinned with a cinch buckle. Game as he was, too—it's a scandal among snakes—lemme tell you what he done. First night in camp the boys started to initiate him in the leather breeches degree. Ross Hargis busted him one swipe with his chaparreras, and what do you reckon the poor child did? Got up, the little skeeter, and licked Ross. Licked Ross Hargis. Licked him good. Hit him plenty and everywhere and hard. Ross'd just get up and pick out a fresh place to lay down on agin.

"Then that McGuire goes off there and lays down with his head in the grass and bleeds. A hem'ridge they calls it. He lays there eighteen hours by the watch, and they can't budge him. Then Ross Hargis, who loves any man who can lick him, goes to work and damns the doctors from Greenland to Poland Chiny; and him and Green Branch Johnson they gets McGuire into a tent, and spells each other feedin' him chopped raw meat and whisky.

"But it looks like the kid ain't got no appetite to git well, for they misses him from the tent in the night and finds him rootin' in the grass, and likewise a drizzle fallin'. 'G'wan,' he says, 'lemme go and die like I wanter. He said I was a liar and a fake and I was playin' sick. Lemme alone.'

"Two weeks," went on the cook, "he laid around, not noticin' nobody, and then—"

A sudden thunder filled the air, and a score of galloping centaurs crashed through the brush into camp.

"Illustrious rattlesnakes!" exclaimed Pete, springing all ways at once; "here's the boys come, and I'm an assassinated man if supper ain't ready in three minutes."

But Raidler saw only one thing. A little, brown-faced, grinning chap, springing from his saddle in the full light of the fire. McGuire was not like that, and yet—

In another instant the cattleman was holding him by the hand and shoulder.

"Son, son, how goes it?" was all he found to say.

"Close to the ground, says you," shouted McGuire, crunching Raidler's fingers in a grip of steel; "and dat's where I found it—healt' and strengt', and tumbled to what a cheap skate I been actin'. T'anks fer kickin' me out, old man. And—say! de joke's on dat croaker, ain't it? I looked t'rough the window and see him playin' tag on dat Dago kid's solar plexus."

"You son of a tinker," growled the cattleman, "whyn't you talk up and say the doctor never examined you?"

"Ah—g'wan!" said McGuire, with a flash of his old asperity, "nobody can't bluff me. You never ast me. You made your spiel, and you t'rowed me out, and I let it go at dat. And, say, friend, dis chasin' cows is outer sight. Dis is de whitest bunch of sports I ever travelled with. You'll let me stay, won't yer, old man?"

Raidler looked wonderingly toward Ross Hargis.

"That cussed little runt," remarked Ross tenderly, "is the Jo-dartin'est hustler—and the hardest hitter in anybody's cow camp."

VIII

An Afternoon Miracle

A t the United States end of an international river bridge, four armed rangers sweltered in a little 'dobe hut, keeping a fairly faithful espionage upon the lagging trail of passengers from the Mexican side.

Bud Dawson, proprietor of the Top Notch Saloon, had, on the evening previous, violently ejected from his premises one Leandro Garcia, for alleged violation of the Top Notch code of behaviour. Garcia had mentioned twenty-four hours as a limit, by which time he would call and collect a painful indemnity for personal satisfaction.

This Mexican, although a tremendous braggart, was thoroughly courageous, and each side of the river respected him for one of these attributes. He and a following of similar bravoes were addicted to the pastime of retrieving towns from stagnation.

The day designated by Garcia for retribution was to be further signalised on the American side by a cattlemen's convention, a bull fight, and an old settlers' barbecue and picnic. Knowing the avenger to be a man of his word, and believing it prudent to court peace while three such gently social relaxations were in progress, Captain McNulty, of the ranger company stationed there, detailed his lieutenant and three men for duty at the end of the bridge. Their instructions were to prevent the invasion of Garcia, either alone or attended by his gang.

Travel was slight that sultry afternoon, and the rangers swore gently, and mopped their brows in their convenient but close quarters. For an hour no one had crossed save an old woman enveloped in a brown wrapper and a black mantilla, driving before her a burro loaded with kindling wood tied in small bundles for peddling. Then three shots were fired down the street, the sound coming clear and snappy through the still air.

The four rangers quickened from sprawling, symbolic figures of indolence to alert life, but only one rose to his feet. Three turned their eyes beseechingly but hopelessly upon the fourth, who had gotten nimbly up and was buckling his cartridge-belt around him. The three knew that Lieutenant Bob Buckley, in command, would allow no man of them the privilege of investigating a row when he himself might go.

The agile, broad-chested lieutenant, without a change of expression in his smooth, yellow-brown, melancholy face, shot the belt strap through the guard of the buckle, hefted his sixes in their holsters as a belle gives the finishing touches to her toilette, caught up his Winchester, and dived for the door. There he paused long enough to caution his comrades to maintain their watch upon the bridge, and then plunged into the broiling highway.

The three relapsed into resigned inertia and plaintive comment.

"I've heard of fellows," grumbled Broncho Leathers, "what was wedded to danger, but if Bob Buckley ain't committed bigamy with trouble, I'm a son of a gun."

"Peculiarness of Bob is," inserted the Nueces Kid, "he ain't had proper trainin'. He never learned how to git skeered. Now, a man ought to be skeered enough when he tackles a fuss to hanker after readin' his name on the list of survivors, anyway."

"Buckley," commented Ranger No. 3, who was a misguided Eastern man, burdened with an education, "scraps in such a solemn manner that I have been led to doubt its spontaneity. I'm not quite onto his system, but he fights, like Tybalt, by the book of arithmetic."

"I never heard," mentioned Broncho, "about any of Dibble's ways of mixin' scrappin' and cipherin'."

"Triggernometry?" suggested the Nueces infant.

"That's rather better than I hoped from you," nodded the Easterner, approvingly. "The other meaning is that Buckley never goes into a fight without giving away weight. He seems to dread taking the slightest advantage. That's quite close to foolhardiness when you are dealing with horse-thieves and fence-cutters who would ambush you any night, and shoot you in the back if they could. Buckley's too full of sand. He'll play Horatius and hold the bridge once too often some day."

"I'm on there," drawled the Kid; "I mind that bridge gang in the reader. Me, I go instructed for the other chap—Spurious Somebody—the one that fought and pulled his freight, to fight 'em on some other day."

"Anyway," summed up Broncho, "Bob's about the gamest man I ever see along the Rio Bravo. Great Sam Houston! If she gets any hotter she'll sizzle!" Broncho whacked at a scorpion with his four-pound Stetson felt, and the three watchers relapsed into comfortless silence.

How well Bob Buckley had kept his secret, since these men, for two years his side comrades in countless border raids and dangers, thus spake of him, not knowing that he was the most arrant physical coward in all that Rio Bravo country! Neither his friends nor his enemies had suspected him of aught else than the finest courage. It was purely a physical cowardice, and only by an extreme, grim effort of will had he forced his craven body to do the bravest deeds. Scourging himself always, as a monk whips his besetting sin, Buckley threw himself with apparent recklessness into every danger, with the hope of some day ridding himself of the despised affliction. But each successive test brought no relief, and the ranger's face, by nature adapted to cheerfulness and good-humour, became set to the guise of gloomy melancholy. Thus, while the frontier admired his deeds, and his prowess was celebrated in print and by word of mouth in many camp-fires in the valley of the Bravo, his heart was sick within him. Only himself knew of the horrible tightening of the chest, the dry mouth, the weakening of the spine, the agony of the strung nerves—the never-failing symptoms of his shameful malady.

One mere boy in his company was wont to enter a fray with a leg perched flippantly about the horn of his saddle, a cigarette hanging from his lips, which emitted smoke and original slogans of clever invention. Buckley would have given a year's pay to attain that devil-may-care method. Once the debonair youth said to him: "Buck, you go into a scrap like it was a funeral. Not," he added, with a complimentary wave of his tin cup, "but what it generally is."

Buckley's conscience was of the New England order with Western adjustments, and he continued to get his rebellious body into as many difficulties as possible; wherefore, on that sultry afternoon he chose to drive his own protesting limbs to investigation of that sudden alarm that had startled the peace and dignity of the State.

Two squares down the street stood the Top Notch Saloon. Here Buckley came upon signs of recent upheaval. A few curious spectators pressed about its front entrance, grinding beneath their heels the fragments of a plate-glass window. Inside, Buckley found Bud Dawson utterly ignoring a bullet wound in his shoulder, while he feelingly wept at having to explain why he failed to drop the "blamed masquerooter," who shot him. At the entrance of the ranger Bud turned appealingly to him for confirmation of the devastation he might have dealt.

"You know, Buck, I'd 'a' plum got him, first rattle, if I'd thought a minute. Come in a-masque-rootin', playin' female till he got the drop, and turned loose. I never reached for a gun, thinkin' it was sure

Chihuahua Betty, or Mrs. Atwater, or anyhow one of the Mayfield girls comin' a-gunnin', which they might, liable as not. I never thought of that blamed Garcia until—"

"Garcia!" snapped Buckley. "How did he get over here?"

Bud's bartender took the ranger by the arm and led him to the side door. There stood a patient grey burro cropping the grass along the gutter, with a load of kindling wood tied across its back. On the ground lay a black shawl and a voluminous brown dress.

"Masquerootin' in them things," called Bud, still resisting attempted ministrations to his wounds. "Thought he was a lady till he gave a yell and winged me."

"He went down this side street," said the bartender. "He was alone, and he'll hide out till night when his gang comes over. You ought to find him in that Mexican lay-out below the depot. He's got a girl down there—Pancha Sales."

"How was he armed?" asked Buckley.

"Two pearl-handled sixes, and a knife."

"Keep this for me, Billy," said the ranger, handing over his Winchester. Quixotic, perhaps, but it was Bob Buckley's way. Another man—and a braver one—might have raised a posse to accompany him. It was Buckley's rule to discard all preliminary advantage.

The Mexican had left behind him a wake of closed doors and an empty street, but now people were beginning to emerge from their places of refuge with assumed unconsciousness of anything having happened. Many citizens who knew the ranger pointed out to him with alacrity the course of Garcia's retreat.

As Buckley swung along upon the trail he felt the beginning of the suffocating constriction about his throat, the cold sweat under the brim of his hat, the old, shameful, dreaded sinking of his heart as it went down, down, down in his bosom.

THE MORNING TRAIN OF THE Mexican Central had that day been three hours late, thus failing to connect with the I. & G.N. on the other side of the river. Passengers for *Los Estados Unidos* grumblingly sought entertainment in the little swaggering mongrel town of two nations, for, until the morrow, no other train would come to rescue them. Grumblingly, because two days later would begin the great fair and races in San Antone. Consider that at that time San Antone was the hub of the wheel of Fortune, and the names of its spokes were Cattle,

Wool, Faro, Running Horses, and Ozone. In those times cattlemen played at crack-loo on the sidewalks with double-eagles, and gentlemen backed their conception of the fortuitous card with stacks limited in height only by the interference of gravity. Wherefore, thither journeyed the sowers and the reapers—they who stampeded the dollars, and they who rounded them up. Especially did the caterers to the amusement of the people haste to San Antone. Two greatest shows on earth were already there, and dozens of smallest ones were on the way.

On a side track near the mean little 'dobe depot stood a private car, left there by the Mexican train that morning and doomed by an ineffectual schedule to ignobly await, amid squalid surroundings, connection with the next day's regular.

The car had been once a common day-coach, but those who had sat in it and gringed to the conductor's hat-band slips would never have recognised it in its transformation. Paint and gilding and certain domestic touches had liberated it from any suspicion of public servitude. The whitest of lace curtains judiciously screened its windows. From its fore end drooped in the torrid air the flag of Mexico. From its rear projected the Stars and Stripes and a busy stovepipe, the latter reinforcing in its suggestion of culinary comforts the general suggestion of privacy and ease. The beholder's eye, regarding its gorgeous sides, found interest to culminate in a single name in gold and blue letters extending almost its entire length—a single name, the audacious privilege of royalty and genius. Doubly, then, was this arrogant nomenclature here justified; for the name was that of "Alvarita, Queen of the Serpent Tribe." This, her car, was back from a triumphant tour of the principal Mexican cities, and now headed for San Antonio, where, according to promissory advertisement, she would exhibit her "Marvellous Dominion and Fearless Control over Deadly and Venomous Serpents, Handling them with Ease as they Coil and Hiss to the Terror of Thousands of Tongue-tied Tremblers!"

One hundred in the shade kept the vicinity somewhat depeopled. This quarter of the town was a ragged edge; its denizens the bubbling froth of five nations; its architecture tent, *jacal*, and 'dobe; its distractions the hurdy-gurdy and the informal contribution to the sudden stranger's store of experience. Beyond this dishonourable fringe upon the old town's jowl rose a dense mass of trees, surmounting and filling a little hollow. Through this bickered a small stream that perished down the sheer and disconcerting side of the great canon of the Rio Bravo del Norte.

In this sordid spot was condemned to remain for certain hours the impotent transport of the Queen of the Serpent Tribe.

The front door of the car was open. Its forward end was curtained off into a small reception-room. Here the admiring and propitiatory reporters were wont to sit and transpose the music of Senorita Alvarita's talk into the more florid key of the press. A picture of Abraham Lincoln hung against a wall; one of a cluster of school-girls grouped upon stone steps was in another place; a third was Easter lilies in a blood-red frame. A neat carpet was under foot. A pitcher, sweating cold drops, and a glass stood on a fragile stand. In a willow rocker, reading a newspaper, sat Alvarita.

Spanish, you would say; Andalusian, or, better still, Basque; that compound, like the diamond, of darkness and fire. Hair, the shade of purple grapes viewed at midnight. Eyes, long, dusky, and disquieting with their untroubled directness of gaze. Face, haughty and bold, touched with a pretty insolence that gave it life. To hasten conviction of her charm, but glance at the stacks of handbills in the corner, green, and yellow, and white. Upon them you see an incompetent presentment of the senorita in her professional garb and pose. Irresistible, in black lace and yellow ribbons, she faces you; a blue racer is spiralled upon each bare arm; coiled twice about her waist and once about her neck, his horrid head close to hers, you perceive Kuku, the great eleven-foot Asian python.

A hand drew aside the curtain that partitioned the car, and a middle-aged, faded woman holding a knife and a half-peeled potato looked in and said:

"Alviry, are you right busy?"

"I'm reading the home paper, ma. What do you think! that pale, tow-headed Matilda Price got the most votes in the *News* for the prettiest girl in Gallipo—*lees*."

"Shush! She wouldn't of done it if *you'd* been home, Alviry. Lord knows, I hope we'll be there before fall's over. I'm tired gallopin' round the world playin' we are dagoes, and givin' snake shows. But that ain't what I wanted to say. That there biggest snake's gone again. I've looked all over the car and can't find him. He must have been gone an hour. I remember hearin' somethin' rustlin' along the floor, but I thought it was you."

"Oh, blame that old rascal!" exclaimed the Queen, throwing down her paper. "This is the third time he's got away. George never *will* fasten down the lid to his box properly. I do believe he's *afraid* of Kuku. Now I've got to go hunt him."

"Better hurry; somebody might hurt him."

The Queen's teeth showed in a gleaming, contemptuous smile. "No danger. When they see Kuku outside they simply scoot away and buy bromides. There's a crick over between here and the river. That old scamp'd swap his skin any time for a drink of running water. I guess I'll find him there, all right."

A few minutes later Alvarita stopped upon the forward platform, ready for her quest. Her handsome black skirt was shaped to the most recent proclamation of fashion. Her spotless shirt-waist gladdened the eye in that desert of sunshine, a swelling oasis, cool and fresh. A man's split-straw hat sat firmly on her coiled, abundant hair. Beneath her serene, round, impudent chin a man's four-in-hand tie was jauntily knotted about a man's high, stiff collar. A parasol she carried, of white silk, and its fringe was lace, yellowly genuine.

I will grant Gallipolis as to her costume, but firmly to Seville or Valladolid I am held by her eyes; castanets, balconies, mantillas, serenades, ambuscades, escapades—all these their dark depths guaranteed.

"Ain't you afraid to go out alone, Alviry?" queried the Queen-mother anxiously. "There's so many rough people about. Mebbe you'd better—"

"I never saw anything I was afraid of yet, ma. 'Specially people. And men in particular. Don't you fret. I'll trot along back as soon as I find that runaway scamp."

The dust lay thick upon the bare ground near the tracks. Alvarita's eye soon discovered the serrated trail of the escaped python. It led across the depot grounds and away down a smaller street in the direction of the little canon, as predicted by her. A stillness and lack of excitement in the neighbourhood encouraged the hope that, as yet, the inhabitants were unaware that so formidable a guest traversed their highways. The heat had driven them indoors, whence outdrifted occasional shrill laughs, or the depressing whine of a maltreated concertina. In the shade a few Mexican children, like vivified stolid idols in clay, stared from their play, vision-struck and silent, as Alvarita came and went. Here and there a woman peeped from a door and stood dumb, reduced to silence by the aspect of the white silk parasol.

A hundred yards and the limits of the town were passed, scattered chaparral succeeding, and then a noble grove, overflowing the bijou canon. Through this a small bright stream meandered. Park-like it was, with a kind of cockney ruralness further endorsed by the waste papers and rifled tins of picnickers. Up this stream, and down it, among its pseudo-sylvan glades and depressions, wandered the bright and unruffled Alvarita. Once she saw evidence of the recreant reptile's progress in his distinctive trail across a spread of fine sand in the arroyo. The living water was bound to lure him; he could not be far away.

So sure was she of his immediate proximity that she perched herself to idle for a time in the curve of a great creeper that looped down from a giant water-elm. To reach this she climbed from the pathway a little distance up the side of a steep and rugged incline. Around her chaparral grew thick and high. A late-blooming ratama tree dispensed from its yellow petals a sweet and persistent odour. Adown the ravine rustled a seductive wind, melancholy with the taste of sodden, fallen leaves.

Alvarita removed her hat, and undoing the oppressive convolutions of her hair, began to slowly arrange it in two long, dusky plaits.

From the obscure depths of a thick clump of evergreen shrubs five feet away, two small jewel-bright eyes were steadfastly regarding her. Coiled there lay Kuku, the great python; Kuku, the magnificent, he of the plated muzzle, the grooved lips, the eleven-foot stretch of elegantly and brilliantly mottled skin. The great python was viewing his mistress without a sound or motion to disclose his presence. Perhaps the splendid truant forefelt his capture, but, screened by the foliage, thought to prolong the delight of his escapade. What pleasure it was, after the hot and dusty car, to lie thus, smelling the running water, and feeling the agreeable roughness of the earth and stones against his body! Soon, very soon the Queen would find him, and he, powerless as a worm in her audacious hands, would be returned to the dark chest in the narrow house that ran on wheels.

Alvarita heard a sudden crunching of the gravel below her. Turning her head she saw a big, swarthy Mexican, with a daring and evil expression, contemplating her with an ominous, dull eye.

"What do you want?" she asked as sharply as five hairpins between her lips would permit, continuing to plait her hair, and looking him over with placid contempt. The Mexican continued to gaze at her, and showed his teeth in a white, jagged smile.

"I no hurt-y you, Senorita," he said.

"You bet you won't," answered the Queen, shaking back one finished, massive plait. "But don't you think you'd better move on?"

O. HENRY

"Not hurt-y you—no. But maybeso take one *beso*—one li'l kees, you call him."

The man smiled again, and set his foot to ascend the slope. Alvarita leaned swiftly and picked up a stone the size of a cocoanut.

"Vamoose, quick," she ordered peremptorily, "you *coon!*"

The red of insult burned through the Mexican's dark skin.

"*Hidalgo, Yo!*" he shot between his fangs. "I am not neg-r-ro! *Diabla bonita*, for that you shall pay me."

He made two quick upward steps this time, but the stone, hurled by no weak arm, struck him square in the chest. He staggered back to the footway, swerved half around, and met another sight that drove all thoughts of the girl from his head. She turned her eyes to see what had diverted his interest. A man with red-brown, curling hair and a melancholy, sunburned, smooth-shaven face was coming up the path, twenty yards away. Around the Mexican's waist was buckled a pistol belt with two empty holsters. He had laid aside his sixes—possibly in the *jacal* of the fair Pancha—and had forgotten them when the passing of the fairer Alvarita had enticed him to her trail. His hands now flew instinctively to the holsters, but finding the weapons gone, he spread his fingers outward with the eloquent, abjuring, deprecating Latin gesture, and stood like a rock. Seeing his plight, the newcomer unbuckled his own belt containing two revolvers, threw it upon the ground, and continued to advance.

"Splendid!" murmured Alvarita, with flashing eyes.

As Bob Buckley, according to the mad code of bravery that his sensitive conscience imposed upon his cowardly nerves, abandoned his guns and closed in upon his enemy, the old, inevitable nausea of abject fear wrung him. His breath whistled through his constricted air passages. His feet seemed like lumps of lead. His mouth was dry as dust. His heart, congested with blood, hurt his ribs as it thumped against them. The hot June day turned to moist November. And still he advanced, spurred by a mandatory pride that strained its uttermost against his weakling flesh.

The distance between the two men slowly lessened. The Mexican stood, immovable, waiting. When scarce five yards separated them a little shower of loosened gravel rattled down from above to the ranger's feet. He glanced upward with instinctive caution. A pair of dark eyes, brilliantly soft, and fierily tender, encountered and held his own. The most fearful heart and the boldest one in all the Rio Bravo country exchanged a silent and inscrutable communication. Alvarita, still seated within her vine, leaned forward above the breast-high chaparral. One hand was laid across her bosom. One great dark braid curved forward over her shoulder. Her lips were parted; her face was lit with what seemed but wonder—great and absolute wonder. Her eyes lingered upon Buckley's. Let no one ask or presume to tell through what subtle medium the miracle was performed. As by a lightning flash two clouds will accomplish counterpoise and compensation of electric surcharge, so on that eyeglance the man received his complement of manhood, and the maid conceded what enriched her womanly grace by its loss.

The Mexican, suddenly stirring, ventilated his attitude of apathetic waiting by conjuring swiftly from his bootleg a long knife. Buckley cast aside his hat, and laughed once aloud, like a happy school-boy at a frolic. Then, empty-handed, he sprang nimbly, and Garcia met him without default.

So soon was the engagement ended that disappointment imposed upon the ranger's warlike ecstasy. Instead of dealing the traditional downward stroke, the Mexican lunged straight with his knife. Buckley took the precarious chance, and caught his wrist, fair and firm. Then he delivered the good Saxon knock-out blow—always so pathetically disastrous to the fistless Latin races—and Garcia was down and out, with his head under a clump of prickly pears. The ranger looked up again to the Queen of the Serpents.

Alvarita scrambled down to the path.

"I'm mighty glad I happened along when I did," said the ranger.

"He—he frightened me so!" cooed Alvarita.

They did not hear the long, low hiss of the python under the shrubs. Wiliest of the beasts, no doubt he was expressing the humiliation he felt at having so long dwelt in subjection to this trembling and colouring mistress of his whom he had deemed so strong and potent and fearsome.

Then came galloping to the spot the civic authorities; and to them the ranger awarded the prostrate disturber of the peace, whom they bore away limply across the saddle of one of their mounts. But Buckley and Alvarita lingered.

Slowly, slowly they walked. The ranger regained his belt of weapons. With a fine timidity she begged the indulgence of fingering the great .45's, with little "Ohs" and "Ahs" of new-born, delicious shyness.

The *canoncito* was growing dusky. Beyond its terminus in the river bluff they could see the outer world yet suffused with the waning glory of sunset.

A scream—a piercing scream of fright from Alvarita. Back she cowered, and the ready, protecting arm of Buckley formed her refuge. What terror so dire as to thus beset the close of the reign of the never-before-daunted Queen?

Across the path there crawled a *caterpillar*—a horrid, fuzzy, two-inch caterpillar! Truly, Kuku, thou went avenged. Thus abdicated the Queen of the Serpent Tribe—*viva la reina*!

IX

The Higher Abdication

C urly the tramp sidled toward the free-lunch counter. He caught a fleeting glance from the bartender's eye, and stood still, trying to look like a business man who had just dined at the Menger and was waiting for a friend who had promised to pick him up in his motor car. Curly's histrionic powers were equal to the impersonation; but his make-up was wanting.

The bartender rounded the bar in a casual way, looking up at the ceiling as though he was pondering some intricate problem of kalsomining, and then fell upon Curly so suddenly that the roadster had no excuses ready. Irresistibly, but so composedly that it seemed almost absendmindedness on his part, the dispenser of drinks pushed Curly to the swinging doors and kicked him out, with a nonchalance that almost amounted to sadness. That was the way of the Southwest.

Curly arose from the gutter leisurely. He felt no anger or resentment toward his ejector. Fifteen years of tramphood spent out of the twenty-two years of his life had hardened the fibres of his spirit. The slings and arrows of outrageous fortune fell blunted from the buckler of his armoured pride. With especial resignation did he suffer contumely and injury at the hands of bartenders. Naturally, they were his enemies; and unnaturally, they were often his friends. He had to take his chances with them. But he had not yet learned to estimate these cool, languid, Southwestern knights of the bungstarter, who had the manners of an Earl of Pawtucket, and who, when they disapproved of your presence, moved you with the silence and despatch of a chess automaton advancing a pawn.

Curly stood for a few moments in the narrow, mesquite-paved street. San Antonio puzzled and disturbed him. Three days he had been a non-paying guest of the town, having dropped off there from a box car of an I. & G.N. freight, because Greaser Johnny had told him in Des Moines that the Alamo City was manna fallen, gathered, cooked, and served free with cream and sugar. Curly had found the tip partly a good one. There was hospitality in plenty of a careless, liberal, irregular sort. But the town itself was a weight upon his spirits after his experience with the rushing, business-like, systematised cities of the North and East. Here he was often flung a dollar, but too frequently a good-natured kick would follow it. Once a band of hilarious cowboys had roped him on Military Plaza and dragged him across the black soil until no respectable rag-bag would have stood sponsor for his clothes. The winding, doubling streets, leading nowhere, bewildered him. And then there was a little river, crooked as a pot-hook, that crawled through the middle of the town, crossed by a hundred little bridges so nearly alike that they got on Curly's nerves. And the last bartender wore a number nine shoe.

The saloon stood on a corner. The hour was eight o'clock. Homefarers and outgoers jostled Curly on the narrow stone sidewalk. Between the buildings to his left he looked down a cleft that proclaimed itself another thoroughfare. The alley was dark except for one patch of light. Where there was light there were sure to be human beings. Where there were human beings after nightfall in San Antonio there might be food, and there was sure to be drink. So Curly headed for the light.

The illumination came from Schwegel's Cafe. On the sidewalk in front of it Curly picked up an old envelope. It might have contained a check for a million. It was empty; but the wanderer read the address, "Mr. Otto Schwegel," and the name of the town and State. The postmark was Detroit.

Curly entered the saloon. And now in the light it could be perceived that he bore the stamp of many years of vagabondage. He had none of the tidiness of the calculating and shrewd professional tramp. His wardrobe represented the cast-off specimens of half a dozen fashions and eras. Two factories had combined their efforts in providing shoes for his feet. As you gazed at him there passed through your mind vague impressions of mummies, wax figures, Russian exiles, and men lost on desert islands. His face was covered almost to his eyes with a curly brown beard that he kept trimmed short with a pocket-knife, and that had furnished him with his *nom de route*. Light-blue eyes, full of sullenness, fear, cunning, impudence, and fawning, witnessed the stress that had been laid upon his soul.

The saloon was small, and in its atmosphere the odours of meat and drink struggled for the ascendancy. The pig and the cabbage wrestled with hydrogen and oxygen. Behind the bar Schwegel laboured with an assistant whose epidermal pores showed no signs of being obstructed. Hot weinerwurst and sauerkraut were being served to purchasers of beer. Curly shuffled to the end of the bar, coughed hollowly, and told Schwegel that he was a Detroit cabinet-maker out of a job.

It followed as the night the day that he got his schooner and lunch.

"Was you acquainted maybe with Heinrich Strauss in Detroit?" asked Schwegel.

"Did I know Heinrich Strauss?" repeated Curly, affectionately. "Why, say, 'Bo, I wish I had a dollar for every game of pinochle me and Heine has played on Sunday afternoons."

More beer and a second plate of steaming food was set before the diplomat. And then Curly, knowing to a fluid-drachm how far a "con" game would go, shuffled out into the unpromising street.

And now he began to perceive the inconveniences of this stony Southern town. There was none of the outdoor gaiety and brilliancy and music that provided distraction even to the poorest in the cities of the North. Here, even so early, the gloomy, rock-walled houses were closed and barred against the murky dampness of the night. The streets were mere fissures through which flowed grey wreaths of river mist. As he walked he heard laughter and the chink of coin and chips behind darkened windows, and music coming from every chink of wood and stone. But the diversions were selfish; the day of popular pastimes had not yet come to San Antonio.

But at length Curly, as he strayed, turned the sharp angle of another lost street and came upon a rollicking band of stockmen from the outlying ranches celebrating in the open in front of an ancient wooden hotel. One great roisterer from the sheep country who had just instigated a movement toward the bar, swept Curly in like a stray goat with the rest of his flock. The princes of kine and wool hailed him as a new zoological discovery, and uproariously strove to preserve him in the diluted alcohol of their compliments and regards.

An hour afterward Curly staggered from the hotel barroom dismissed by his fickle friends, whose interest in him had subsided as quickly as it had risen. Full—stoked with alcoholic fuel and cargoed with food, the only question remaining to disturb him was that of shelter and bed.

A drizzling, cold Texas rain had begun to fall—an endless, lazy, unintermittent downfall that lowered the spirits of men and raised a reluctant steam from the warm stones of the streets and houses. Thus comes the "norther" dousing gentle spring and amiable autumn with the chilling salutes and adieux of coming and departing winter.

Curly followed his nose down the first tortuous street into which his irresponsible feet conducted him. At the lower end of it, on the bank of the serpentine stream, he perceived an open gate in a cemented rock wall. Inside he saw camp fires and a row of low wooden sheds built against three sides of the enclosing wall. He entered the enclosure. Under the sheds many horses were champing at their oats and corn. Many wagons and buckboards stood about with their teams' harness thrown carelessly upon the shafts and doubletrees. Curly recognised the place as a wagon-yard, such as is provided by merchants for their out-of-town friends and customers. No one was in sight. No doubt the drivers of those wagons were scattered about the town "seeing the elephant and hearing the owl." In their haste to become patrons of the town's dispensaries of mirth and good cheer the last ones to depart must have left the great wooden gate swinging open.

Curly had satisfied the hunger of an anaconda and the thirst of a camel, so he was neither in the mood nor the condition of an explorer. He zigzagged his way to the first wagon that his eyesight distinguished in the semi-darkness under the shed. It was a two-horse wagon with a top of white canvas. The wagon was half filled with loose piles of wool sacks, two or three great bundles of grey blankets, and a number of bales, bundles, and boxes. A reasoning eye would have estimated the load at once as ranch supplies, bound on the morrow for some outlying hacienda. But to the drowsy intelligence of Curly they represented only warmth and softness and protection against the cold humidity of the night. After several unlucky efforts, at last he conquered gravity so far as to climb over a wheel and pitch forward upon the best and warmest bed he had fallen upon in many a day. Then he became instinctively a burrowing animal, and dug his way like a prairie-dog down among the sacks and blankets, hiding himself from the cold air as snug and safe as a bear in his den. For three nights sleep had visited Curly only in broken and shivering doses. So now, when Morpheus condescended to pay him a call, Curly got such a strangle hold on the mythological old gentleman that it was a wonder that anyone else in the whole world got a wink of sleep that night.

SIX COWPUNCHERS OF THE CIBOLO Ranch were waiting around the door of the ranch store. Their ponies cropped grass near by, tied in the Texas fashion—which is not tied at all. Their bridle reins had been dropped to the earth, which is a more effectual way of securing them (such is the power of habit and imagination) than you could devise out of a half-inch rope and a live-oak tree.

These guardians of the cow lounged about, each with a brown cigarette paper in his hand, and gently but unceasingly cursed Sam Revell, the storekeeper. Sam stood in the door, snapping the red elastic bands on his pink madras shirtsleeves and looking down affectionately at the only pair of tan shoes within a forty-mile radius. His offence had been serious, and he was divided between humble apology and admiration for the beauty of his raiment. He had allowed the ranch stock of "smoking" to become exhausted.

"I thought sure there was another case of it under the counter, boys," he explained. "But it happened to be catterdges."

"You've sure got a case of happenedicitis," said Poky Rodgers, fency rider of the Largo Verde *potrero*. "Somebody ought to happen to give you a knock on the head with the butt end of a quirt. I've rode in nine miles for some tobacco; and it don't appear natural and seemly that you ought to be allowed to live."

"The boys was smokin' cut plug and dried mesquite leaves mixed when I left," sighed Mustang Taylor, horse wrangler of the Three Elm camp. "They'll be lookin' for me back by nine. They'll be settin' up, with their papers ready to roll a whiff of the real thing before bedtime. And I've got to tell 'em that this pink-eyed, sheep-headed, sulphur-footed, shirt-waisted son of a calico broncho, Sam Revell, hasn't got no tobacco on hand."

Gregorio Falcon, Mexican vaquero and best thrower of the rope on the Cibolo, pushed his heavy, silver-embroidered straw sombrero back upon his thicket of jet black curls, and scraped the bottoms of his pockets for a few crumbs of the precious weed.

"Ah, Don Samuel," he said, reproachfully, but with his touch of Castilian manners, "escuse me. Dthey say dthe jackrabbeet and dthe sheep have dthe most leetle *sesos*—how you call dthem—brain-es? Ah don't believe dthat, Don Samuel—escuse me. Ah dthink people w'at don't keep esmokin' tobacco, dthey—bot you weel escuse me, Don Samuel."

"Now, what's the use of chewin' the rag, boys," said the untroubled Sam, stooping over to rub the toes of his shoes with a red-and-yellow handkerchief. "Ranse took the order for some more smokin' to San Antone with him Tuesday. Pancho rode Ranse's hoss back yesterday; and Ranse is goin' to drive the wagon back himself. There wa'n't much of a load—just some woolsacks and blankets and nails and canned peaches and a few things we was out of. I look for Ranse to roll in to-day sure. He's an early starter and a hell-to-split driver, and he ought to be here not far from sundown."

"What plugs is he drivin'?" asked Mustang Taylor, with a smack of hope in his tones.

"The buckboard greys," said Sam.

"I'll wait a spell, then," said the wrangler. "Them plugs eat up a trail like a road-runner swallowin' a whip snake. And you may bust me open a can of greengage plums, Sam, while I'm waitin' for somethin' better."

"Open me some yellow clings," ordered Poky Rodgers. "I'll wait, too."

The tobaccoless punchers arranged themselves comfortably on the steps of the store. Inside Sam chopped open with a hatchet the tops of the cans of fruit.

The store, a big, white wooden building like a barn, stood fifty yards from the ranch-house. Beyond it were the horse corrals; and still farther the wool sheds and the brush-topped shearing pens—for the Rancho Cibolo raised both cattle and sheep. Behind the store, at a little distance, were the grass-thatched *jacals* of the Mexicans who bestowed their allegiance upon the Cibolo.

The ranch-house was composed of four large rooms, with plastered adobe walls, and a two-room wooden ell. A twenty-feet-wide "gallery" circumvented the structure. It was set in a grove of immense live-oaks and water-elms near a lake—a long, not very wide, and tremendously deep lake in which at nightfall, great gars leaped to the surface and plunged with the noise of hippopotamuses frolicking at their bath. From the trees hung garlands and massive pendants of the melancholy grey moss of the South. Indeed, the Cibolo ranch-house seemed more of the South than of the West. It looked as if old "Kiowa" Truesdell might have brought it with him from the lowlands of Mississippi when he came to Texas with his rifle in the hollow of his arm in '55.

But, though he did not bring the family mansion, Truesdell did bring something in the way of a family inheritance that was more lasting than brick or stone. He brought one end of the Truesdell-Curtis family feud. And when a Curtis bought the Rancho de los Olmos, sixteen miles from the Cibolo, there were lively times on the pear flats and in the chaparral thickets off the Southwest. In those days Truesdell cleaned the brush of many a wolf and tiger cat and Mexican lion; and one or two Curtises fell heirs to notches on his rifle stock. Also he buried a brother with a Curtis bullet in him on the bank of the lake at Cibolo. And then the Kiowa Indians made their last raid upon the ranches between the Frio and the Rio Grande, and Truesdell at the head of his rangers rid the earth of them to the last brave, earning his sobriquet. Then came prosperity in the form of waxing herds and broadening lands. And then old age and bitterness, when he sat, with his great mane of hair as white as the Spanish-dagger blossoms and his fierce, pale-blue eyes, on the shaded gallery at Cibolo, growling like the pumas that he had slain. He snapped his fingers at old age; the bitter taste to life did not come from that. The cup that stuck at his lips was that his only son Ransom wanted to marry a Curtis, the last youthful survivor of the other end of the feud.

For a while the only sounds to be heard at the store were the rattling of the tin spoons and the gurgling intake of the juicy fruits by the cowpunchers, the stamping of the grazing ponies, and the singing of a doleful song by Sam as he contentedly brushed his stiff auburn hair for the twentieth time that day before a crinkly mirror.

From the door of the store could be seen the irregular, sloping stretch of prairie to the south, with its reaches of light-green, billowy mesquite flats in the lower places, and its rises crowned with nearly black masses of short chaparral. Through the mesquite flat wound the ranch road that, five miles away, flowed into the old government trail to San Antonio. The sun was so low that the gentlest elevation cast its grey shadow miles into the green-gold sea of sunshine.

That evening ears were quicker than eyes.

The Mexican held up a tawny finger to still the scraping of tin against tin.

"One waggeen," said he, "cross dthe Arroyo Hondo. Ah hear dthe wheel. Verree rockee place, dthe Hondo."

"You've got good ears, Gregorio," said Mustang Taylor. "I never heard nothin' but the song-bird in the bush and the zephyr skallyhootin' across the peaceful dell."

In ten minutes Taylor remarked: "I see the dust of a wagon risin' right above the fur end of the flat."

"You have verree good eyes, senor," said Gregorio, smiling.

Two miles away they saw a faint cloud dimming the green ripples of the mesquites. In twenty minutes they heard the clatter of the horses' hoofs: in five minutes more the grey plugs dashed out of the thicket, whickering for oats and drawing the light wagon behind them like a toy.

From the *jacals* came a cry of: "El Amo! El Amo!" Four Mexican youths raced to unharness the greys. The cowpunchers gave a yell of greeting and delight.

Ranse Truesdell, driving, threw the reins to the ground and laughed.

"It's under the wagon sheet, boys," he said. "I know what you're waiting for. If Sam lets it run out again we'll use those yellow shoes of his for a target. There's two cases. Pull 'em out and light up. I know you all want a smoke."

After striking dry country Ranse had removed the wagon sheet from the bows and thrown it over the goods in the wagon. Six pair of hasty hands dragged it off and grabbled beneath the sacks and blankets for the cases of tobacco.

Long Collins, tobacco messenger from the San Gabriel outfit, who rode with the longest stirrups west of the Mississippi, delved with an arm like the tongue of a wagon. He caught something harder than a blanket and pulled out a fearful thing—a shapeless, muddy bunch of leather tied together with wire and twine. From its ragged end, like the head and claws of a disturbed turtle, protruded human toes.

"Who-ee!" yelled Long Collins. "Ranse, are you a-packin' around of corpuses? Here's a—howlin' grasshoppers!"

Up from his long slumber popped Curly, like some vile worm from its burrow. He clawed his way out and sat blinking like a disreputable, drunken owl. His face was as bluish-red and puffed and seamed and cross-lined as the cheapest round steak of the butcher. His eyes were swollen slits; his nose a pickled beet; his hair would have made the wildest thatch of a Jack-in-the-box look like the satin poll of a Cleo de Merode. The rest of him was scarecrow done to the life.

Ranse jumped down from his seat and looked at his strange cargo with wide-open eyes.

"Here, you maverick, what are you doing in my wagon? How did you get in there?"

The punchers gathered around in delight. For the time they had forgotten tobacco.

Curly looked around him slowly in every direction. He snarled like a Scotch terrier through his ragged beard.

"Where is this?" he rasped through his parched throat. "It's a damn farm in an old field. What'd you bring me here for—say? Did I say I wanted to come here? What are you Reubs rubberin' at—hey? G'wan or I'll punch some of yer faces."

"Drag him out, Collins," said Ranse.

Curly took a slide and felt the ground rise up and collide with his shoulder blades. He got up and sat on the steps of the store shivering from outraged nerves, hugging his knees and sneering. Taylor lifted out a case of tobacco and wrenched off its top. Six cigarettes began to glow, bringing peace and forgiveness to Sam.

"How'd you come in my wagon?" repeated Ranse, this time in a voice that drew a reply.

Curly recognised the tone. He had heard it used by freight brakemen and large persons in blue carrying clubs.

"Me?" he growled. "Oh, was you talkin' to me? Why, I was on my way to the Menger, but my valet had forgot to pack my pyjamas. So I crawled into that wagon in the wagon-yard—see? I never told you to bring me out to this bloomin' farm—see?"

"What is it, Mustang?" asked Poky Rodgers, almost forgetting to smoke in his ecstasy. "What do it live on?"

"It's a galliwampus, Poky," said Mustang. "It's the thing that hollers 'willi-walloo' up in ellum trees in the low grounds of nights. I don't know if it bites."

"No, it ain't, Mustang," volunteered Long Collins. "Them galliwampuses has fins on their backs, and eighteen toes. This here is a hicklesnifter. It lives under the ground and eats cherries. Don't stand so close to it. It wipes out villages with one stroke of its prehensile tail."

Sam, the cosmopolite, who called bartenders in San Antone by their first name, stood in the door. He was a better zoologist.

"Well, ain't that a Willie for your whiskers?" he commented. "Where'd you dig up the hobo, Ranse? Goin' to make an auditorium for inbreviates out of the ranch?"

"Say," said Curly, from whose panoplied breast all shafts of wit fell blunted. "Any of you kiddin' guys got a drink on you? Have your fun. Say, I've been hittin' the stuff till I don't know straight up."

He turned to Ranse. "Say, you shanghaied me on your d—d old prairie schooner—did I tell you to drive me to a farm? I want a drink. I'm goin' all to little pieces. What's doin'?"

Ranse saw that the tramp's nerves were racking him. He despatched one of the Mexican boys to the ranch-house for a glass of whisky. Curly gulped it down; and into his eyes came a brief, grateful glow—as human as the expression in the eye of a faithful setter dog.

"Thanky, boss," he said, quietly.

"You're thirty miles from a railroad, and forty miles from a saloon," said Ranse.

Curly fell back weakly against the steps.

"Since you are here," continued the ranchman, "come along with me. We can't turn you out on the prairie. A rabbit might tear you to pieces."

He conducted Curly to a large shed where the ranch vehicles were kept. There he spread out a canvas cot and brought blankets.

"I don't suppose you can sleep," said Ranse, "since you've been pounding your ear for twenty-four hours. But you can camp here till morning. I'll have Pedro fetch you up some grub."

"Sleep!" said Curly. "I can sleep a week. Say, sport, have you got a coffin nail on you?"

FIFTY MILES HAD RANSOM TRUESDELL driven that day. And yet this is what he did.

Old "Kiowa" Truesdell sat in his great wicker chair reading by the light of an immense oil lamp. Ranse laid a bundle of newspapers fresh from town at his elbow.

"Back, Ranse?" said the old man, looking up.

"Son," old "Kiowa" continued, "I've been thinking all day about a certain matter that we have talked about. I want you to tell me again. I've lived for you. I've fought wolves and Indians and worse white men to protect you. You never had any mother that you can remember. I've taught you to shoot straight, ride hard, and live clean. Later on I've worked to pile up dollars that'll be yours. You'll be a rich man, Ranse, when my chunk goes out. I've made you. I've licked you into shape like a leopard cat licks its cubs. You don't belong to yourself—you've got to be a Truesdell first. Now, is there to be any more nonsense about this Curtis girl?"

"I'll tell you once more," said Ranse, slowly. "As I am a Truesdell and as you are my father, I'll never marry a Curtis."

"Good boy," said old "Kiowa." "You'd better go get some supper."

Ranse went to the kitchen at the rear of the house. Pedro, the Mexican cook, sprang up to bring the food he was keeping warm in the stove.

"Just a cup of coffee, Pedro," he said, and drank it standing. And then:

"There's a tramp on a cot in the wagon-shed. Take him something to eat. Better make it enough for two."

Ranse walked out toward the *jacals*. A boy came running.

"Manuel, can you catch Vaminos, in the little pasture, for me?"

"Why not, senor? I saw him near the *puerta* but two hours past. He bears a drag-rope."

"Get him and saddle him as quick as you can."

"*Prontito, senor.*"

Soon, mounted on Vaminos, Ranse leaned in the saddle, pressed with his knees, and galloped eastward past the store, where sat Sam trying his guitar in the moonlight.

Vaminos shall have a word—Vaminos the good dun horse. The Mexicans, who have a hundred names for the colours of a horse, called him *gruyo*. He was a mouse-coloured, slate-coloured, flea-bitten roan-dun, if you can conceive it. Down his back from his mane to his tail went a line of black. He would live forever; and surveyors have not laid off as many miles in the world as he could travel in a day.

Eight miles east of the Cibolo ranch-house Ranse loosened the pressure of his knees, and Vaminos stopped under a big ratama tree. The yellow ratama blossoms showered fragrance that would have undone the roses of France. The moon made the earth a great concave bowl with a crystal sky for a lid. In a glade five jack-rabbits leaped and played together like kittens. Eight miles farther east shone a faint star that appeared to have dropped below the horizon. Night riders, who often steered their course by it, knew it to be the light in the Rancho de los Olmos.

In ten minutes Yenna Curtis galloped to the tree on her sorrel pony Dancer. The two leaned and clasped hands heartily.

"I ought to have ridden nearer your home," said Ranse. "But you never will let me."

Yenna laughed. And in the soft light you could see her strong white teeth and fearless eyes. No sentimentality there, in spite of the moonlight, the odour of the ratamas, and the admirable figure of Ranse Truesdell, the lover. But she was there, eight miles from her home, to meet him.

"How often have I told you, Ranse," she said, "that I am your half-way girl? Always half-way."

"Well?" said Ranse, with a question in his tones.

"I did," said Yenna, with almost a sigh. "I told him after dinner when I thought he would be in a good humour. Did you ever wake up a lion, Ranse, with the mistaken idea that he would be a kitten? He almost tore the ranch to pieces. It's all up. I love my daddy, Ranse, and I'm afraid—I'm afraid of him too. He ordered me to promise that I'd never marry a Truesdell. I promised. That's all. What luck did you have?"

"The same," said Ranse, slowly. "I promised him that his son would never marry a Curtis. Somehow I couldn't go against him. He's mighty old. I'm sorry, Yenna."

The girl leaned in her saddle and laid one hand on Ranse's, on the horn of his saddle.

"I never thought I'd like you better for giving me up," she said ardently, "but I do. I must ride back now, Ranse. I slipped out of the house and saddled Dancer myself. Good-night, neighbour."

"Good-night," said Ranse. "Ride carefully over them badger holes."

They wheeled and rode away in opposite directions. Yenna turned in her saddle and called clearly:

"Don't forget I'm your half-way girl, Ranse."

"Damn all family feuds and inherited scraps," muttered Ranse vindictively to the breeze as he rode back to the Cibolo.

Ranse turned his horse into the small pasture and went to his own room. He opened the lowest drawer of an old bureau to get out the packet of letters that Yenna had written him one summer when she had gone to Mississippi for a visit. The drawer stuck, and he yanked at it savagely—as a man will. It came out of the bureau, and bruised both his shins—as a drawer will. An old, folded yellow letter without an envelope fell from somewhere—probably from where it had lodged in one of the upper drawers. Ranse took it to the lamp and read it curiously.

Then he took his hat and walked to one of the Mexican *jacals*.

"Tia Juana," he said, "I would like to talk with you a while."

An old, old Mexican woman, white-haired and wonderfully wrinkled, rose from a stool.

"Sit down," said Ranse, removing his hat and taking the one chair in the *jacal*. "Who am I, Tia Juana?" he asked, speaking Spanish.

"Don Ransom, our good friend and employer. Why do you ask?" answered the old woman wonderingly.

"Tia Juana, who am I?" he repeated, with his stern eyes looking into hers.

A frightened look came in the old woman's face. She fumbled with her black shawl.

"Who am I, Tia Juana?" said Ranse once more.

"Thirty-two years I have lived on the Rancho Cibolo," said Tia Juana. "I thought to be buried under the coma mott beyond the garden before these things should be known. Close the door, Don Ransom, and I will speak. I see in your face that you know."

An hour Ranse spent behind Tia Juana's closed door. As he was on his way back to the house Curly called to him from the wagon-shed.

The tramp sat on his cot, swinging his feet and smoking.

"Say, sport," he grumbled. "This is no way to treat a man after kidnappin' him. I went up to the store and borrowed a razor from that fresh guy and had a shave. But that ain't all a man needs. Say—can't you loosen up for about three fingers more of that booze? I never asked you to bring me to your d—d farm."

"Stand up out here in the light," said Ranse, looking at him closely.

Curly got up sullenly and took a step or two.

His face, now shaven smooth, seemed transformed. His hair had been combed, and it fell back from the right side of his forehead with a peculiar wave. The moonlight charitably softened the ravages of drink; and his aquiline, well-shaped nose and small, square cleft chin almost gave distinction to his looks.

Ranse sat on the foot of the cot and looked at him curiously.

"Where did you come from—have you got any home or folks anywhere?"

"Me? Why, I'm a dook," said Curly. "I'm Sir Reginald—oh, cheese it. No; I don't know anything about my ancestors. I've been a tramp ever since I can remember. Say, old pal, are you going to set 'em up again to-night or not?"

"You answer my questions and maybe I will. How did you come to be a tramp?"

"Me?" answered Curly. "Why, I adopted that profession when I was an infant. Case of had to. First thing I can remember, I belonged to a big, lazy hobo called Beefsteak Charley. He sent me around to houses to beg. I wasn't hardly big enough to reach the latch of a gate."

"Did he ever tell you how he got you?" asked Ranse.

"Once when he was sober he said he bought me for an old six-shooter and six bits from a band of drunken Mexican sheep-shearers. But what's the diff? That's all I know."

"All right," said Ranse. "I reckon you're a maverick for certain. I'm going to put the Rancho Cibolo brand on you. I'll start you to work in one of the camps to-morrow."

"Work!" sniffed Curly, disdainfully. "What do you take me for? Do you think I'd chase cows, and hop-skip-and-jump around after crazy sheep like that pink and yellow guy at the store says these Reubs do? Forget it."

"Oh, you'll like it when you get used to it," said Ranse. "Yes, I'll send you up one more drink by Pedro. I think you'll make a first-class cowpuncher before I get through with you."

"Me?" said Curly. "I pity the cows you set me to chaperon. They can go chase themselves. Don't forget my nightcap, please, boss."

Ranse paid a visit to the store before going to the house. Sam Rivell was taking off his tan shoes regretting and preparing for bed.

"Any of the boys from the San Gabriel camp riding in early in the morning?" asked Ranse.

"Long Collins," said Sam briefly. "For the mail."

"Tell him," said Ranse, "to take that tramp out to camp with him and keep him till I get there."

Curly was sitting on his blankets in the San Gabriel camp cursing talentedly when Ranse Truesdell rode up and dismounted on the next afternoon. The cowpunchers were ignoring the stray. He was grimy with dust and black dirt. His clothes were making their last stand in favour of the conventions.

Ranse went up to Buck Rabb, the camp boss, and spoke briefly.

"He's a plumb buzzard," said Buck. "He won't work, and he's the low-downest passel of inhumanity I ever see. I didn't know what you wanted done with him, Ranse, so I just let him set. That seems to suit him. He's been condemned to death by the boys a dozen times, but I told 'em maybe you was savin' him for the torture."

Ranse took off his coat.

"I've got a hard job before me, Buck, I reckon, but it has to be done. I've got to make a man out of that thing. That's what I've come to camp for."

He went up to Curly.

"Brother," he said, "don't you think if you had a bath it would allow you to take a seat in the company of your fellow-man with less injustice to the atmosphere."

"Run away, farmer," said Curly, sardonically. "Willie will send for nursey when he feels like having his tub."

The *charco*, or water hole, was twelve yards away. Ranse took one of Curly's ankles and dragged him like a sack of potatoes to the brink.

Then with the strength and sleight of a hammer-throw he hurled the offending member of society far into the lake.

Curly crawled out and up the bank spluttering like a porpoise.

Ranse met him with a piece of soap and a coarse towel in his hands.

"Go to the other end of the lake and use this," he said. "Buck will give you some dry clothes at the wagon."

The tramp obeyed without protest. By the time supper was ready he had returned to camp. He was hardly to be recognised in his new shirt and brown duck clothes. Ranse observed him out of the corner of his eye.

"Lordy, I hope he ain't a coward," he was saying to himself. "I hope he won't turn out to be a coward."

His doubts were soon allayed. Curly walked straight to where he stood. His light-blue eyes were blazing.

"Now I'm clean," he said meaningly, "maybe you'll talk to me. Think you've got a picnic here, do you? You clodhoppers think you can run over a man because you know he can't get away. All right. Now, what do you think of that?"

Curly planted a stinging slap against Ranse's left cheek. The print of his hand stood out a dull red against the tan.

Ranse smiled happily.

The cowpunchers talk to this day of the battle that followed.

Somewhere in his restless tour of the cities Curly had acquired the art of self-defence. The ranchman was equipped only with the splendid strength and equilibrium of perfect health and the endurance conferred by decent living. The two attributes nearly matched. There were no formal rounds. At last the fibre of the clean liver prevailed. The last time Curly went down from one of the ranchman's awkward but powerful blows he remained on the grass, but looking up with an unquenched eye.

Ranse went to the water barrel and washed the red from a cut on his chin in the stream from the faucet.

On his face was a grin of satisfaction.

Much benefit might accrue to educators and moralists if they could know the details of the curriculum of reclamation through which Ranse put his waif during the month that he spent in the San Gabriel camp. The ranchman had no fine theories to work out—perhaps his whole stock of pedagogy embraced only a knowledge of horse-breaking and a belief in heredity.

The cowpunchers saw that their boss was trying to make a man out of the strange animal that he had sent among them; and they tacitly organised themselves into a faculty of assistants. But their system was their own.

Curly's first lesson stuck. He became on friendly and then on intimate terms with soap and water. And the thing that pleased Ranse most was that his "subject" held his ground at each successive higher step. But the steps were sometimes far apart.

Once he got at the quart bottle of whisky kept sacredly in the grub tent for rattlesnake bites, and spent sixteen hours on the grass, magnificently drunk. But when he staggered to his feet his first move was to find his soap and towel and start for the *charco*. And once, when a treat came from the ranch in the form of a basket of fresh tomatoes and young onions, Curly devoured the entire consignment before the punchers reached the camp at supper time.

And then the punchers punished him in their own way. For three days they did not speak to him, except to reply to his own questions or remarks. And they spoke with absolute and unfailing politeness. They played tricks on one another; they pounded one another hurtfully and affectionately; they heaped upon one another's heads friendly curses and obloquy; but they were polite to Curly. He saw it, and it stung him as much as Ranse hoped it would.

Then came a night that brought a cold, wet norther. Wilson, the youngest of the outfit, had lain in camp two days, ill with fever. When Joe got up at daylight to begin breakfast he found Curly sitting asleep against a wheel of the grub wagon with only a saddle blanket around him, while Curly's blankets were stretched over Wilson to protect him from the rain and wind.

Three nights after that Curly rolled himself in his blanket and went to sleep. Then the other punchers rose up softly and began to make preparations. Ranse saw Long Collins tie a rope to the horn of a saddle. Others were getting out their six-shooters.

"Boys," said Ranse, "I'm much obliged. I was hoping you would. But I didn't like to ask."

Half a dozen six-shooters began to pop—awful yells rent the air—Long Collins galloped wildly across Curly's bed, dragging the saddle after him. That was merely their way of gently awaking their victim. Then they hazed him for an hour, carefully and ridiculously, after the code of cow camps. Whenever he uttered protest they held him stretched over a roll of blankets and thrashed him woefully with a pair of leather leggings.

And all this meant that Curly had won his spurs, that he was receiving the puncher's accolade. Nevermore would they be polite to him. But he would be their "pardner" and stirrup-brother, foot to foot.

When the fooling was ended all hands made a raid on Joe's big coffee-pot by the fire for a Java nightcap. Ranse watched the new knight carefully to see if he understood and was worthy. Curly limped with his cup of coffee to a log and sat upon it. Long Collins followed and sat by his side. Buck Rabb went and sat at the other. Curly—grinned.

And then Ranse furnished Curly with mounts and saddle and equipment, and turned him over to Buck Rabb, instructing him to finish the job.

Three weeks later Ranse rode from the ranch into Rabb's camp, which was then in Snake Valley. The boys were saddling for the day's ride. He sought out Long Collins among them.

"How about that bronco?" he asked.

Long Collins grinned.

"Reach out your hand, Ranse Truesdell," he said, "and you'll touch him. And you can shake his'n, too, if you like, for he's plumb white and there's none better in no camp."

Ranse looked again at the clear-faced, bronzed, smiling cowpuncher who stood at Collins's side. Could that be Curly? He held out his hand, and Curly grasped it with the muscles of a bronco-buster.

"I want you at the ranch," said Ranse.

"All right, sport," said Curly, heartily. "But I want to come back again. Say, pal, this is a dandy farm. And I don't want any better fun than hustlin' cows with this bunch of guys. They're all to the merry-merry."

At the Cibolo ranch-house they dismounted. Ranse bade Curly wait at the door of the living room. He walked inside. Old "Kiowa" Truesdell was reading at a table.

"Good-morning, Mr. Truesdell," said Ranse.

The old man turned his white head quickly.

"How is this?" he began. "Why do you call me 'Mr.—'?"

When he looked at Ranse's face he stopped, and the hand that held his newspaper shook slightly.

"Boy," he said slowly, "how did you find it out?"

"It's all right," said Ranse, with a smile. "I made Tia Juana tell me. It was kind of by accident, but it's all right."

"You've been like a son to me," said old "Kiowa," trembling.

"Tia Juana told me all about it," said Ranse. "She told me how you adopted me when I was knee-high to a puddle duck out of a wagon train of prospectors that was bound West. And she told me how the kid—your own kid, you know—got lost or was run away with. And she said it was the same day that the sheep-shearers got on a bender and left the ranch."

"Our boy strayed from the house when he was two years old," said the old man. "And then along came those emigrant wagons with a youngster they didn't want; and we took you. I never intended you to know, Ranse. We never heard of our boy again."

"He's right outside, unless I'm mighty mistaken," said Ranse, opening the door and beckoning.

Curly walked in.

No one could have doubted. The old man and the young had the same sweep of hair, the same nose, chin, line of face, and prominent light-blue eyes.

Old "Kiowa" rose eagerly.

Curly looked about the room curiously. A puzzled expression came over his face. He pointed to the wall opposite.

"Where's the tick-tock?" he asked, absent-mindedly.

"The clock," cried old "Kiowa" loudly. "The eight-day clock used to stand there. Why—"

He turned to Ranse, but Ranse was not there.

Already a hundred yards away, Vaminos, the good flea-bitten dun, was bearing him eastward like a racer through dust and chaparral towards the Rancho de los Olmos.

X

Cupid a la Carte

"The dispositions of woman," said Jeff Peters, after various opinions on the subject had been advanced, "run, regular, to diversions. What a woman wants is what you're out of. She wants more of a thing when it's scarce. She likes to have souvenirs of things that never happened. She likes to be reminded of things she never heard of. A one-sided view of objects is disjointing to the female composition.

"'Tis a misfortune of mine, begotten by nature and travel," continued Jeff, looking thoughtfully between his elevated feet at the grocery stove, "to look deeper into some subjects than most people do. I've breathed gasoline smoke talking to street crowds in nearly every town in the United States. I've held 'em spellbound with music, oratory, sleight of hand, and prevarications, while I've sold 'em jewelry, medicine, soap, hair tonic, and junk of other nominations. And during my travels, as a matter of recreation and expiation, I've taken cognisance some of women. It takes a man a lifetime to find out about one particular woman; but if he puts in, say, ten years, industrious and curious, he can acquire the general rudiments of the sex. One lesson I picked up was when I was working the West with a line of Brazilian diamonds and a patent fire kindler just after my trip from Savannah down through the cotton belt with Dalby's Anti-explosive Lamp Oil Powder. 'Twas when the Oklahoma country was in first bloom. Guthrie was rising in the middle of it like a lump of self-raising dough. It was a boom town of the regular kind—you stood in line to get a chance to wash your face; if you ate over ten minutes you had a lodging bill added on; if you slept on a plank at night they charged it to you as board the next morning.

"By nature and doctrines I am addicted to the habit of discovering choice places wherein to feed. So I looked around and found a proposition that exactly cut the mustard. I found a restaurant tent just opened up by an outfit that had drifted in on the tail of the boom. They had knocked together a box house, where they lived and did the cooking, and served the meals in a tent pitched against the side. That tent was joyful with placards on it calculated to redeem the world-worn pilgrim from the sinfulness of boarding houses and pick-me-up hotels. 'Try Mother's Home-Made Biscuits,' 'What's the Matter with Our Apple Dumplings and Hard Sauce?' 'Hot Cakes and Maple Syrup Like You Ate When a Boy,' 'Our Fried Chicken Never Was Heard to Crow'—there was literature doomed to please the digestions of man! I said to myself that mother's wandering boy should munch there that night. And so it came to pass. And there is where I contracted my case of Mame Dugan.

"Old Man Dugan was six feet by one of Indiana loafer, and he spent his time sitting on his shoulder blades in a rocking-chair in the shanty memorialising the great corn-crop failure of '96. Ma Dugan did the cooking, and Mame waited on the table.

"As soon as I saw Mame I knew there was a mistake in the census reports. There wasn't but one girl in the United States. When you come to specifications it isn't easy. She was about the size of an angel, and she had eyes, and ways about her. When you come to the kind of a girl she was, you'll find a belt of 'em reaching from the Brooklyn Bridge west as far as the courthouse in Council Bluffs, Ia. They earn their own living in stores, restaurants, factories, and offices. They're chummy and honest and free and tender and sassy, and they look life straight in the eye. They've met man face to face, and discovered that he's a poor creature. They've dropped to it that the reports in the Seaside Library about his being a fairy prince lack confirmation.

"Mame was that sort. She was full of life and fun, and breezy; she passed the repartee with the boarders quick as a wink; you'd have smothered laughing. I am disinclined to make excavations into the insides of a personal affection. I am glued to the theory that the diversions and discrepancies of the indisposition known as love should be as private a sentiment as a toothbrush. 'Tis my opinion that the biographies of the heart should be confined with the historical romances of the liver to the advertising pages of the magazines. So, you'll excuse the lack of an itemised bill of my feelings toward Mame.

"Pretty soon I got a regular habit of dropping into the tent to eat at irregular times when there wasn't so many around. Mame would sail in with a smile, in a black dress and white apron, and say: 'Hello, Jeff—why don't you come at mealtime? Want to see how much trouble you can be, of course. Friedchickenbeefsteakporkchopshamandeggspotpie'— and so on. She called me Jeff, but there was no significations attached. Designations was all she meant. The front names of any of us she used as they came to hand. I'd eat about two meals before I left, and string 'em out like a society spread where they changed plates and wives, and josh one another festively between bites. Mame stood for it, pleasant, for it wasn't up to her to take any canvas off the tent by declining dollars just because they were whipped in after meal times.

"It wasn't long until there was another fellow named Ed Collier got the between-meals affliction, and him and me put in bridges between breakfast and dinner, and dinner and supper, that made a three-ringed circus of that tent, and Mame's turn as waiter a continuous performance. That Collier man was saturated with designs and contrivings. He was in well-boring or insurance or claim-jumping, or something—I've forgotten which. He was a man well lubricated with gentility, and his words were such as recommended you to his point of view. So, Collier and me infested the grub tent with care and activity. Mame was level full of impartiality. 'Twas like a casino hand the way she dealt out her favours—one to Collier and one to me and one to the board, and not a card up her sleeve.

"Me and Collier naturally got acquainted, and gravitated together some on the outside. Divested of his stratagems, he seemed to be a pleasant chap, full of an amiable sort of hostility.

"'I notice you have an affinity for grubbing in the banquet hall after the guests have fled,' says I to him one day, to draw his conclusions.

"'Well, yes,' says Collier, reflecting; 'the tumult of a crowded board seems to harass my sensitive nerves.'

"'It exasperates mine some, too,' says I. 'Nice little girl, don't you think?'

"'I see,' says Collier, laughing. 'Well, now that you mention it, I have noticed that she doesn't seem to displease the optic nerve.'

"'She's a joy to mine,' says I, 'and I'm going after her. Notice is hereby served.'

"'I'll be as candid as you,' admits Collier, 'and if the drug stores don't run out of pepsin I'll give you a run for your money that'll leave you a dyspeptic at the wind-up.'

"So Collier and me begins the race; the grub department lays in new supplies; Mame waits on us, jolly and kind and agreeable, and it looks like an even break, with Cupid and the cook working overtime in Dugan's restaurant.

"'Twas one night in September when I got Mame to take a walk after supper when the things were all cleared away. We strolled out a distance and sat on a pile of lumber at the edge of town. Such opportunities was seldom, so I spoke my piece, explaining how the Brazilian diamonds and the fire kindler were laying up sufficient treasure to guarantee the happiness of two, and that both of 'em together couldn't equal the light from somebody's eyes, and that the name of Dugan should be changed to Peters, or reasons why not would be in order.

"Mame didn't say anything right away. Directly she gave a kind of shudder, and I began to learn something.

"'Jeff,' she says, 'I'm sorry you spoke. I like you as well as any of them, but there isn't a man in the world I'd ever marry, and there never will be. Do you know what a man is in my eye? He's a tomb. He's a sarcophagus for the interment of Beafsteakporkchopsliver'nbaconham-andeggs. He's that and nothing more. For two years I've watched men eat, eat, eat, until they represent nothing on earth to me but ruminant bipeds. They're absolutely nothing but something that goes in front of a knife and fork and plate at the table. They're fixed that way in my mind and memory. I've tried to overcome it, but I can't. I've heard girls rave about their sweethearts, but I never could understand it. A man and a sausage grinder and a pantry awake in me exactly the same sentiments. I went a matinee once to see an actor the girls were crazy about. I got interested enough to wonder whether he liked his steak rare, medium, or well done, and his eggs over or straight up. That was all. No, Jeff; I'll marry no man and see him sit at the breakfast table and eat, and come back to dinner and eat, and happen in again at supper to eat, eat, eat.'

"'But, Mame,' says I, 'it'll wear off. You've had too much of it. You'll marry some time, of course. Men don't eat always.'

"'As far as my observation goes, they do. No, I'll tell you what I'm going to do.' Mame turns, sudden, to animation and bright eyes. 'There's a girl named Susie Foster in Terre Haute, a chum of mine. She waits in the railroad eating house there. I worked two years in a restaurant in that town. Susie has it worse than I do, because the men who eat at railroad stations gobble. They try to flirt and gobble at the same time. Whew! Susie and I have it all planned out. We're saving our money, and when we get enough we're going to buy a little cottage and five acres we know of, and live together, and grow violets for the Eastern market. A man better not bring his appetite within a mile of that ranch.'

"'Don't girls ever—' I commenced, but Mame heads me off, sharp.

"'No, they don't. They nibble a little bit sometimes; that's all.'

"'I thought the confect—'

"'For goodness' sake, change the subject,' says Mame.

"As I said before, that experience puts me wise that the feminine arrangement ever struggles after deceptions and illusions. Take England—beef made her; wieners elevated Germany; Uncle Sam owes his greatness to fried chicken and pie, but the young ladies of the Shetalkyou schools, they'll never believe it. Shakespeare, they allow, and Rubinstein, and the Rough Riders is what did the trick.

"'Twas a situation calculated to disturb. I couldn't bear to give up Mame; and yet it pained me to think of abandoning the practice of eating. I had acquired the habit too early. For twenty-seven years I had been blindly rushing upon my fate, yielding to the insidious lures of that deadly monster, food. It was too late. I was a ruminant biped for keeps. It was lobster salad to a doughnut that my life was going to be blighted by it.

"I continued to board at the Dugan tent, hoping that Mame would relent. I had sufficient faith in true love to believe that since it has often outlived the absence of a square meal it might, in time, overcome the presence of one. I went on ministering to my fatal vice, although I felt that each time I shoved a potato into my mouth in Mame's presence I might be burying my fondest hopes.

"I think Collier must have spoken to Mame and got the same answer, for one day he orders a cup of coffee and a cracker, and sits nibbling the corner of it like a girl in the parlour, that's filled up in the kitchen, previous, on cold roast and fried cabbage. I caught on and did the same, and maybe we thought we'd made a hit! The next day we tried it again, and out comes old man Dugan fetching in his hands the fairy viands.

"'Kinder off yer feed, ain't ye, gents?' he asks, fatherly and some sardonic. 'Thought I'd spell Mame a bit, seein' the work was light, and my rheumatiz can stand the strain.'

"So back me and Collier had to drop to the heavy grub again. I noticed about that time that I was seized by a most uncommon and devastating appetite. I ate until Mame must have hated to see me darken the door. Afterward I found out that I had been made the victim of the first dark and irreligious trick played on me by Ed Collier. Him and me had been taking drinks together uptown regular, trying to drown our thirst for food. That man had bribed about ten bartenders to always put a big slug of Appletree's Anaconda Appetite Bitters in every one of my drinks. But the last trick he played me was hardest to forget.

"One day Collier failed to show up at the tent. A man told me he left town that morning. My only rival now was the bill of fare. A few days before he left Collier had presented me with a two-gallon jug of fine whisky which he said a cousin had sent him from Kentucky. I now have reason to believe that it contained Appletree's Anaconda Appetite Bitters almost exclusively. I continued to devour tons of provisions. In Mame's eyes I remained a mere biped, more ruminant than ever.

"About a week after Collier pulled his freight there came a kind of side-show to town, and hoisted a tent near the railroad. I judged it was a sort of fake museum and curiosity business. I called to see Mame one night, and Ma Dugan said that she and Thomas, her younger brother, had gone to the show. That same thing happened for three nights that week. Saturday night I caught her on the way coming back, and got to sit on the steps a while and talk to her. I noticed she looked different. Her eyes were softer, and shiny like. Instead of a Mame Dugan to fly from the voracity of man and raise violets, she seemed to be a Mame more in line as God intended her, approachable, and suited to bask in the light of the Brazilians and the Kindler.

"'You seem to be right smart inveigled,' says I, 'with the Unparalleled Exhibition of the World's Living Curiosities and Wonders.'

"'It's a change,' says Mame.

"'You'll need another,' says I, 'if you keep on going every night.'

"'Don't be cross, Jeff,' says she; 'it takes my mind off business.'

"'Don't the curiosities eat?' I ask.

"'Not all of them. Some of them are wax.'

"'Look out, then, that you don't get stuck,' says I, kind of flip and foolish.

"Mame blushed. I didn't know what to think about her. My hopes raised some that perhaps my attentions had palliated man's awful crime of visibly introducing nourishment into his system. She talked some about the stars, referring to them with respect and politeness, and I drivelled a quantity about united hearts, homes made bright by true affection, and the Kindler. Mame listened without scorn, and I says to myself, 'Jeff, old man, you're removing the hoodoo that has clung to the consumer of victuals; you're setting your heel upon the serpent that lurks in the gravy bowl.'

"Monday night I drop around. Mame is at the Unparalleled Exhibition with Thomas.

"'Now, may the curse of the forty-one seven-sided sea cooks,' says I, 'and the bad luck of the nine impenitent grasshoppers rest upon this self-same sideshow at once and forever more. Amen. I'll go to see it myself to-morrow night and investigate its baleful charm. Shall man that was made to inherit the earth be bereft of his sweetheart first by a knife and fork and then by a ten-cent circus?'

"The next night before starting out for the exhibition tent I inquire and find out that Mame is not at home. She is not at the circus with Thomas this time, for Thomas waylays me in the grass outside of the grub tent with a scheme of his own before I had time to eat supper.

"'What'll you give me, Jeff,' says he, 'if I tell you something?'

"'The value of it, son,' I says.

"'Sis is stuck on a freak,' says Thomas, 'one of the side-show freaks. I don't like him. She does. I overheard 'em talking. Thought maybe you'd like to know. Say, Jeff, does it put you wise two dollars' worth? There's a target rifle up town that—'

"I frisked my pockets and commenced to dribble a stream of halves and quarters into Thomas's hat. The information was of the pile-driver system of news, and it telescoped my intellects for a while. While I was leaking small change and smiling foolish on the outside, and suffering disturbances internally, I was saying, idiotically and pleasantly:

"'Thank you, Thomas—thank you—er—a freak, you said, Thomas. Now, could you make out the monstrosity's entitlements a little clearer, if you please, Thomas?'

"'This is the fellow,' says Thomas, pulling out a yellow handbill from his pocket and shoving it under my nose. 'He's the Champion Faster of the Universe. I guess that's why Sis got soft on him. He don't eat nothing. He's going to fast forty-nine days. This is the sixth. That's him.'

"I looked at the name Thomas pointed out—'Professor Eduardo Collieri.' 'Ah!' says I, in admiration, 'that's not so bad, Ed Collier. I give you credit for the trick. But I don't give you the girl until she's Mrs. Freak.'

"I hit the sod in the direction of the show. I came up to the rear of the tent, and, as I did so, a man wiggled out like a snake from under the bottom of the canvas, scrambled to his feet, and ran into me like a locoed bronco. I gathered him by the neck and investigated him by the light of the stars. It is Professor Eduardo Collieri, in human habiliments, with a desperate look in one eye and impatience in the other.

"'Hello, Curiosity,' says I. 'Get still a minute and let's have a look at your freakship. How do you like being the willopus-wallopus or the bim-bam from Borneo, or whatever name you are denounced by in the side-show business?'

"'Jeff Peters,' says Collier, in a weak voice. 'Turn me loose, or I'll slug you one. I'm in the extremest kind of a large hurry. Hands off!'

"'Tut, tut, Eddie,' I answers, holding him hard; 'let an old friend gaze on the exhibition of your curiousness. It's an eminent graft you fell onto, my son. But don't speak of assaults and battery, because you're not fit. The best you've got is a lot of nerve and a mighty empty stomach.' And so it was. The man was as weak as a vegetarian cat.

"'I'd argue this case with you, Jeff,' says he, regretful in his style, 'for an unlimited number of rounds if I had half an hour to train in and a slab of beefsteak two feet square to train with. Curse the man, I say, that invented the art of going foodless. May his soul in eternity be chained up within two feet of a bottomless pit of red-hot hash. I'm abandoning the conflict, Jeff; I'm deserting to the enemy. You'll find Miss Dugan inside contemplating the only living mummy and the informed hog. She's a fine girl, Jeff. I'd have beat you out if I could have kept up the grubless habit a little while longer. You'll have to admit that the fasting dodge was aces-up for a while. I figured it out that way. But say, Jeff, it's said that love makes the world go around. Let me tell you, the announcement lacks verification. It's the wind from the dinner horn that does it. I love that Mame Dugan. I've gone six days without food in order to coincide with her sentiments. Only one bite did I have. That was when I knocked the tattooed man down with a war club and got a sandwich he was gobbling. The manager fined me all my salary; but salary wasn't what I was after. 'Twas that girl. I'd give my life for her, but I'd endanger my immortal soul for a beef stew. Hunger is a horrible thing, Jeff. Love and business and family and religion and art and patriotism are nothing but shadows of words when a man's starving!'

"In such language Ed Collier discoursed to me, pathetic. I gathered the diagnosis that his affections and his digestions had been implicated in a scramble and the commissary had won out. I never disliked Ed Collier. I searched my internal admonitions of suitable etiquette to see if I could find a remark of a consoling nature, but there was none convenient.

"'I'd be glad, now,' says Ed, 'if you'll let me go. I've been hard hit, but I'll hit the ration supply harder. I'm going to clean out every restaurant in town. I'm going to wade waist deep in sirloins and swim in ham and eggs. It's an awful thing, Jeff Peters, for a man to come to this pass—to give up his girl for something to eat—it's worse than that man Esau, that swapped his copyright for a partridge—but then, hunger's a fierce thing. You'll excuse me, now, Jeff, for I smell a pervasion of ham frying in the distance, and my legs are crying out to stampede in that direction.'

"'A hearty meal to you, Ed Collier,' I says to him, 'and no hard feelings. For myself, I am projected to be an unseldom eater, and I have condolence for your predicaments.'

"There was a sudden big whiff of frying ham smell on the breeze; and the Champion Faster gives a snort and gallops off in the dark toward fodder.

"I wish some of the cultured outfit that are always advertising the extenuating circumstances of love and romance had been there to see. There was Ed Collier, a fine man full of contrivances and flirtations, abandoning the girl of his heart and ripping out into the contiguous territory in the pursuit of sordid grub. 'Twas a rebuke to the poets and a slap at the best-paying element of fiction. An empty stomach is a sure antidote to an overfull heart.

"I was naturally anxious to know how far Mame was infatuated with Collier and his stratagems. I went inside the Unparalleled Exhibition, and there she was. She looked surprised to see me, but unguilty.

"'It's an elegant evening outside,' says I. 'The coolness is quite nice and gratifying, and the stars are lined out, first class, up where they belong. Wouldn't you shake these by-products of the animal kingdom long enough to take a walk with a common human who never was on a programme in his life?'

"Mame gave a sort of sly glance around, and I knew what that meant.

"'Oh,' says I, 'I hate to tell you; but the curiosity that lives on wind has flew the coop. He just crawled out under the tent. By this time he has amalgamated himself with half the delicatessen truck in town.'

"'You mean Ed Collier?' says Mame.

"'I do,' I answers; 'and a pity it is that he has gone back to crime again. I met him outside the tent, and he exposed his intentions of devastating the food crop of the world. 'Tis enormously sad when one's ideal descends from his pedestal to make a seventeen-year locust of himself.'

"Mame looked me straight in the eye until she had corkscrewed my reflections.

"'Jeff,' says she, 'it isn't quite like you to talk that way. I don't care to hear Ed Collier ridiculed. A man may do ridiculous things, but they don't look ridiculous to the girl he does 'em for. That was one man in a hundred. He stopped eating just to please me. I'd be hard-hearted and ungrateful if I didn't feel kindly toward him. Could you do what he did?'

"'I know,' says I, seeing the point, 'I'm condemned. I can't help it. The brand of the consumer is upon my brow. Mrs. Eve settled that business for me when she made the dicker with the snake. I fell from the fire into the frying-pan. I guess I'm the Champion Feaster of the Universe.' I spoke humble, and Mame mollified herself a little.

"'Ed Collier and I are good friends,' she said, 'the same as me and you. I gave him the same answer I did you—no marrying for me. I liked to be with Ed and talk with him. There was something mighty pleasant to me in the thought that here was a man who never used a knife and fork, and all for my sake.'

"'Wasn't you in love with him?' I asks, all injudicious. 'Wasn't there a deal on for you to become Mrs. Curiosity?'

"All of us do it sometimes. All of us get jostled out of the line of profitable talk now and then. Mame put on that little lemon *glace* smile that runs between ice and sugar, and says, much too pleasant: 'You're short on credentials for asking that question, Mr. Peters. Suppose you do a forty-nine day fast, just to give you ground to stand on, and then maybe I'll answer it.'

"So, even after Collier was kidnapped out of the way by the revolt of his appetite, my own prospects with Mame didn't seem to be improved. And then business played out in Guthrie.

"I had stayed too long there. The Brazilians I had sold commenced to show signs of wear, and the Kindler refused to light up right frequent on wet mornings. There is always a time, in my business, when the star of success says, 'Move on to the next town.' I was travelling by wagon at that time so as not to miss any of the small towns; so I hitched up a few days later and went down to tell Mame good-bye. I wasn't abandoning the game; I intended running over to Oklahoma City and work it for a week or two. Then I was coming back to institute fresh proceedings against Mame.

"What do I find at the Dugans' but Mame all conspicuous in a blue travelling dress, with her little trunk at the door. It seems that sister Lottie Bell, who is a typewriter in Terre Haute, is going to be married next Thursday, and Mame is off for a week's visit to be an accomplice at the ceremony. Mame is waiting for a freight wagon that is going to take her to Oklahoma, but I condemns the freight wagon with promptness and scorn, and offers to deliver the goods myself. Ma Dugan sees no reason why not, as Mr. Freighter wants pay for the job; so, thirty minutes later Mame and I pull out in my light spring wagon with white canvas cover, and head due south.

"That morning was of a praiseworthy sort. The breeze was lively, and smelled excellent of flowers and grass, and the little cottontail rabbits entertained themselves with skylarking across the road. My two Kentucky bays went for the horizon until it come sailing in so fast you wanted to dodge it like a clothesline. Mame was full of talk and rattled on like a kid about her old home and her school pranks and the things she liked and the hateful ways of those Johnson girls just across the street, 'way up in Indiana. Not a word was said about Ed Collier or victuals or such solemn subjects. About noon Mame looks and finds that the lunch she had put up in a basket had been left behind. I could have managed quite a collation, but Mame didn't seem to be grieving over nothing to eat, so I made no lamentations. It was a sore subject with me, and I ruled provender in all its branches out of my conversation.

"I am minded to touch light on explanations how I came to lose the way. The road was dim and well grown with grass; and there was Mame by my side confiscating my intellects and attention. The excuses are good or they are not, as they may appear to you. But I lost it, and at dusk that afternoon, when we should have been in Oklahoma City, we were seesawing along the edge of nowhere in some undiscovered river bottom, and the rain was falling in large, wet bunches. Down there in the swamps we saw a little log house on a small knoll of high ground. The bottom grass and the chaparral and the lonesome timber crowded all around it. It seemed to be a melancholy little house, and you felt sorry for it. 'Twas that house for the night, the way I reasoned it. I explained to Mame, and she leaves it to me to decide. She doesn't become galvanic and prosecuting, as most women would, but she says it's all right; she knows I didn't mean to do it.

"We found the house was deserted. It had two empty rooms. There was a little shed in the yard where beasts had once been kept. In a loft of it was a lot of old hay. I put my horses in there and gave them some of it, for which they looked at me sorrowful, expecting apologies. The rest of the hay I carried into the house by armfuls, with a view to accommodations. I also brought in the patent kindler and the Brazilians, neither of which are guaranteed against the action of water.

"Mame and I sat on the wagon seats on the floor, and I lit a lot of the kindler on the hearth, for the night was chilly. If I was any judge, that girl enjoyed it. It was a change for her. It gave her a different point of view. She laughed and talked, and the kindler made a dim light compared to her eyes. I had a pocketful of cigars, and as far as I was concerned there had never been any fall of man. We were at the same old stand in the Garden of Eden. Out there somewhere in the rain and the dark was the river of Zion, and the angel with the flaming sword had not yet put up the keep-off-the-grass sign. I opened up a gross or two of the Brazilians and made Mame put them on—rings, brooches, necklaces, eardrops, bracelets, girdles, and lockets. She flashed and sparkled like a million-dollar princess until she had pink spots in her cheeks and almost cried for a looking-glass.

"When it got late I made a fine bunk on the floor for Mame with the hay and my lap robes and blankets out of the wagon, and persuaded her to lie down. I sat in the other room burning tobacco and listening to the pouring rain and meditating on the many vicissitudes that came to a man during the seventy years or so immediately preceding his funeral.

"I must have dozed a little while before morning, for my eyes were shut, and when I opened them it was daylight, and there stood Mame with her hair all done up neat and correct, and her eyes bright with admiration of existence.

"'Gee whiz, Jeff!' she exclaims, 'but I'm hungry. I could eat a—'

"I looked up and caught her eye. Her smile went back in and she gave me a cold look of suspicion. Then I laughed, and laid down on the floor to laugh easier. It seemed funny to me. By nature and geniality I am a hearty laugher, and I went the limit. When I came to, Mame was sitting with her back to me, all contaminated with dignity.

"'Don't be angry, Mame,' I says, 'for I couldn't help it. It's the funny way you've done up your hair. If you could only see it!'

"'You needn't tell stories, sir,' said Mame, cool and advised. 'My hair is all right. I know what you were laughing about. Why, Jeff, look outside,' she winds up, peeping through a chink between the logs. I opened the little wooden window and looked out. The entire river bottom was flooded, and the knob of land on which the house stood was an island in the middle of a rushing stream of yellow water a hundred yards wide. And it was still raining hard. All we could do was to stay there till the doves brought in the olive branch.

"I am bound to admit that conversations and amusements languished during that day. I was aware that Mame was getting a too prolonged one-sided view of things again, but I had no way to change it. Personally, I was wrapped up in the desire to eat. I had hallucinations of hash and visions of ham, and I kept saying to myself all the time, 'What'll you have to eat, Jeff?—what'll you order now, old man, when the waiter comes?' I picks out to myself all sorts of favourites from the bill of fare, and imagines them coming. I guess it's that way with all hungry men. They can't get their cogitations trained on anything but something to eat. It shows that the little table with the broken-legged caster and the imitation Worcester sauce and the napkin covering up the coffee stains is the paramount issue, after all, instead of the question of immortality or peace between nations.

"I sat there, musing along, arguing with myself quite heated as to how I'd have my steak—with mushrooms, or *a la creole*. Mame was on the other seat, pensive, her head leaning on her hand. 'Let the potatoes come home-fried,' I states in my mind, 'and brown the hash in the pan, with nine poached eggs on the side.' I felt, careful, in my own pockets to see if I could find a peanut or a grain or two of popcorn.

"Night came on again with the river still rising and the rain still falling. I looked at Mame and I noticed that desperate look on her face that a girl always wears when she passes an ice-cream lair. I knew that poor girl was hungry—maybe for the first time in her life. There was that anxious look in her eye that a woman has only when she has missed a meal or feels her skirt coming unfastened in the back.

"It was about eleven o'clock or so on the second night when we sat, gloomy, in our shipwrecked cabin. I kept jerking my mind away from the subject of food, but it kept flopping back again before I could fasten it. I thought of everything good to eat I had ever heard of. I went away back to my kidhood and remembered the hot biscuit sopped in sorghum and bacon gravy with partiality and respect. Then I trailed along up the years, pausing at green apples and salt, flapjacks and maple, lye hominy, fried chicken Old Virginia style, corn on the cob, spareribs and sweet potato pie, and wound up with Georgia Brunswick stew, which is the top notch of good things to eat, because it comprises 'em all.

"They say a drowning man sees a panorama of his whole life pass before him. Well, when a man's starving he sees the ghost of every meal he ever ate set out before him, and he invents new dishes that would make the fortune of a chef. If somebody would collect the last words of men who starved to death, they'd have to sift 'em mighty fine to discover the sentiment, but they'd compile into a cook book that would sell into the millions.

"I guess I must have had my conscience pretty well inflicted with culinary meditations, for, without intending to do so, I says, out loud, to the imaginary waiter, 'Cut it thick and have it rare, with the French fried, and six, soft-scrambled, on toast.'

"Mame turned her head quick as a wing. Her eyes were sparkling and she smiled sudden.

"'Medium for me,' she rattles out, 'with the Juliennes, and three, straight up. Draw one, and brown the wheats, double order to come. Oh, Jeff, wouldn't it be glorious! And then I'd like to have a half fry, and a little chicken curried with rice, and a cup custard with ice cream, and—'

"'Go easy,' I interrupts; 'where's the chicken liver pie, and the kidney *saute* on toast, and the roast lamb, and—'

"'Oh,' cuts in Mame, all excited, 'with mint sauce, and the turkey salad, and stuffed olives, and raspberry tarts, and—'

"'Keep it going,' says I. 'Hurry up with the fried squash, and the hot corn pone with sweet milk, and don't forget the apple dumpling with hard sauce, and the cross-barred dew-berry pie—'

"Yes, for ten minutes we kept up that kind of restaurant repartee. We ranges up and down and backward and forward over the main trunk lines and the branches of the victual subject, and Mame leads the game, for she is apprised in the ramifications of grub, and the dishes she nominates aggravates my yearnings. It seems that there is a feeling that Mame will line up friendly again with food. It seems that she looks upon the obnoxious science of eating with less contempt than before.

"The next morning we find that the flood has subsided. I geared up the bays, and we splashed out through the mud, some precarious, until we found the road again. We were only a few miles wrong, and in two hours we were in Oklahoma City. The first thing we saw was a big restaurant sign, and we piled into there in a hurry. Here I finds myself sitting with Mame at table, with knives and forks and plates between us, and she not scornful, but smiling with starvation and sweetness.

"'Twas a new restaurant and well stocked. I designated a list of quotations from the bill of fare that made the waiter look out toward the wagon to see how many more might be coming.

"There we were, and there was the order being served. 'Twas a banquet for a dozen, but we felt like a dozen. I looked across the table at Mame and smiled, for I had recollections. Mame was looking at the table like a boy looks at his first stem-winder. Then she looked at me, straight in the face, and two big tears came in her eyes. The waiter was gone after more grub.

"'Jeff,' she says, soft like, 'I've been a foolish girl. I've looked at things from the wrong side. I never felt this way before. Men get hungry every day like this, don't they? They're big and strong, and they do the hard work of the world, and they don't eat just to spite silly waiter girls in restaurants, do they, Jeff? You said once—that is, you asked me—you wanted me to—well, Jeff, if you still care—I'd be glad and willing to have you always sitting across the table from me. Now give me something to eat, quick, please.'

"So, as I've said, a woman needs to change her point of view now and then. They get tired of the same old sights—the same old dinner table, washtub, and sewing machine. Give 'em a touch of the various—a little travel and a little rest, a little tomfoolery along with the tragedies of keeping house, a little petting after the blowing-up, a little upsetting and a little jostling around—and everybody in the game will have chips added to their stack by the play."

XI

THE CABALLERO'S WAY

The Cisco Kid had killed six men in more or less fair scrimmages, had murdered twice as many (mostly Mexicans), and had winged a larger number whom he modestly forbore to count. Therefore a woman loved him.

The Kid was twenty-five, looked twenty; and a careful insurance company would have estimated the probable time of his demise at, say, twenty-six. His habitat was anywhere between the Frio and the Rio Grande. He killed for the love of it—because he was quick-tempered—to avoid arrest—for his own amusement—any reason that came to his mind would suffice. He had escaped capture because he could shoot five-sixths of a second sooner than any sheriff or ranger in the service, and because he rode a speckled roan horse that knew every cow-path in the mesquite and pear thickets from San Antonio to Matamoras.

Tonia Perez, the girl who loved the Cisco Kid, was half Carmen, half Madonna, and the rest—oh, yes, a woman who is half Carmen and half Madonna can always be something more—the rest, let us say, was humming-bird. She lived in a grass-roofed *jacal* near a little Mexican settlement at the Lone Wolf Crossing of the Frio. With her lived a father or grandfather, a lineal Aztec, somewhat less than a thousand years old, who herded a hundred goats and lived in a continuous drunken dream from drinking *mescal*. Back of the *jacal* a tremendous forest of bristling pear, twenty feet high at its worst, crowded almost to its door. It was along the bewildering maze of this spinous thicket that the speckled roan would bring the Kid to see his girl. And once, clinging like a lizard to the ridge-pole, high up under the peaked grass roof, he had heard Tonia, with her Madonna face and Carmen beauty and humming-bird soul, parley with the sheriff's posse, denying knowledge of her man in her soft *melange* of Spanish and English.

One day the adjutant-general of the State, who is, *ex offico*, commander of the ranger forces, wrote some sarcastic lines to Captain Duval of Company X, stationed at Laredo, relative to the serene and undisturbed existence led by murderers and desperadoes in the said captain's territory.

The captain turned the colour of brick dust under his tan, and forwarded the letter, after adding a few comments, per ranger Private Bill Adamson, to ranger Lieutenant Sandridge, camped at a water hole on the Nueces with a squad of five men in preservation of law and order.

Lieutenant Sandridge turned a beautiful *couleur de rose* through his ordinary strawberry complexion, tucked the letter in his hip pocket, and chewed off the ends of his gamboge moustache.

The next morning he saddled his horse and rode alone to the Mexican settlement at the Lone Wolf Crossing of the Frio, twenty miles away.

Six feet two, blond as a Viking, quiet as a deacon, dangerous as a machine gun, Sandridge moved among the *Jacales*, patiently seeking news of the Cisco Kid.

Far more than the law, the Mexicans dreaded the cold and certain vengeance of the lone rider that the ranger sought. It had been one of the Kid's pastimes to shoot Mexicans "to see them kick": if he demanded from them moribund Terpsichorean feats, simply that he might be entertained, what terrible and extreme penalties would be certain to follow should they anger him! One and all they lounged with upturned palms and shrugging shoulders, filling the air with "*quien sabes*" and denials of the Kid's acquaintance.

But there was a man named Fink who kept a store at the Crossing—a man of many nationalities, tongues, interests, and ways of thinking.

"No use to ask them Mexicans," he said to Sandridge. "They're afraid to tell. This *hombre* they call the Kid—Goodall is his name, ain't it?— he's been in my store once or twice. I have an idea you might run across him at—but I guess I don't keer to say, myself. I'm two seconds later in pulling a gun than I used to be, and the difference is worth thinking about. But this Kid's got a half-Mexican girl at the Crossing that he comes to see. She lives in that *jacal* a hundred yards down the arroyo at the edge of the pear. Maybe she—no, I don't suppose she would, but that *jacal* would be a good place to watch, anyway."

Sandridge rode down to the *jacal* of Perez. The sun was low, and the broad shade of the great pear thicket already covered the grass-thatched hut. The goats were enclosed for the night in a brush corral near by. A few kids walked the top of it, nibbling the chaparral leaves. The old Mexican lay upon a blanket on the grass, already in a stupor from his mescal, and dreaming, perhaps, of the nights when he and Pizarro touched glasses to their New World fortunes—so old his wrinkled face seemed to proclaim him to be. And in the door of the *jacal* stood Tonia.

And Lieutenant Sandridge sat in his saddle staring at her like a gannet agape at a sailorman.

The Cisco Kid was a vain person, as all eminent and successful assassins are, and his bosom would have been ruffled had he known that at a simple exchange of glances two persons, in whose minds he had been looming large, suddenly abandoned (at least for the time) all thought of him.

Never before had Tonia seen such a man as this. He seemed to be made of sunshine and blood-red tissue and clear weather. He seemed to illuminate the shadow of the pear when he smiled, as though the sun were rising again. The men she had known had been small and dark. Even the Kid, in spite of his achievements, was a stripling no larger than herself, with black, straight hair and a cold, marble face that chilled the noonday.

As for Tonia, though she sends description to the poorhouse, let her make a millionaire of your fancy. Her blue-black hair, smoothly divided in the middle and bound close to her head, and her large eyes full of the Latin melancholy, gave her the Madonna touch. Her motions and air spoke of the concealed fire and the desire to charm that she had inherited from the *gitanas* of the Basque province. As for the humming-bird part of her, that dwelt in her heart; you could not perceive it unless her bright red skirt and dark blue blouse gave you a symbolic hint of the vagarious bird.

The newly lighted sun-god asked for a drink of water. Tonia brought it from the red jar hanging under the brush shelter. Sandridge considered it necessary to dismount so as to lessen the trouble of her ministrations.

I play no spy; nor do I assume to master the thoughts of any human heart; but I assert, by the chronicler's right, that before a quarter of an hour had sped, Sandridge was teaching her how to plait a six-strand rawhide stake-rope, and Tonia had explained to him that were it not for her little English book that the peripatetic *padre* had given her and the little crippled *chivo*, that she fed from a bottle, she would be very, very lonely indeed.

Which leads to a suspicion that the Kid's fences needed repairing, and that the adjutant-general's sarcasm had fallen upon unproductive soil.

In his camp by the water hole Lieutenant Sandridge announced and reiterated his intention of either causing the Cisco Kid to nibble the black loam of the Frio country prairies or of haling him before a judge and jury. That sounded business-like. Twice a week he rode over to the Lone Wolf Crossing of the Frio, and directed Tonia's slim, slightly lemon-tinted fingers among the intricacies of the slowly growing lariata. A six-strand plait is hard to learn and easy to teach.

The ranger knew that he might find the Kid there at any visit. He kept his armament ready, and had a frequent eye for the pear thicket at the rear of the *jacal*. Thus he might bring down the kite and the humming-bird with one stone.

While the sunny-haired ornithologist was pursuing his studies the Cisco Kid was also attending to his professional duties. He moodily shot up a saloon in a small cow village on Quintana Creek, killed the town marshal (plugging him neatly in the centre of his tin badge), and then rode away, morose and unsatisfied. No true artist is uplifted by shooting an aged man carrying an old-style .38 bulldog.

On his way the Kid suddenly experienced the yearning that all men feel when wrong-doing loses its keen edge of delight. He yearned for the woman he loved to reassure him that she was his in spite of it. He wanted her to call his bloodthirstiness bravery and his cruelty devotion. He wanted Tonia to bring him water from the red jar under the brush shelter, and tell him how the *chivo* was thriving on the bottle.

The Kid turned the speckled roan's head up the ten-mile pear flat that stretches along the Arroyo Hondo until it ends at the Lone Wolf Crossing of the Frio. The roan whickered; for he had a sense of locality and direction equal to that of a belt-line street-car horse; and he knew he would soon be nibbling the rich mesquite grass at the end of a forty-foot stake-rope while Ulysses rested his head in Circe's straw-roofed hut.

More weird and lonesome than the journey of an Amazonian explorer is the ride of one through a Texas pear flat. With dismal monotony and startling variety the uncanny and multiform shapes of the cacti lift their twisted trunks, and fat, bristly hands to encumber the way. The demon plant, appearing to live without soil or rain, seems to taunt the parched traveller with its lush grey greenness. It warps itself a thousand times about what look to be open and inviting paths, only to lure the rider into blind and impassable spine-defended "bottoms of the bag," leaving him to retreat, if he can, with the points of the compass whirling in his head.

To be lost in the pear is to die almost the death of the thief on the cross, pierced by nails and with grotesque shapes of all the fiends hovering about.

O. HENRY

But it was not so with the Kid and his mount. Winding, twisting, circling, tracing the most fantastic and bewildering trail ever picked out, the good roan lessened the distance to the Lone Wolf Crossing with every coil and turn that he made.

While they fared the Kid sang. He knew but one tune and sang it, as he knew but one code and lived it, and but one girl and loved her. He was a single-minded man of conventional ideas. He had a voice like a coyote with bronchitis, but whenever he chose to sing his song he sang it. It was a conventional song of the camps and trail, running at its beginning as near as may be to these words:

> Don't you monkey with my Lulu girl
> Or I'll tell you what I'll do—

and so on. The roan was inured to it, and did not mind.

But even the poorest singer will, after a certain time, gain his own consent to refrain from contributing to the world's noises. So the Kid, by the time he was within a mile or two of Tonia's *jacal*, had reluctantly allowed his song to die away—not because his vocal performance had become less charming to his own ears, but because his laryngeal muscles were aweary.

As though he were in a circus ring the speckled roan wheeled and danced through the labyrinth of pear until at length his rider knew by certain landmarks that the Lone Wolf Crossing was close at hand. Then, where the pear was thinner, he caught sight of the grass roof of the *jacal* and the hackberry tree on the edge of the arroyo. A few yards farther the Kid stopped the roan and gazed intently through the prickly openings. Then he dismounted, dropped the roan's reins, and proceeded on foot, stooping and silent, like an Indian. The roan, knowing his part, stood still, making no sound.

The Kid crept noiselessly to the very edge of the pear thicket and reconnoitred between the leaves of a clump of cactus.

Ten yards from his hiding-place, in the shade of the *jacal*, sat his Tonia calmly plaiting a rawhide lariat. So far she might surely escape condemnation; women have been known, from time to time, to engage in more mischievous occupations. But if all must be told, there is to be added that her head reposed against the broad and comfortable chest of a tall red-and-yellow man, and that his arm was about her, guiding her nimble fingers that required so many lessons at the intricate six-strand plait.

Sandridge glanced quickly at the dark mass of pear when he heard a slight squeaking sound that was not altogether unfamiliar. A gun-scabbard will make that sound when one grasps the handle of a six-shooter suddenly. But the sound was not repeated; and Tonia's fingers needed close attention.

And then, in the shadow of death, they began to talk of their love; and in the still July afternoon every word they uttered reached the ears of the Kid.

"Remember, then," said Tonia, "you must not come again until I send for you. Soon he will be here. A *vaquero* at the *tienda* said to-day he saw him on the Guadalupe three days ago. When he is that near he always comes. If he comes and finds you here he will kill you. So, for my sake, you must come no more until I send you the word."

"All right," said the stranger. "And then what?"

"And then," said the girl, "you must bring your men here and kill him. If not, he will kill you."

"He ain't a man to surrender, that's sure," said Sandridge. "It's kill or be killed for the officer that goes up against Mr. Cisco Kid."

"He must die," said the girl. "Otherwise there will not be any peace in the world for thee and me. He has killed many. Let him so die. Bring your men, and give him no chance to escape."

"You used to think right much of him," said Sandridge.

Tonia dropped the lariat, twisted herself around, and curved a lemon-tinted arm over the ranger's shoulder.

"But then," she murmured in liquid Spanish, "I had not beheld thee, thou great, red mountain of a man! And thou art kind and good, as well as strong. Could one choose him, knowing thee? Let him die; for then I will not be filled with fear by day and night lest he hurt thee or me."

"How can I know when he comes?" asked Sandridge.

"When he comes," said Tonia, "he remains two days, sometimes three. Gregorio, the small son of old Luisa, the *lavendera*, has a swift pony. I will write a letter to thee and send it by him, saying how it will be best to come upon him. By Gregorio will the letter come. And bring many men with thee, and have much care, oh, dear red one, for the rattlesnake is not quicker to strike than is '*El Chivato*,' as they call him, to send a ball from his *pistola*."

"The Kid's handy with his gun, sure enough," admitted Sandridge, "but when I come for him I shall come alone. I'll get him by myself or not at all. The Cap wrote one or two things to me that make me want to do the trick without any help. You let me know when Mr. Kid arrives, and I'll do the rest."

"I will send you the message by the boy Gregorio," said the girl. "I knew you were braver than that small slayer of men who never smiles. How could I ever have thought I cared for him?"

It was time for the ranger to ride back to his camp on the water hole. Before he mounted his horse he raised the slight form of Tonia with one arm high from the earth for a parting salute. The drowsy stillness of the torpid summer air still lay thick upon the dreaming afternoon. The smoke from the fire in the *jacal*, where the *frijoles* blubbered in the iron pot, rose straight as a plumb-line above the clay-daubed chimney. No sound or movement disturbed the serenity of the dense pear thicket ten yards away.

When the form of Sandridge had disappeared, loping his big dun down the steep banks of the Frio crossing, the Kid crept back to his own horse, mounted him, and rode back along the tortuous trail he had come.

But not far. He stopped and waited in the silent depths of the pear until half an hour had passed. And then Tonia heard the high, untrue notes of his unmusical singing coming nearer and nearer; and she ran to the edge of the pear to meet him.

The Kid seldom smiled; but he smiled and waved his hat when he saw her. He dismounted, and his girl sprang into his arms. The Kid looked at her fondly. His thick, black hair clung to his head like a wrinkled mat. The meeting brought a slight ripple of some undercurrent of feeling to his smooth, dark face that was usually as motionless as a clay mask.

"How's my girl?" he asked, holding her close.

"Sick of waiting so long for you, dear one," she answered. "My eyes are dim with always gazing into that devil's pincushion through which you come. And I can see into it such a little way, too. But you are here, beloved one, and I will not scold. *Que mal muchacho*! not to come to see your *alma* more often. Go in and rest, and let me water your horse and stake him with the long rope. There is cool water in the jar for you."

The Kid kissed her affectionately.

"Not if the court knows itself do I let a lady stake my horse for me," said he. "But if you'll run in, *chica*, and throw a pot of coffee together while I attend to the *caballo*, I'll be a good deal obliged."

Besides his marksmanship the Kid had another attribute for which he admired himself greatly. He was *muy caballero*, as the Mexicans express it, where the ladies were concerned. For them he had always gentle words and consideration. He could not have spoken a harsh word to a woman. He might ruthlessly slay their husbands and brothers, but he could not have laid the weight of a finger in anger upon a woman. Wherefore many of that interesting division of humanity who had come under the spell of his politeness declared their disbelief in the stories circulated about Mr. Kid. One shouldn't believe everything one heard, they said. When confronted by their indignant men folk with proof of the *caballero's* deeds of infamy, they said maybe he had been driven to it, and that he knew how to treat a lady, anyhow.

Considering this extremely courteous idiosyncrasy of the Kid and the pride he took in it, one can perceive that the solution of the problem that was presented to him by what he saw and heard from his hiding-place in the pear that afternoon (at least as to one of the actors) must have been obscured by difficulties. And yet one could not think of the Kid overlooking little matters of that kind.

At the end of the short twilight they gathered around a supper of *frijoles*, goat steaks, canned peaches, and coffee, by the light of a lantern in the *jacal*. Afterward, the ancestor, his flock corralled, smoked a cigarette and became a mummy in a grey blanket. Tonia washed the few dishes while the Kid dried them with the flour-sacking towel. Her eyes shone; she chatted volubly of the inconsequent happenings of her small world since the Kid's last visit; it was as all his other home-comings had been.

Then outside Tonia swung in a grass hammock with her guitar and sang sad *canciones de amor*.

"Do you love me just the same, old girl?" asked the Kid, hunting for his cigarette papers.

"Always the same, little one," said Tonia, her dark eyes lingering upon him.

"I must go over to Fink's," said the Kid, rising, "for some tobacco. I thought I had another sack in my coat. I'll be back in a quarter of an hour."

"Hasten," said Tonia, "and tell me—how long shall I call you my own this time? Will you be gone again to-morrow, leaving me to grieve, or will you be longer with your Tonia?"

"Oh, I might stay two or three days this trip," said the Kid, yawning. "I've been on the dodge for a month, and I'd like to rest up."

He was gone half an hour for his tobacco. When he returned Tonia was still lying in the hammock.

"It's funny," said the Kid, "how I feel. I feel like there was somebody lying behind every bush and tree waiting to shoot me. I never had mullygrubs like them before. Maybe it's one of them presumptions. I've got half a notion to light out in the morning before day. The Guadalupe country is burning up about that old Dutchman I plugged down there."

"You are not afraid—no one could make my brave little one fear."

"Well, I haven't been usually regarded as a jack-rabbit when it comes to scrapping; but I don't want a posse smoking me out when I'm in your *jacal*. Somebody might get hurt that oughtn't to."

"Remain with your Tonia; no one will find you here."

The Kid looked keenly into the shadows up and down the arroyo and toward the dim lights of the Mexican village.

"I'll see how it looks later on," was his decision.

At midnight a horseman rode into the rangers' camp, blazing his way by noisy "halloes" to indicate a pacific mission. Sandridge and one or two others turned out to investigate the row. The rider announced himself to be Domingo Sales, from the Lone Wolf Crossing. he bore a letter for Senor Sandridge. Old Luisa, the *lavendera*, had persuaded him to bring it, he said, her son Gregorio being too ill of a fever to ride.

Sandridge lighted the camp lantern and read the letter. These were its words:

Dear One

He has come. Hardly had you ridden away when he came out of the pear. When he first talked he said he would stay three days or more. Then as it grew later he was like a wolf or a fox, and walked about without rest, looking and listening. Soon he said he must leave before daylight when it is dark and stillest. And then he seemed to suspect that I be not true to him. He looked at me so strange that I am frightened. I swear to him that I love him, his own Tonia. Last of all he said I must prove to him I am true. He thinks that even now men are waiting to kill him as he rides from my house. To escape he says he will dress in my clothes, my red skirt and the blue waist I wear and the brown mantilla over the head, and thus ride away. But before that he says that I must put on his clothes, his *pantalones* and *camisa* and hat, and ride away on his horse from the *jacal* as far as the big road beyond the crossing and back again. This before he goes, so he can tell if I am true and if men are hidden to shoot him. It is a terrible thing. An hour before daybreak this is to be. Come, my dear one, and kill this man and take me for your Tonia. Do not try to take hold of him alive, but kill him quickly. Knowing all, you should do that. You must come long before the time and hide yourself in the little shed near the *jacal* where the wagon and saddles are kept. It is dark in there. He will wear my red skirt and blue waist and brown mantilla. I send you a hundred kisses. Come surely and shoot quickly and straight.

Thine Own Tonia

Sandridge quickly explained to his men the official part of the missive. The rangers protested against his going alone.

"I'll get him easy enough," said the lieutenant. "The girl's got him trapped. And don't even think he'll get the drop on me."

Sandridge saddled his horse and rode to the Lone Wolf Crossing. He tied his big dun in a clump of brush on the arroyo, took his Winchester from its scabbard, and carefully approached the Perez *jacal*. There was only the half of a high moon drifted over by ragged, milk-white gulf clouds.

The wagon-shed was an excellent place for ambush; and the ranger got inside it safely. In the black shadow of the brush shelter in front of the *jacal* he could see a horse tied and hear him impatiently pawing the hard-trodden earth.

He waited almost an hour before two figures came out of the *jacal*. One, in man's clothes, quickly mounted the horse and galloped past the wagon-shed toward the crossing and village. And then the other figure, in skirt, waist, and mantilla over its head, stepped out into the faint moonlight, gazing after the rider. Sandridge thought he would take his chance then before Tonia rode back. He fancied she might not care to see it.

"Throw up your hands," he ordered loudly, stepping out of the wagon-shed with his Winchester at his shoulder.

There was a quick turn of the figure, but no movement to obey, so the ranger pumped in the bullets—one—two—three—and then twice more; for you never could be too sure of bringing down the Cisco Kid. There was no danger of missing at ten paces, even in that half moonlight.

The old ancestor, asleep on his blanket, was awakened by the shots. Listening further, he heard a great cry from some man in mortal distress or anguish, and rose up grumbling at the disturbing ways of moderns.

The tall, red ghost of a man burst into the *jacal*, reaching one hand, shaking like a *tule* reed, for the lantern hanging on its nail. The other spread a letter on the table.

"Look at this letter, Perez," cried the man. "Who wrote it?"

"*Ah, Dios*! it is Senor Sandridge," mumbled the old man, approaching. "*Pues, senor*, that letter was written by '*El Chivato*,' as he is called—by the man of Tonia. They say he is a bad man; I do not know. While Tonia slept he wrote the letter and sent it by this old hand of mine to Domingo Sales to be brought to you. Is there anything wrong in the letter? I am very old; and I did not know. *Valgame Dios*! it is a very foolish world; and there is nothing in the house to drink—nothing to drink."

Just then all that Sandridge could think of to do was to go outside and throw himself face downward in the dust by the side of his humming-bird, of whom not a feather fluttered. He was not a *caballero* by instinct, and he could not understand the niceties of revenge.

A mile away the rider who had ridden past the wagon-shed struck up a harsh, untuneful song, the words of which began:

> *Don't you monkey with my Lulu girl*
> *Or I'll tell you what I'll do—*

XII

THE SPHINX APPLE

Twenty miles out from Paradise, and fifteen miles short of Sunrise City, Bildad Rose, the stage-driver, stopped his team. A furious snow had been falling all day. Eight inches it measured now, on a level. The remainder of the road was not without peril in daylight, creeping along the ribs of a bijou range of ragged mountains. Now, when both snow and night masked its dangers, further travel was not to be thought of, said Bildad Rose. So he pulled up his four stout horses, and delivered to his five passengers oral deductions of his wisdom.

Judge Menefee, to whom men granted leadership and the initiatory as upon a silver salver, sprang from the coach at once. Four of his fellow-passengers followed, inspired by his example, ready to explore, to objurgate, to resist, to submit, to proceed, according as their prime factor might be inclined to sway them. The fifth passenger, a young woman, remained in the coach.

Bildad had halted upon the shoulder of the first mountain spur. Two rail-fences, ragged-black, hemmed the road. Fifty yards above the upper fence, showing a dark blot in the white drifts, stood a small house. Upon this house descended—or rather ascended—Judge Menefee and his cohorts with boyish whoops born of the snow and stress. They called; they pounded at window and door. At the inhospitable silence they waxed restive; they assaulted and forced the pregnable barriers, and invaded the premises.

The watchers from the coach heard stumblings and shoutings from the interior of the ravaged house. Before long a light within flickered, glowed, flamed high and bright and cheerful. Then came running back through the driving flakes the exuberant explorers. More deeply pitched than the clarion—even orchestral in volume—the voice of Judge Menefee proclaimed the succour that lay in apposition with their state of travail. The one room of the house was uninhabited, he said, and bare of furniture; but it contained a great fireplace, and they had discovered an ample store of chopped wood in a lean-to at the rear. Housing and warmth against the shivering night were thus assured. For the placation of Bildad Rose there was news of a stable, not ruined beyond service, with hay in a loft, near the house.

"Gentlemen," cried Bildad Rose from his seat, swathed in coats and robes, "tear me down two panels of that fence, so I can drive in. That is old man Redruth's shanty. I thought we must be nigh it. They took him to the foolish house in August."

Cheerfully the four passengers sprang at the snow-capped rails. The exhorted team tugged the coach up the slant to the door of the edifice from which a mid-summer madness had ravished its proprietor. The driver and two of the passengers began to unhitch. Judge Menefee opened the door of the coach, and removed his hat.

"I have to announce, Miss Garland," said he, "the enforced suspension of our journey. The driver asserts that the risk in travelling the mountain road by night is too great even to consider. It will be necessary to remain in the shelter of this house until morning. I beg that you will feel that there is nothing to fear beyond a temporary inconvenience. I have personally inspected the house, and find that there are means to provide against the rigour of the weather, at least. You shall be made as comfortable as possible. Permit me to assist you to alight."

To the Judge's side came the passenger whose pursuit in life was the placing of the Little Goliath windmill. His name was Dunwoody; but that matters not much. In travelling merely from Paradise to Sunrise City one needs little or no name. Still, one who would seek to divide honours with Judge Madison L. Menefee deserves a cognomenal peg upon which Fame may hang a wreath. Thus spake, loudly and buoyantly, the aerial miller:

"Guess you'll have to climb out of the ark, Mrs. McFarland. This wigwam isn't exactly the Palmer House, but it turns snow, and they won't search your grip for souvenir spoons when you leave. *We've* got a fire going; and *we'll* fix you up with dry Tilbys and keep the mice away, anyhow, all right, all right."

One of the two passengers who were struggling in a melee of horses, harness, snow, and the sarcastic injunctions of Bildad Rose, called loudly from the whirl of his volunteer duties: "Say! some of you fellows get Miss Solomon into the house, will you? Whoa, there! you confounded brute!"

Again must it be gently urged that in travelling from Paradise to Sunrise City an accurate name is prodigality. When Judge Menefee— sanctioned to the act by his grey hair and widespread repute—had introduced himself to the lady passenger, she had, herself, sweetly breathed a name, in response, that the hearing of the male passengers had variously interpreted. In the not unjealous spirit of rivalry that eventuated, each clung stubbornly to his own theory. For the lady passenger to have reasseverated or corrected would have seemed didactic if not unduly solicitous of a specific acquaintance. Therefore the lady passenger permitted herself to be Garlanded and McFarlanded and Solomoned with equal and discreet complacency. It is thirty-five miles from Paradise to Sunrise City. *Compagnon de voyage* is name enough, by the gripsack of the Wandering Jew! for so brief a journey.

Soon the little party of wayfarers were happily seated in a cheerful arc before the roaring fire. The robes, cushions, and removable portions of the coach had been brought in and put to service. The lady passenger chose a place near the hearth at one end of the arc. There she graced almost a throne that her subjects had prepared. She sat upon cushions and leaned against an empty box and barrel, robe bespread, which formed a defence from the invading draughts. She extended her feet, delectably shod, to the cordial heat. She ungloved her hands, but retained about her neck her long fur boa. The unstable flames half revealed, while the warding boa half submerged, her face—a youthful face, altogether feminine, clearly moulded and calm with beauty's unchallenged confidence. Chivalry and manhood were here vying to please and comfort her. She seemed to accept their devoirs—not piquantly, as one courted and attended; nor preeningly, as many of her sex unworthily reap their honours; not yet stolidly, as the ox receives his hay; but concordantly with nature's own plan—as the lily ingests the drop of dew foreordained to its refreshment.

Outside the wind roared mightily, the fine snow whizzed through the cracks, the cold besieged the backs of the immolated six; but the elements did not lack a champion that night. Judge Menefee was attorney for the storm. The weather was his client, and he strove by special pleading to convince his companions in that frigid jury-box that they sojourned in a bower of roses, beset only by benignant zephyrs. He drew upon a fund of gaiety, wit, and anecdote, sophistical, but crowned with success. His cheerfulness communicated itself irresistibly. Each one hastened to contribute his own quota toward the general optimism. Even the lady passenger was moved to expression.

"I think it is quite charming," she said, in her slow, crystal tones.

At intervals some one of the passengers would rise and humorously explore the room. There was little evidence to be collected of its habitation by old man Redruth.

Bildad Rose was called upon vivaciously for the ex-hermit's history. Now, since the stage-driver's horses were fairly comfortable and his passengers appeared to be so, peace and comity returned to him.

"The old didapper," began Bildad, somewhat irreverently, "infested this here house about twenty year. He never allowed nobody to come nigh him. He'd duck his head inside and slam the door whenever a team drove along. There was spinning-wheels up in his loft, all right. He used to buy his groceries and tobacco at Sam Tilly's store, on the Little Muddy. Last August he went up there dressed in a red bedquilt, and told Sam he was King Solomon, and that the Queen of Sheba was coming to visit him. He fetched along all the money he had—a little bag full of silver—and dropped it in Sam's well. 'She won't come,' says old man Redruth to Sam, 'if she knows I've got any money.'

"As soon as folks heard he had that sort of a theory about women and money they knowed he was crazy; so they sent down and packed him to the foolish asylum."

"Was there a romance in his life that drove him to a solitary existence?" asked one of the passengers, a young man who had an Agency.

"No," said Bildad, "not that I ever heard spoke of. Just ordinary trouble. They say he had had unfortunateness in the way of love derangements with a young lady when he was young; before he contracted red bed-quilts and had his financial conclusions disqualified. I never heard of no romance."

"Ah!" exclaimed Judge Menefee, impressively; "a case of unrequited affection, no doubt."

"No, sir," returned Bildad, "not at all. She never married him. Marmaduke Mulligan, down at Paradise, seen a man once that come from old Redruth's town. He said Redruth was a fine young man, but when you kicked him on the pocket all you could hear jingle was a cuff-fastener and a bunch of keys. He was engaged to this young lady—Miss Alice—something was her name; I've forgot. This man said she was the kind of girl you like to have reach across you in a car to pay the fare. Well, there come to the town a young chap all affluent and easy, and fixed up with buggies and mining stock and leisure time. Although she was a staked claim, Miss Alice and the new entry seemed to strike a mutual kind of a clip. They had calls and coincidences of going to the post office and such things as sometimes make a girl send back the engagement ring and other presents—'a rift within the loot,' the poetry man calls it.

"One day folks seen Redruth and Miss Alice standing talking at the gate. Then he lifts his hat and walks away, and that was the last anybody in that town seen of him, as far as this man knew."

"What about the young lady?" asked the young man who had an Agency.

"Never heard," answered Bildad. "Right there is where my lode of information turns to an old spavined crowbait, and folds its wings, for I've pumped it dry."

"A very sad—" began Judge Menefee, but his remark was curtailed by a higher authority.

"What a charming story!" said the lady passenger, in flute-like tones.

A little silence followed, except for the wind and the crackling of the fire.

The men were seated upon the floor, having slightly mitigated its inhospitable surface with wraps and stray pieces of boards. The man who was placing Little Goliath windmills arose and walked about to ease his cramped muscles.

Suddenly a triumphant shout came from him. He hurried back from a dusky corner of the room, bearing aloft something in his hand. It was an apple—a large, red-mottled, firm pippin, pleasing to behold. In a paper bag on a high shelf in that corner he had found it. It could have been no relic of the lovewrecked Redruth, for its glorious soundness repudiated the theory that it had lain on that musty shelf since August. No doubt some recent bivouackers, lunching in the deserted house, had left it there.

Dunwoody—again his exploits demand for him the honours of nomenclature—flaunted his apple in the faces of his fellow-marooners. "See what I found, Mrs. McFarland!" he cried, vaingloriously. He held the apple high up in the light of the fire, where it glowed a still richer red. The lady passenger smiled calmly—always calmly.

"What a charming apple!" she murmured, clearly.

For a brief space Judge Menefee felt crushed, humiliated, relegated. Second place galled him. Why had this blatant, obtrusive, unpolished man of windmills been selected by Fate instead of himself to discover the sensational apple? He could have made of the act a scene, a function, a setting for some impromptu, fanciful discourse or piece of comedy— and have retained the role of cynosure. Actually, the lady passenger was regarding this ridiculous Dunboddy or Woodbundy with an admiring smile, as if the fellow had performed a feat! And the windmill man swelled and gyrated like a sample of his own goods, puffed up with the wind that ever blows from the chorus land toward the domain of the star.

While the transported Dunwoody, with his Aladdin's apple, was receiving the fickle attentions of all, the resourceful jurist formed a plan to recover his own laurels.

With his courtliest smile upon his heavy but classic features, Judge Menefee advanced, and took the apple, as if to examine it, from the hand of Dunwoody. In his hand it became Exhibit A.

"A fine apple," he said, approvingly. "Really, my dear Mr. Dudwindy, you have eclipsed all of us as a forager. But I have an idea. This apple shall become an emblem, a token, a symbol, a prize bestowed by the mind and heart of beauty upon the most deserving."

The audience, except one, applauded. "Good on the stump, ain't he?" commented the passenger who was nobody in particular to the young man who had an Agency.

The unresponsive one was the windmill man. He saw himself reduced to the ranks. Never would the thought have occurred to him to declare his apple an emblem. He had intended, after it had been divided and eaten, to create diversion by sticking the seeds against his forehead and naming them for young ladies of his acquaintance. One he was going to name Mrs. McFarland. The seed that fell off first would be—but 'twas too late now.

"The apple," continued Judge Menefee, charging his jury, "in modern days occupies, though undeservedly, a lowly place in our esteem. Indeed, it is so constantly associated with the culinary and the commercial that it is hardly to be classed among the polite fruits. But in ancient times this was not so. Biblical, historical, and mythological lore abounds with evidences that the apple was the aristocrat of fruits. We still say 'the apple of the eye' when we wish to describe something superlatively precious. We find in Proverbs the comparison to 'apples of silver.' No other product of tree or vine has been so utilised in figurative speech. Who has not heard of and longed for the 'apples of the Hesperides'? I need not call your attention to the most tremendous and significant instance of the apple's ancient prestige when its consumption by our first parents occasioned the fall of man from his state of goodness and perfection."

"Apples like them," said the windmill man, lingering with the objective article, "are worth $3.50 a barrel in the Chicago market."

"Now, what I have to propose," said Judge Menefee, conceding an indulgent smile to his interrupter, "is this: We must remain here, perforce, until morning. We have wood in plenty to keep us warm. Our next need is to entertain ourselves as best we can, in order that the time shall not pass too slowly. I propose that we place this apple in the hands of Miss Garland. It is no longer a fruit, but, as I said, a prize, in award, representing a great human idea. Miss Garland, herself, shall cease to be an individual—but only temporarily, I am happy to add"—(a low bow, full of the old-time grace). "She shall represent her sex; she shall be the embodiment, the epitome of womankind—the heart and brain, I may say, of God's masterpiece of creation. In this guise she shall judge and decide the question which follows:

"But a few minutes ago our friend, Mr. Rose, favoured us with an entertaining but fragmentary sketch of the romance in the life of the former professor of this habitation. The few facts that we have learned seem to me to open up a fascinating field for conjecture, for the study of human hearts, for the exercise of the imagination—in short, for story-telling. Let us make use of the opportunity. Let each one of us relate his own version of the story of Redruth, the hermit, and his lady-love, beginning where Mr. Rose's narrative ends—at the parting of the lovers at the gate. This much should be assumed and conceded—that the young lady was not necessarily to blame for Redruth's becoming a crazed and world-hating hermit. When we have done, Miss Garland shall render the JUDGEMENT OF WOMAN. As the Spirit of her Sex she shall decide which version of the story best and most truly depicts human and love interest, and most faithfully estimates the character and acts of Redruth's betrothed according to the feminine view. The apple shall be bestowed upon him who is awarded the decision. If you are all agreed, we shall be pleased to hear the first story from Mr. Dinwiddie."

The last sentence captured the windmill man. He was not one to linger in the dumps.

"That's a first-rate scheme, Judge," he said, heartily. "Be a regular short-story vaudeville, won't it? I used to be correspondent for a paper in Springfield, and when there wasn't any news I faked it. Guess I can do my turn all right."

"I think the idea is charming," said the lady passenger, brightly. "It will be almost like a game."

Judge Menefee stepped forward and placed the apple in her hand impressively.

"In olden days," he said, orotundly, "Paris awarded the golden apple to the most beautiful."

"I was at the Exposition," remarked the windmill man, now cheerful again, "but I never heard of it. And I was on the Midway, too, all the time I wasn't at the machinery exhibit."

"But now," continued the Judge, "the fruit shall translate to us the mystery and wisdom of the feminine heart. Take the apple, Miss Garland. Hear our modest tales of romance, and then award the prize as you may deem it just."

The lady passenger smiled sweetly. The apple lay in her lap beneath her robes and wraps. She reclined against her protecting bulwark, brightly and cosily at ease. But for the voices and the wind one might have listened hopefully to hear her purr. Someone cast fresh logs upon the fire. Judge Menefee nodded suavely. "Will you oblige us with the initial story?" he asked.

The windmill man sat as sits a Turk, with his hat well back on his head on account of the draughts.

"Well," he began, without any embarrassment, "this is about the way I size up the difficulty: Of course Redruth was jostled a good deal by this duck who had money to play ball with who tried to cut him out of his girl. So he goes around, naturally, and asks her if the game is still square. Well, nobody wants a guy cutting in with buggies and gold bonds when he's got an option on a girl. Well, he goes around to see her. Well, maybe he's hot, and talks like the proprietor, and forgets that an engagement ain't always a lead-pipe cinch. Well, I guess that makes Alice warm under the lacy yoke. Well, she answers back sharp. Well, he—"

"Say!" interrupted the passenger who was nobody in particular, "if you could put up a windmill on every one of them 'wells' you're using, you'd be able to retire from business, wouldn't you?"

The windmill man grinned good-naturedly.

"Oh, I ain't no *Guy de Mopassong*," he said, cheerfully. "I'm giving it to you in straight American. Well, she says something like this: 'Mr. Gold Bonds is only a friend,' says she; 'but he takes me riding and buys me theatre tickets, and that's what you never do. Ain't I to never have any pleasure in life while I can?' 'Pass this chatfield-chatfield thing along,' says Redruth;—'hand out the mitt to the Willie with creases in it or you don't put your slippers under my wardrobe.'

"Now that kind of train orders don't go with a girl that's got any spirit. I bet that girl loved her honey all the time. Maybe she only wanted, as girls do, to work the good thing for a little fun and caramels before she settled down to patch George's other pair, and be a good wife. But he is glued to the high horse, and won't come down. Well, she hands him back the ring, proper enough; and George goes away and hits the booze. Yep. That's what done it. I bet that girl fired the cornucopia with the fancy vest two days after her steady left. George boards a freight and checks his bag of crackers for parts unknown. He sticks to Old Booze for a number of years; and then the aniline and aquafortis gets the decision. 'Me for the hermit's hut,' says George, 'and the long whiskers, and the buried can of money that isn't there.'

"But that Alice, in my mind, was on the level. She never married, but took up typewriting as soon as the wrinkles began to show, and kept a cat that came when you said 'weeny—weeny—weeny!' I got too much faith in good women to believe they throw down the fellow they're stuck on every time for the dough." The windmill man ceased.

"I think," said the lady passenger, slightly moving upon her lowly throne, "that that is a char—"

"Oh, Miss Garland!" interposed Judge Menefee, with uplifted hand, "I beg of you, no comments! It would not be fair to the other contestants. Mr.—er—will you take the next turn?" The Judge addressed the young man who had the Agency.

"My version of the romance," began the young man, diffidently clasping his hands, "would be this: They did not quarrel when they parted. Mr. Redruth bade her good-by and went out into the world to seek his fortune. He knew his love would remain true to him. He scorned the thought that his rival could make an impression upon a heart so fond and faithful. I would say that Mr. Redruth went out to the Rocky Mountains in Wyoming to seek for gold. One day a crew of pirates landed and captured him while at work, and—"

"Hey! what's that?" sharply called the passenger who was nobody in particular—"a crew of pirates landed in the Rocky Mountains! Will you tell us how they sailed—"

"Landed from a train," said the narrator, quietly and not without some readiness. "They kept him prisoner in a cave for months, and then they took him hundreds of miles away to the forests of Alaska. There a beautiful Indian girl fell in love with him, but he remained true to

Alice. After another year of wandering in the woods, he set out with the diamonds—"

"What diamonds?" asked the unimportant passenger, almost with acerbity.

"The ones the saddlemaker showed him in the Peruvian temple," said the other, somewhat obscurely. "When he reached home, Alice's mother led him, weeping, to a green mound under a willow tree. 'Her heart was broken when you left,' said her mother. 'And what of my rival—of Chester McIntosh?' asked Mr. Redruth, as he knelt sadly by Alice's grave. 'When he found out,' she answered, 'that her heart was yours, he pined away day by day until, at length, he started a furniture store in Grand Rapids. We heard lately that he was bitten to death by an infuriated moose near South Bend, Ind., where he had gone to try to forget scenes of civilisation.' With which, Mr. Redruth forsook the face of mankind and became a hermit, as we have seen.

"My story," concluded the young man with an Agency, "may lack the literary quality; but what I wanted it to show is that the young lady remained true. She cared nothing for wealth in comparison with true affection. I admire and believe in the fair sex too much to think otherwise."

The narrator ceased, with a sidelong glance at the corner where reclined the lady passenger.

Bildad Rose was next invited by Judge Menefee to contribute his story in the contest for the apple of judgment. The stage-driver's essay was brief.

"I'm not one of them lobo wolves," he said, "who are always blaming on women the calamities of life. My testimony in regards to the fiction story you ask for, Judge, will be about as follows: What ailed Redruth was pure laziness. If he had up and slugged this Percival De Lacey that tried to give him the outside of the road, and had kept Alice in the grape-vine swing with the blind-bridle on, all would have been well. The woman you want is sure worth taking pains for.

"'Send for me if you want me again,' says Redruth, and hoists his Stetson, and walks off. He'd have called it pride, but the nixycomlogical name for it is laziness. No woman don't like to run after a man. 'Let him come back, hisself,' says the girl; and I'll be bound she tells the boy with the pay ore to trot; and then spends her time watching out the window for the man with the empty pocket-book and the tickly moustache.

"I reckon Redruth waits about nine year expecting her to send him a note by a nigger asking him to forgive her. But she don't. 'This game won't work,' says Redruth; 'then so won't I.' And he goes in the hermit business and raises whiskers. Yes; laziness and whiskers was what done the trick. They travel together. You ever hear of a man with long whiskers and hair striking a bonanza? No. Look at the Duke of Marlborough and this Standard Oil snoozer. Have they got 'em?

"Now, this Alice didn't never marry, I'll bet a hoss. If Redruth had married somebody else she might have done so, too. But he never turns up. She has these here things they call fond memories, and maybe a lock of hair and a corset steel that he broke, treasured up. Them sort of articles is as good as a husband to some women. I'd say she played out a lone hand. I don't blame no woman for old man Redruth's abandonment of barber shops and clean shirts."

Next in order came the passenger who was nobody in particular. Nameless to us, he travels the road from Paradise to Sunrise City.

But him you shall see, if the firelight be not too dim, as he responds to the Judge's call.

A lean form, in rusty-brown clothing, sitting like a frog, his arms wrapped about his legs, his chin resting upon his knees. Smooth, oakum-coloured hair; long nose; mouth like a satyr's, with upturned, tobacco-stained corners. An eye like a fish's; a red necktie with a horseshoe pin. He began with a rasping chuckle that gradually formed itself into words.

"Everybody wrong so far. What! a romance without any orange blossoms! Ho, ho! My money on the lad with the butterfly tie and the certified checks in his trouserings.

"Take 'em as they parted at the gate? All right. 'You never loved me,' says Redruth, wildly, 'or you wouldn't speak to a man who can buy you the ice-cream.' 'I hate him,' says she. 'I loathe his side-bar buggy; I despise the elegant cream bonbons he sends me in gilt boxes covered with real lace; I feel that I could stab him to the heart when he presents me with a solid medallion locket with turquoises and pearls running in a vine around the border. Away with him! 'Tis only you I love.' 'Back to the cosey corner!' says Redruth. 'Was I bound and lettered in East Aurora? Get platonic, if you please. No jack-pots for mine. Go and hate your friend some more. For me the Nickerson girl on Avenue B, and gum, and a trolley ride.'

"Around that night comes John W. Croesus. 'What! tears?' says he, arranging his pearl pin. 'You have driven my lover away,' says little

Alice, sobbing: 'I hate the sight of you.' 'Marry me, then,' says John W., lighting a Henry Clay. 'What!' she cries indignantly, 'marry you! Never,' she says, 'until this blows over, and I can do some shopping, and you see about the licence. There's a telephone next door if you want to call up the county clerk.'"

The narrator paused to give vent to his cynical chuckle.

"Did they marry?" he continued. "Did the duck swallow the June-bug? And then I take up the case of Old Boy Redruth. There's where you are all wrong again, according to my theory. What turned him into a hermit? One says laziness; one says remorse; one says booze. I say women did it. How old is the old man now?" asked the speaker, turning to Bildad Rose.

"I should say about sixty-five."

"All right. He conducted his hermit shop here for twenty years. Say he was twenty-five when he took off his hat at the gate. That leaves twenty years for him to account for, or else be docked. Where did he spend that ten and two fives? I'll give you my idea. Up for bigamy. Say there was the fat blonde in Saint Jo, and the panatela brunette at Skillet Ridge, and the gold tooth down in the Kaw valley. Redruth gets his cases mixed, and they send him up the road. He gets out after they are through with him, and says: 'Any line for me except the crinoline. The hermit trade is not overdone, and the stenographers never apply to 'em for work. The jolly hermit's life for me. No more long hairs in the comb or dill pickles lying around in the cigar tray.' You tell me they pinched old Redruth for the noodle villa just because he said he was King Solomon? Figs! He *was* Solomon. That's all of mine. I guess it don't call for any apples. Enclosed find stamps. It don't sound much like a prize winner."

Respecting the stricture laid by Judge Menefee against comments upon the stories, all were silent when the passenger who was nobody in particular had concluded. And then the ingenious originator of the contest cleared his throat to begin the ultimate entry for the prize. Though seated with small comfort upon the floor, you might search in vain for any abatement of dignity in Judge Menefee. The now diminishing firelight played softly upon his face, as clearly chiselled as a Roman emperor's on some old coin, and upon the thick waves of his honourable grey hair.

"A woman's heart!" he began, in even but thrilling tones—"who can hope to fathom it? The ways and desires of men are various. I think that the hearts of all women beat with the same rhythm, and to the same old tune of love. Love, to a woman, means sacrifice. If she be worthy of the name, no gold or rank will outweigh with her a genuine devotion.

"Gentlemen of the—er—I should say, my friends, the case of Redruth *versus* love and affection has been called. Yet, who is on trial? Not Redruth, for he has been punished. Not those immortal passions that clothe our lives with the joy of the angels. Then who? Each man of us here to-night stands at the bar to answer if chivalry or darkness inhabits his bosom. To judge us sits womankind in the form of one of its fairest flowers. In her hand she holds the prize, intrinsically insignificant, but worthy of our noblest efforts to win as a guerdon of approval from so worthy a representative of feminine judgment and taste.

"In taking up the imaginary history of Redruth and the fair being to whom he gave his heart, I must, in the beginning, raise my voice against the unworthy insinuation that the selfishness or perfidy or love of luxury of any woman drove him to renounce the world. I have not found woman to be so unspiritual or venal. We must seek elsewhere, among man's baser nature and lower motives for the cause.

"There was, in all probability, a lover's quarrel as they stood at the gate on that memorable day. Tormented by jealousy, young Redruth vanished from his native haunts. But had he just cause to do so? There is no evidence for or against. But there is something higher than evidence; there is the grand, eternal belief in woman's goodness, in her steadfastness against temptation, in her loyalty even in the face of proffered riches.

"I picture to myself the rash lover, wandering, self-tortured, about the world. I picture his gradual descent, and, finally, his complete despair when he realises that he has lost the most precious gift life had to offer him. Then his withdrawal from the world of sorrow and the subsequent derangement of his faculties becomes intelligible.

"But what do I see on the other hand? A lonely woman fading away as the years roll by; still faithful, still waiting, still watching for a form and listening for a step that will come no more. She is old now. Her hair is white and smoothly banded. Each day she sits at the door and gazes longingly down the dusty road. In spirit she is waiting there at the gate, just as he left her—his forever, but not here below. Yes; my belief in woman paints that picture in my mind. Parted forever on earth, but waiting! She in anticipation of a meeting in Elysium; he in the Slough of Despond."

O. HENRY

"I thought he was in the bughouse," said the passenger who was nobody in particular.

Judge Menefee stirred, a little impatiently. The men sat, drooping, in grotesque attitudes. The wind had abated its violence; coming now in fitful, virulent puffs. The fire had burned to a mass of red coals which shed but a dim light within the room. The lady passenger in her cosey nook looked to be but a formless dark bulk, crowned by a mass of coiled, sleek hair and showing but a small space of snowy forehead above her clinging boa.

Judge Menefee got stiffly to his feet.

"And now, Miss Garland," he announced, "we have concluded. It is for you to award the prize to the one of us whose argument—especially, I may say, in regard to his estimate of true womanhood—approaches nearest to your own conception."

No answer came from the lady passenger. Judge Menefee bent over solicitously. The passenger who was nobody in particular laughed low and harshly. The lady was sleeping sweetly. The Judge essayed to take her hand to awaken her. In doing so he touched a small, cold, round, irregular something in her lap.

"She has eaten the apple," announced Judge Menefee, in awed tones, as he held up the core for them to see.

XIII

The Missing Chord

I stopped overnight at the sheep-ranch of Rush Kinney, on the Sandy Fork of the Nueces. Mr. Kinney and I had been strangers up to the time when I called "Hallo!" at his hitching-rack; but from that moment until my departure on the next morning we were, according to the Texas code, undeniable friends.

After supper the ranchman and I lugged our chairs outside the two-room house, to its floorless gallery roofed with chaparral and sacuista grass. With the rear legs of our chairs sinking deep into the hardpacked loam, each of us reposed against an elm pillar of the structure and smoked El Toro tobacco, while we wrangled amicably concerning the affairs of the rest of the world.

As for conveying adequate conception of the engaging charm of that prairie evening, despair waits upon it. It is a bold chronicler who will undertake the description of a Texas night in the early spring. An inventory must suffice.

The ranch rested upon the summit of a lenient slope. The ambient prairie, diversified by arroyos and murky patches of brush and pear, lay around us like a darkened bowl at the bottom of which we reposed as dregs. Like a turquoise cover the sky pinned us there. The miraculous air, heady with ozone and made memorably sweet by leagues of wild flowerets, gave tang and savour to the breath. In the sky was a great, round, mellow searchlight which we knew to be no moon, but the dark lantern of summer, who came to hunt northward the cowering spring. In the nearest corral a flock of sheep lay silent until a groundless panic would send a squad of them huddling together with a drumming rush. For other sounds a shrill family of coyotes yapped beyond the shearing-pen, and whippoorwills twittered in the long grass. But even these dissonances hardly rippled the clear torrent of the mocking-birds' notes that fell from a dozen neighbouring shrubs and trees. It would not have been preposterous for one to tiptoe and essay to touch the stars, they hung so bright and imminent.

Mr. Kinney's wife, a young and capable woman, we had left in the house. She remained to busy herself with the domestic round of duties, in which I had observed that she seemed to take a buoyant and contented pride. In one room we had supped. Presently, from the other, as Kinney and I sat without, there burst a volume of sudden and brilliant music. If I could justly estimate the art of piano-playing, the construer of that rollicking fantasia had creditably mastered the secrets of the keyboard. A piano, and one so well played, seemed to me to be an unusual thing to find in that small and unpromising ranch-house. I must have looked my surprise at Rush Kinney, for he laughed in his soft, Southern way, and nodded at me through the moonlit haze of our cigarettes.

"You don't often hear as agreeable a noise as that on a sheep-ranch," he remarked; "but I never see any reason for not playing up to the arts and graces just because we happen to live out in the brush. It's a lonesome life for a woman; and if a little music can make it any better, why not have it? That's the way I look at it."

"A wise and generous theory," I assented. "And Mrs. Kinney plays well. I am not learned in the science of music, but I should call her an uncommonly good performer. She has technic and more than ordinary power."

The moon was very bright, you will understand, and I saw upon Kinney's face a sort of amused and pregnant expression, as though there were things behind it that might be expounded.

"You came up the trail from the Double-Elm Fork," he said promisingly. "As you crossed it you must have seen an old deserted *jacal* to your left under a comma mott."

"I did," said I. "There was a drove of *javalis* rooting around it. I could see by the broken corrals that no one lived there."

"That's where this music proposition started," said Kinney. "I don't mind telling you about it while we smoke. That's where old Cal Adams lived. He had about eight hundred graded merinos and a daughter that was solid silk and as handsome as a new stake-rope on a thirty-dollar pony. And I don't mind telling you that I was guilty in the second degree of hanging around old Cal's ranch all the time I could spare away from lambing and shearing. Miss Marilla was her name; and I had figured it out by the rule of two that she was destined to become the chatelaine and lady superior of Rancho Lomito, belonging to R. Kinney, Esq., where you are now a welcome and honoured guest.

"I will say that old Cal wasn't distinguished as a sheepman. He was a little, old stoop-shouldered *hombre* about as big as a gun scabbard, with scraggy white whiskers, and condemned to the continuous use of language. Old Cal was so obscure in his chosen profession that he wasn't even hated by the cowmen. And when a sheepman don't get eminent enough to acquire the hostility of the cattlemen, he is mighty apt to die unwept and considerably unsung.

"But that Marilla girl was a benefit to the eye. And she was the most elegant kind of a housekeeper. I was the nearest neighbour, and I used to ride over to the Double-Elm anywhere from nine to sixteen times a week with fresh butter or a quarter of venison or a sample of new sheep-dip just as a frivolous excuse to see Marilla. Marilla and me got to be extensively inveigled with each other, and I was pretty sure I was going to get my rope around her neck and lead her over to the Lomito. Only she was so everlastingly permeated with filial sentiments toward old Cal that I never could get her to talk about serious matters.

"You never saw anybody in your life that was as full of knowledge and had less sense than old Cal. He was advised about all the branches of information contained in learning, and he was up to all the rudiments of doctrines and enlightenment. You couldn't advance him any ideas on any of the parts of speech or lines of thought. You would have thought he was a professor of the weather and politics and chemistry and natural history and the origin of derivations. Any subject you brought up old Cal could give you an abundant synopsis of it from the Greek root up to the time it was sacked and on the market.

"One day just after the fall shearing I rides over to the Double-Elm with a lady's magazine about fashions for Marilla and a scientific paper for old Cal.

"While I was tying my pony to a mesquite, out runs Marilla, 'tickled to death' with some news that couldn't wait.

"'Oh, Rush,' she says, all flushed up with esteem and gratification, 'what do you think! Dad's going to buy me a piano. Ain't it grand? I never dreamed I'd ever have one.'

"'It's sure joyful,' says I. 'I always admired the agreeable uproar of a piano. It'll be lots of company for you. That's mighty good of Uncle Cal to do that.'

"'I'm all undecided,' says Marilla, 'between a piano and an organ. A parlour organ is nice.'

"'Either of 'em,' says I, 'is first-class for mitigating the lack of noise around a sheep-ranch. For my part,' I says, 'I shouldn't like anything better than to ride home of an evening and listen to a few waltzes and jigs, with somebody about your size sitting on the piano-stool and rounding up the notes.'

"'Oh, hush about that,' says Marilla, 'and go on in the house. Dad hasn't rode out to-day. He's not feeling well.'

"Old Cal was inside, lying on a cot. He had a pretty bad cold and cough. I stayed to supper.

"'Going to get Marilla a piano, I hear,' says I to him.

"'Why, yes, something of the kind, Rush,' says he. 'She's been hankering for music for a long spell; and I allow to fix her up with something in that line right away. The sheep sheared six pounds all round this fall; and I'm going to get Marilla an instrument if it takes the price of the whole clip to do it.'

"'*Star wayno*,' says I. 'The little girl deserves it.'

"'I'm going to San Antone on the last load of wool,' says Uncle Cal, 'and select an instrument for her myself.'

"'Wouldn't it be better,' I suggests, 'to take Marilla along and let her pick out one that she likes?'

"I might have known that would set Uncle Cal going. Of course, a man like him, that knew everything about everything, would look at that as a reflection on his attainments.

"'No, sir, it wouldn't,' says he, pulling at his white whiskers. 'There ain't a better judge of musical instruments in the whole world than what I am. I had an uncle,' says he, 'that was a partner in a piano-factory, and I've seen thousands of 'em put together. I know all about musical instruments from a pipe-organ to a corn-stalk fiddle. There ain't a man lives, sir, that can tell me any news about any instrument that has to be pounded, blowed, scraped, grinded, picked, or wound with a key.'

"'You get me what you like, dad,' says Marilla, who couldn't keep her feet on the floor from joy. 'Of course you know what to select. I'd just as lief it was a piano or a organ or what.'

"'I see in St. Louis once what they call a orchestrion,' says Uncle Cal, 'that I judged was about the finest thing in the way of music ever invented. But there ain't room in this house for one. Anyway, I imagine they'd cost a thousand dollars. I reckon something in the piano line would suit Marilla the best. She took lessons in that respect for two years over at Birdstail. I wouldn't trust the buying of an instrument to anybody else but myself. I reckon if I hadn't took up sheep-raising I'd have been one of the finest composers or piano-and-organ manufacturers in the world.'

"That was Uncle Cal's style. But I never lost any patience with him, on account of his thinking so much of Marilla. And she thought just as much of him. He sent her to the academy over at Birdstail for two years when it took nearly every pound of wool to pay the expenses.

"Along about Tuesday Uncle Cal put out for San Antone on the last wagonload of wool. Marilla's uncle Ben, who lived in Birdstail, come over and stayed at the ranch while Uncle Cal was gone.

"It was ninety miles to San Antone, and forty to the nearest railroad-station, so Uncle Cal was gone about four days. I was over at the Double-Elm when he came rolling back one evening about sundown. And up there in the wagon, sure enough, was a piano or a organ—we couldn't tell which—all wrapped up in woolsacks, with a wagon-sheet tied over it in case of rain. And out skips Marilla, hollering, 'Oh, oh!' with her eyes shining and her hair a-flying. 'Dad—dad,' she sings out, 'have you brought it—have you brought it?'—and it right there before her eyes, as women will do.

"'Finest piano in San Antone,' says Uncle Cal, waving his hand, proud. 'Genuine rosewood, and the finest, loudest tone you ever listened to. I heard the storekeeper play it, and I took it on the spot and paid cash down.'

"Me and Ben and Uncle Cal and a Mexican lifted it out of the wagon and carried it in the house and set it in a corner. It was one of them upright instruments, and not very heavy or very big.

"And then all of a sudden Uncle Cal flops over and says he's mighty sick. He's got a high fever, and he complains of his lungs. He gets into bed, while me and Ben goes out to unhitch and put the horses in the pasture, and Marilla flies around to get Uncle Cal something hot to drink. But first she puts both arms on that piano and hugs it with a soft kind of a smile, like you see kids doing with their Christmas toys.

"When I came in from the pasture, Marilla was in the room where the piano was. I could see by the strings and woolsacks on the floor that she had had it unwrapped. But now she was tying the wagon-sheet over it again, and there was a kind of solemn, whitish look on her face.

"'Ain't wrapping up the music again, are you, Marilla?' I asks. 'What's the matter with just a couple of tunes for to see how she goes under the saddle?'

"'Not to-night, Rush,' says she. 'I don't want to play any to-night. Dad's too sick. Just think, Rush, he paid three hundred dollars for it—nearly a third of what the wool-clip brought!'

"'Well, it ain't anyways in the neighbourhood of a third of what you are worth,' I told her. 'And I don't think Uncle Cal is too sick to hear a little agitation of the piano-keys just to christen the machine.

"'Not to-night, Rush,' says Marilla, in a way that she had when she wanted to settle things.

"But it seems that Uncle Cal was plenty sick, after all. He got so bad that Ben saddled up and rode over to Birdstail for Doc Simpson. I stayed around to see if I'd be needed for anything.

"When Uncle Cal's pain let up on him a little he called Marilla and says to her: 'Did you look at your instrument, honey? And do you like it?'

"'It's lovely, dad,' says she, leaning down by his pillow; 'I never saw one so pretty. How dear and good it was of you to buy it for me!'

"'I haven't heard you play on it any yet,' says Uncle Cal; 'and I've been listening. My side don't hurt quite so bad now—won't you play a piece, Marilla?'

"But no; she puts Uncle Cal off and soothes him down like you've seen women do with a kid. It seems she's made up her mind not to touch that piano at present.

"When Doc Simpson comes over he tells us that Uncle Cal has pneumonia the worst kind; and as the old man was past sixty and nearly on the lift anyhow, the odds was against his walking on grass any more.

"On the fourth day of his sickness he calls for Marilla again and wants to talk piano. Doc Simpson was there, and so was Ben and Mrs. Ben, trying to do all they could.

"'I'd have made a wonderful success in anything connected with music,' says Uncle Cal. 'I got the finest instrument for the money in San Antone. Ain't that piano all right in every respect, Marilla?'

"'It's just perfect, dad,' says she. 'It's got the finest tone I ever heard. But don't you think you could sleep a little while now, dad?'

"'No, I don't,' says Uncle Cal. 'I want to hear that piano. I don't believe you've even tried it yet. I went all the way to San Antone and picked it out for you myself. It took a third of the fall clip to buy it; but I don't mind that if it makes my good girl happier. Won't you play a little bit for dad, Marilla?'

"Doc Simpson beckoned Marilla to one side and recommended her to do what Uncle Cal wanted, so it would get him quieted. And her uncle Ben and his wife asked her, too.

"'Why not hit out a tune or two with the soft pedal on?' I asks Marilla. 'Uncle Cal has begged you so often. It would please him a good deal to hear you touch up the piano he's bought for you. Don't you think you might?'

"But Marilla stands there with big tears rolling down from her eyes and says nothing. And then she runs over and slips her arm under Uncle Cal's neck and hugs him tight.

"'Why, last night, dad,' we heard her say, 'I played it ever so much. Honest—I have been playing it. And it's such a splendid instrument, you don't know how I love it. Last night I played "Bonnie Dundee" and the "Anvil Polka" and the "Blue Danube"—and lots of pieces. You must surely have heard me playing a little, didn't you, dad? I didn't like to play loud when you was so sick.'

"'Well, well,' says Uncle Cal, 'maybe I did. Maybe I did and forgot about it. My head is a little cranky at times. I heard the man in the store play it fine. I'm mighty glad you like it, Marilla. Yes, I believe I could go to sleep a while if you'll stay right beside me till I do.'

"There was where Marilla had me guessing. Much as she thought of that old man, she wouldn't strike a note on that piano that he'd bought her. I couldn't imagine why she told him she'd been playing it, for the wagon-sheet hadn't ever been off of it since she put it back on the same day it come. I knew she could play a little anyhow, for I'd once heard her snatch some pretty fair dance-music out of an old piano at the Charco Largo Ranch.

"Well, in about a week the pneumonia got the best of Uncle Cal. They had the funeral over at Birdstail, and all of us went over. I brought Marilla back home in my buckboard. Her uncle Ben and his wife were going to stay there a few days with her.

"That night Marilla takes me in the room where the piano was, while the others were out on the gallery.

"'Come here, Rush,' says she; 'I want you to see this now.'

"She unties the rope, and drags off the wagon-sheet.

"If you ever rode a saddle without a horse, or fired off a gun that wasn't loaded, or took a drink out of an empty bottle, why, then you might have been able to scare an opera or two out of the instrument Uncle Cal had bought.

"Instead of a piano, it was one of the machines they've invented to play the piano with. By itself it was about as musical as the holes of a flute without the flute.

"And that was the piano that Uncle Cal had selected; and standing by it was the good, fine, all-wool girl that never let him know it.

"And what you heard playing a while ago," concluded Mr. Kinney, "was that same deputy-piano machine; only just at present it's shoved up against a six-hundred-dollar piano that I bought for Marilla as soon as we was married."

XIV

A CALL LOAN

In those days the cattlemen were the anointed. They were the grandees of the grass, kings of the kine, lords of the lea, barons of beef and bone. They might have ridden in golden chariots had their tastes so inclined. The cattleman was caught in a stampede of dollars. It seemed to him that he had more money than was decent. But when he had bought a watch with precious stones set in the case so large that they hurt his ribs, and a California saddle with silver nails and Angora skin *suaderos*, and ordered everybody up to the bar for whisky—what else was there for him to spend money for?

Not so circumscribed in expedient for the reduction of surplus wealth were those lairds of the lariat who had womenfolk to their name. In the breast of the rib-sprung sex the genius of purse lightening may slumber through years of inopportunity, but never, my brothers, does it become extinct.

So, out of the chaparral came Long Bill Longley from the Bar Circle Branch on the Frio—a wife-driven man—to taste the urban joys of success. Something like half a million dollars he had, with an income steadily increasing.

Long Bill was a graduate of the camp and trail. Luck and thrift, a cool head, and a telescopic eye for mavericks had raised him from cowboy to be a cowman. Then came the boom in cattle, and Fortune, stepping gingerly among the cactus thorns, came and emptied her cornucopia at the doorstep of the ranch.

In the little frontier city of Chaparosa, Longley built a costly residence. Here he became a captive, bound to the chariot of social existence. He was doomed to become a leading citizen. He struggled for a time like a mustang in his first corral, and then he hung up his quirt and spurs. Time hung heavily on his hands. He organised the First National Bank of Chaparosa, and was elected its president.

One day a dyspeptic man, wearing double-magnifying glasses, inserted an official-looking card between the bars of the cashier's window of the First National Bank. Five minutes later the bank force was dancing at the beck and call of a national bank examiner.

This examiner, Mr. J. Edgar Todd, proved to be a thorough one.

At the end of it all the examiner put on his hat, and called the president, Mr. William R. Longley, into the private office.

"Well, how do you find things?" asked Longley, in his slow, deep tones. "Any brands in the round-up you didn't like the looks of?"

"The bank checks up all right, Mr. Longley," said Todd; "and I find your loans in very good shape—with one exception. You are carrying one very bad bit of paper—one that is so bad that I have been thinking that you surely do not realise the serious position it places you in. I refer to a call loan of $10,000 made to Thomas Merwin. Not only is the amount in excess of the maximum sum the bank can loan any individual legally, but it is absolutely without endorsement or security. Thus you have doubly violated the national banking laws, and have laid yourself open to criminal prosecution by the Government. A report of the matter to the Comptroller of the Currency—which I am bound to make—would, I am sure, result in the matter being turned over to the Department of Justice for action. You see what a serious thing it is."

Bill Longley was leaning his lengthy, slowly moving frame back in his swivel chair. His hands were clasped behind his head, and he turned a little to look the examiner in the face. The examiner was surprised to see a smile creep about the rugged mouth of the banker, and a kindly twinkle in his light-blue eyes. If he saw the seriousness of the affair, it did not show in his countenance.

"Of course, you don't know Tom Merwin," said Longley, almost genially. "Yes, I know about that loan. It hasn't any security except Tom Merwin's word. Somehow, I've always found that when a man's word is good it's the best security there is. Oh, yes, I know the Government doesn't think so. I guess I'll see Tom about that note."

Mr. Todd's dyspepsia seemed to grow suddenly worse. He looked at the chaparral banker through his double-magnifying glasses in amazement.

"You see," said Longley, easily explaining the thing away, "Tom heard of 2000 head of two-year-olds down near Rocky Ford on the Rio Grande that could be had for $8 a head. I reckon 'twas one of old Leandro Garcia's outfits that he had smuggled over, and he wanted to make a quick turn on 'em. Those cattle are worth $15 on the hoof in Kansas City. Tom knew it and I knew it. He had $6,000, and I let him have the $10,000 to make the deal with. His brother Ed took 'em on to market three weeks ago. He ought to be back 'most any day now with the money. When he comes Tom'll pay that note."

The bank examiner was shocked. It was, perhaps, his duty to step out to the telegraph office and wire the situation to the Comptroller. But he did not. He talked pointedly and effectively to Longley for three minutes. He succeeded in making the banker understand that he stood upon the border of a catastrophe. And then he offered a tiny loophole of escape.

"I am going to Hilldale's to-night," he told Longley, "to examine a bank there. I will pass through Chaparosa on my way back. At twelve o'clock to-morrow I shall call at this bank. If this loan has been cleared out of the way by that time it will not be mentioned in my report. If not—I will have to do my duty."

With that the examiner bowed and departed.

The President of the First National lounged in his chair half an hour longer, and then he lit a mild cigar, and went over to Tom Merwin's house. Merwin, a ranchman in brown duck, with a contemplative eye, sat with his feet upon a table, plaiting a rawhide quirt.

"Tom," said Longley, leaning against the table, "you heard anything from Ed yet?"

"Not yet," said Merwin, continuing his plaiting. "I guess Ed'll be along back now in a few days."

"There was a bank examiner," said Longley, "nosing around our place to-day, and he bucked a sight about that note of yours. You know I know it's all right, but the thing *is* against the banking laws. I was pretty sure you'd have paid it off before the bank was examined again, but the son-of-a-gun slipped in on us, Tom. Now, I'm short of cash myself just now, or I'd let you have the money to take it up with. I've got till twelve o'clock to-morrow, and then I've got to show the cash in place of that note or—"

"Or what, Bill?" asked Merwin, as Longley hesitated.

"Well, I suppose it means be jumped on with both of Uncle Sam's feet."

"I'll try to raise the money for you on time," said Merwin, interested in his plaiting.

"All right, Tom," concluded Longley, as he turned toward the door; "I knew you would if you could."

Merwin threw down his whip and went to the only other bank in town, a private one, run by Cooper & Craig.

"Cooper," he said, to the partner by that name, "I've got to have $10,000 to-day or to-morrow. I've got a house and lot there that's worth about $6,000 and that's all the actual collateral. But I've got a cattle deal on that's sure to bring me in more than that much profit within a few days."

Cooper began to cough.

"Now, for God's sake don't say no," said Merwin. "I owe that much money on a call loan. It's been called, and the man that called it is a man I've laid on the same blanket with in cow-camps and ranger-camps for ten years. He can call anything I've got. He can call the blood out of my veins and it'll come. He's got to have the money. He's in a devil of a—Well, he needs the money, and I've got to get it for him. You know my word's good, Cooper."

"No doubt of it," assented Cooper, urbanely, "but I've a partner, you know. I'm not free in making loans. And even if you had the best security in your hands, Merwin, we couldn't accommodate you in less than a week. We're just making a shipment of $15,000 to Myer Brothers in Rockdell, to buy cotton with. It goes down on the narrow-gauge to-night. That leaves our cash quite short at present. Sorry we can't arrange it for you."

Merwin went back to his little bare office and plaited at his quirt again. About four o'clock in the afternoon he went to the First National Bank and leaned over the railing of Longley's desk.

"I'll try to get that money for you to-night—I mean to-morrow, Bill."

"All right, Tom," said Longley quietly.

At nine o'clock that night Tom Merwin stepped cautiously out of the small frame house in which he lived. It was near the edge of the little town, and few citizens were in the neighbourhood at that hour. Merwin wore two six-shooters in a belt, and a slouch hat. He moved swiftly down a lonely street, and then followed the sandy road that ran parallel to the narrow-gauge track until he reached the water-tank, two miles below the town. There Tom Merwin stopped, tied a black silk handkerchief about the lower part of his face, and pulled his hat down low.

In ten minutes the night train for Rockdell pulled up at the tank, having come from Chaparosa.

With a gun in each hand Merwin raised himself from behind a clump of chaparral and started for the engine. But before he had taken three steps, two long, strong arms clasped him from behind, and he was lifted from his feet and thrown, face downward upon the grass. There was a heavy knee pressing against his back, and an iron hand grasping each of his wrists. He was held thus, like a child, until the engine had taken water, and until the train had moved, with accelerating speed, out of sight. Then he was released, and rose to his feet to face Bill Longley.

"The case never needed to be fixed up this way, Tom," said Longley. "I saw Cooper this evening, and he told me what you and him talked about. Then I went down to your house to-night and saw you come out with your guns on, and I followed you. Let's go back, Tom."

They walked away together, side by side.

"'Twas the only chance I saw," said Merwin presently. "You called your loan, and I tried to answer you. Now, what'll you do, Bill, if they sock it to you?"

"What would you have done if they'd socked it to you?" was the answer Longley made.

"I never thought I'd lay in a bush to stick up a train," remarked Merwin; "but a call loan's different. A call's a call with me. We've got twelve hours yet, Bill, before this spy jumps onto you. We've got to raise them spondulicks somehow. Maybe we can—Great Sam Houston! do you hear that?"

Merwin broke into a run, and Longley kept with him, hearing only a rather pleasing whistle somewhere in the night rendering the lugubrious air of "The Cowboy's Lament."

"It's the only tune he knows," shouted Merwin, as he ran. "I'll bet—"

They were at the door of Merwin's house. He kicked it open and fell over an old valise lying in the middle of the floor. A sunburned, firm-jawed youth, stained by travel, lay upon the bed puffing at a brown cigarette.

"What's the word, Ed?" gasped Merwin.

"So, so," drawled that capable youngster. "Just got in on the 9:30. Sold the bunch for fifteen, straight. Now, buddy, you want to quit kickin' a valise around that's got $29,000 in greenbacks in its in'ards."

O. HENRY

XV

The Princess and the Puma

There had to be a king and queen, of course. The king was a terrible old man who wore six-shooters and spurs, and shouted in such a tremendous voice that the rattlers on the prairie would run into their holes under the prickly pear. Before there was a royal family they called the man "Whispering Ben." When he came to own 50,000 acres of land and more cattle than he could count, they called him O'Donnell "the Cattle King."

The queen had been a Mexican girl from Laredo. She made a good, mild, Colorado-claro wife, and even succeeded in teaching Ben to modify his voice sufficiently while in the house to keep the dishes from being broken. When Ben got to be king she would sit on the gallery of Espinosa Ranch and weave rush mats. When wealth became so irresistible and oppressive that upholstered chairs and a centre table were brought down from San Antone in the wagons, she bowed her smooth, dark head, and shared the fate of the Danae.

To avoid *lese-majeste* you have been presented first to the king and queen. They do not enter the story, which might be called "The Chronicle of the Princess, the Happy Thought, and the Lion that Bungled his Job."

Josefa O'Donnell was the surviving daughter, the princess. From her mother she inherited warmth of nature and a dusky, semi-tropic beauty. From Ben O'Donnell the royal she acquired a store of intrepidity, common sense, and the faculty of ruling. The combination was one worth going miles to see. Josefa while riding her pony at a gallop could put five out of six bullets through a tomato-can swinging at the end of a string. She could play for hours with a white kitten she owned, dressing it in all manner of absurd clothes. Scorning a pencil, she could tell you out of her head what 1545 two-year-olds would bring on the hoof, at $8.50 per head. Roughly speaking, the Espinosa Ranch is forty miles long and thirty broad—but mostly leased land. Josefa, on her pony, had prospected over every mile of it. Every cow-puncher on the range knew her by sight and was a loyal vassal. Ripley Givens, foreman of one of the Espinosa outfits, saw her one day, and made up his mind to form a royal matrimonial alliance. Presumptuous? No. In those days in the Nueces country a man was a man. And, after all, the title of cattle king does not presuppose blood royalty. Often it only signifies that its owner wears the crown in token of his magnificent qualities in the art of cattle stealing.

One day Ripley Givens rode over to the Double Elm Ranch to inquire about a bunch of strayed yearlings. He was late in setting out on his return trip, and it was sundown when he struck the White Horse Crossing of the Nueces. From there to his own camp it was sixteen miles. To the Espinosa ranch it was twelve. Givens was tired. He decided to pass the night at the Crossing.

There was a fine water hole in the river-bed. The banks were thickly covered with great trees, undergrown with brush. Back from the water hole fifty yards was a stretch of curly mesquite grass—supper for his horse and bed for himself. Givens staked his horse, and spread out his saddle blankets to dry. He sat down with his back against a tree and rolled a cigarette. From somewhere in the dense timber along the river came a sudden, rageful, shivering wail. The pony danced at the end of his rope and blew a whistling snort of comprehending fear. Givens puffed at his cigarette, but he reached leisurely for his pistol-belt, which lay on the grass, and twirled the cylinder of his weapon tentatively. A great gar plunged with a loud splash into the water hole. A little brown rabbit skipped around a bunch of catclaw and sat twitching his whiskers and looking humorously at Givens. The pony went on eating grass.

It is well to be reasonably watchful when a Mexican lion sings soprano along the arroyos at sundown. The burden of his song may be that young calves and fat lambs are scarce, and that he has a carnivorous desire for your acquaintance.

In the grass lay an empty fruit can, cast there by some former sojourner. Givens caught sight of it with a grunt of satisfaction. In his coat pocket tied behind his saddle was a handful or two of ground coffee. Black coffee and cigarettes! What ranchero could desire more?

In two minutes he had a little fire going clearly. He started, with his can, for the water hole. When within fifteen yards of its edge he saw, between the bushes, a side-saddled pony with down-dropped reins cropping grass a little distance to his left. Just rising from her hands and knees on the brink of the water hole was Josefa O'Donnell. She had been drinking water, and she brushed the sand from the palms of her hands. Ten yards away, to her right, half concealed by a clump of sacuista, Givens saw the crouching form of the Mexican lion. His amber eyeballs glared hungrily; six feet from them was the tip of the tail stretched straight, like a pointer's. His hind-quarters rocked with the motion of the cat tribe preliminary to leaping.

Givens did what he could. His six-shooter was thirty-five yards away lying on the grass. He gave a loud yell, and dashed between the lion and the princess.

The "rucus," as Givens called it afterward, was brief and somewhat confused. When he arrived on the line of attack he saw a dim streak in the air, and heard a couple of faint cracks. Then a hundred pounds of Mexican lion plumped down upon his head and flattened him, with a heavy jar, to the ground. He remembered calling out: "Let up, now—no fair gouging!" and then he crawled from under the lion like a worm, with his mouth full of grass and dirt, and a big lump on the back of his head where it had struck the root of a water-elm. The lion lay motionless. Givens, feeling aggrieved, and suspicious of fouls, shook his fist at the lion, and shouted: "I'll rastle you again for twenty—" and then he got back to himself.

Josefa was standing in her tracks, quietly reloading her silver-mounted .38. It had not been a difficult shot. The lion's head made an easier mark than a tomato-can swinging at the end of a string. There was a provoking, teasing, maddening smile upon her mouth and in her dark eyes. The would-be-rescuing knight felt the fire of his fiasco burn down to his soul. Here had been his chance, the chance that he had dreamed of; and Momus, and not Cupid, had presided over it. The satyrs in the wood were, no doubt, holding their sides in hilarious, silent laughter. There had been something like vaudeville—say Signor Givens and his funny knockabout act with the stuffed lion.

"Is that you, Mr. Givens?" said Josefa, in her deliberate, saccharine contralto. "You nearly spoilt my shot when you yelled. Did you hurt your head when you fell?"

"Oh, no," said Givens, quietly; "that didn't hurt." He stooped ignominiously and dragged his best Stetson hat from under the beast. It was crushed and wrinkled to a fine comedy effect. Then he knelt down and softly stroked the fierce, open-jawed head of the dead lion.

"Poor old Bill!" he exclaimed mournfully.

"What's that?" asked Josefa, sharply.

"Of course you didn't know, Miss Josefa," said Givens, with an air of one allowing magnanimity to triumph over grief. "Nobody can blame you. I tried to save him, but I couldn't let you know in time."

"Save who?"

"Why, Bill. I've been looking for him all day. You see, he's been our camp pet for two years. Poor old fellow, he wouldn't have hurt a cottontail rabbit. It'll break the boys all up when they hear about it. But you couldn't tell, of course, that Bill was just trying to play with you."

Josefa's black eyes burned steadily upon him. Ripley Givens met the test successfully. He stood rumpling the yellow-brown curls on his head pensively. In his eye was regret, not unmingled with a gentle reproach. His smooth features were set to a pattern of indisputable sorrow. Josefa wavered.

"What was your pet doing here?" she asked, making a last stand. "There's no camp near the White Horse Crossing."

"The old rascal ran away from camp yesterday," answered Givens readily. "It's a wonder the coyotes didn't scare him to death. You see, Jim Webster, our horse wrangler, brought a little terrier pup into camp last week. The pup made life miserable for Bill—he used to chase him around and chew his hind legs for hours at a time. Every night when bedtime came Bill would sneak under one of the boy's blankets and sleep to keep the pup from finding him. I reckon he must have been worried pretty desperate or he wouldn't have run away. He was always afraid to get out of sight of camp."

Josefa looked at the body of the fierce animal. Givens gently patted one of the formidable paws that could have killed a yearling calf with one blow. Slowly a red flush widened upon the dark olive face of the girl. Was it the signal of shame of the true sportsman who has brought down ignoble quarry? Her eyes grew softer, and the lowered lids drove away all their bright mockery.

"I'm very sorry," she said humbly; "but he looked so big, and jumped so high that—"

"Poor old Bill was hungry," interrupted Givens, in quick defence of the deceased. "We always made him jump for his supper in camp. He would lie down and roll over for a piece of meat. When he saw you he thought he was going to get something to eat from you."

Suddenly Josefa's eyes opened wide.

"I might have shot you!" she exclaimed. "You ran right in between. You risked your life to save your pet! That was fine, Mr. Givens. I like a man who is kind to animals."

Yes; there was even admiration in her gaze now. After all, there was a hero rising out of the ruins of the anti-climax. The look on Givens's face would have secured him a high position in the S.P.C.A.

"I always loved 'em," said he; "horses, dogs, Mexican lions, cows, alligators—"

"I hate alligators," instantly demurred Josefa; "crawly, muddy things!"

"Did I say alligators?" said Givens. "I meant antelopes, of course."

Josefa's conscience drove her to make further amends. She held out her hand penitently. There was a bright, unshed drop in each of her eyes.

"Please forgive me, Mr. Givens, won't you? I'm only a girl, you know, and I was frightened at first. I'm very, very sorry I shot Bill. You don't know how ashamed I feel. I wouldn't have done it for anything."

Givens took the proffered hand. He held it for a time while he allowed the generosity of his nature to overcome his grief at the loss of Bill. At last it was clear that he had forgiven her.

"Please don't speak of it any more, Miss Josefa. 'Twas enough to frighten any young lady the way Bill looked. I'll explain it all right to the boys."

"Are you really sure you don't hate me?" Josefa came closer to him impulsively. Her eyes were sweet—oh, sweet and pleading with gracious penitence. "I would hate anyone who would kill my kitten. And how daring and kind of you to risk being shot when you tried to save him! How very few men would have done that!" Victory wrested from defeat! Vaudeville turned into drama! Bravo, Ripley Givens!

It was now twilight. Of course Miss Josefa could not be allowed to ride on to the ranch-house alone. Givens resaddled his pony in spite of that animal's reproachful glances, and rode with her. Side by side they galloped across the smooth grass, the princess and the man who was kind to animals. The prairie odours of fruitful earth and delicate bloom were thick and sweet around them. Coyotes yelping over there on the hill! No fear. And yet—

Josefa rode closer. A little hand seemed to grope. Givens found it with his own. The ponies kept an even gait. The hands lingered together, and the owner of one explained:

"I never was frightened before, but just think! How terrible it would be to meet a really wild lion! Poor Bill! I'm so glad you came with me!"

O'Donnell was sitting on the ranch gallery.

"Hello, Rip!" he shouted—"that you?"

"He rode in with me," said Josefa. "I lost my way and was late."

"Much obliged," called the cattle king. "Stop over, Rip, and ride to camp in the morning."

But Givens would not. He would push on to camp. There was a bunch of steers to start off on the trail at daybreak. He said good-night, and trotted away.

An hour later, when the lights were out, Josefa, in her night-robe, came to her door and called to the king in his own room across the brick-paved hallway:

"Say, pop, you know that old Mexican lion they call the 'Gotch-eared Devil'—the one that killed Gonzales, Mr. Martin's sheep herder, and about fifty calves on the Salado range? Well, I settled his hash this afternoon over at the White Horse Crossing. Put two balls in his head with my .38 while he was on the jump. I knew him by the slice gone from his left ear that old Gonzales cut off with his machete. You couldn't have made a better shot yourself, daddy."

"Bully for you!" thundered Whispering Ben from the darkness of the royal chamber.

XVI

THE INDIAN SUMMER
OF DRY VALLEY JOHNSON

Dry Valley Johnson shook the bottle. You have to shake the bottle before using; for sulphur will not dissolve. Then Dry Valley saturated a small sponge with the liquid and rubbed it carefully into the roots of his hair. Besides sulphur there was sugar of lead in it and tincture of nux vomica and bay rum. Dry Valley found the recipe in a Sunday newspaper. You must next be told why a strong man came to fall a victim to a Beauty Hint.

Dry Valley had been a sheepman. His real name was Hector, but he had been rechristened after his range to distinguish him from "Elm Creek" Johnson, who ran sheep further down the Frio.

Many years of living face to face with sheep on their own terms wearied Dry Valley Johnson. So, he sold his ranch for eighteen thousand dollars and moved to Santa Rosa to live a life of gentlemanly ease. Being a silent and melancholy person of thirty-five—or perhaps thirty-eight— he soon became that cursed and earth-cumbering thing—an elderlyish bachelor with a hobby. Some one gave him his first strawberry to eat, and he was done for.

Dry Valley bought a four-room cottage in the village, and a library on strawberry culture. Behind the cottage was a garden of which he made a strawberry patch. In his old grey woolen shirt, his brown duck trousers, and high-heeled boots he sprawled all day on a canvas cot under a live-oak tree at his back door studying the history of the seductive, scarlet berry.

The school teacher, Miss De Witt, spoke of him as "a fine, presentable man, for all his middle age." But, the focus of Dry Valley's eyes embraced no women. They were merely beings who flew skirts as a signal for him to lift awkwardly his heavy, round-crowned, broad-brimmed felt Stetson whenever he met them, and then hurry past to get back to his beloved berries.

And all this recitative by the chorus is only to bring us to the point where you may be told why Dry Valley shook up the insoluble sulphur in the bottle. So long-drawn and inconsequential a thing is history—the anamorphous shadow of a milestone reaching down the road between us and the setting sun.

When his strawberries were beginning to ripen Dry Valley bought the heaviest buggy whip in the Santa Rosa store. He sat for many hours under the live oak tree plaiting and weaving in an extension to its lash. When it was done he could snip a leaf from a bush twenty feet away with the cracker. For the bright, predatory eyes of Santa Rosa youth were watching the ripening berries, and Dry Valley was arming himself against their expected raids. No greater care had he taken of his tender lambs during his ranching days than he did of his cherished fruit, warding it from the hungry wolves that whistled and howled and shot their marbles and peered through the fence that surrounded his property.

In the house next to Dry Valley's lived a widow with a pack of children that gave the husbandman frequent anxious misgivings. In the woman there was a strain of the Spanish. She had wedded one of the name of O'Brien. Dry Valley was a connoisseur in cross strains; and he foresaw trouble in the offspring of this union.

Between the two homesteads ran a crazy picket fence overgrown with morning glory and wild gourd vines. Often he could see little heads with mops of black hair and flashing dark eyes dodging in and out between the pickets, keeping tabs on the reddening berries.

Late one afternoon Dry Valley went to the post office. When he came back, like Mother Hubbard he found the deuce to pay. The descendants of Iberian bandits and Hibernian cattle raiders had swooped down upon his strawberry patch. To the outraged vision of Dry Valley there seemed to be a sheep corral full of them; perhaps they numbered five or six. Between the rows of green plants they were stooped, hopping about like toads, gobbling silently and voraciously his finest fruit.

Dry Valley slipped into the house, got his whip, and charged the marauders. The lash curled about the legs of the nearest—a greedy ten-year-old—before they knew they were discovered. His screech gave warning; and the flock scampered for the fence like a drove of *javelis* flushed in the chaparral. Dry Valley's whip drew a toll of two more elfin shrieks before they dived through the vine-clad fence and disappeared.

Dry Valley, less fleet, followed them nearly to the pickets. Checking his useless pursuit, he rounded a bush, dropped his whip and stood, voiceless, motionless, the capacity of his powers consumed by the act of breathing and preserving the perpendicular.

O. HENRY

Behind the bush stood Panchita O'Brien, scorning to fly. She was nineteen, the oldest of the raiders. Her night-black hair was gathered back in a wild mass and tied with a scarlet ribbon. She stood, with reluctant feet, yet nearer the brook than to the river; for childhood had environed and detained her.

She looked at Dry Valley Johnson for a moment with magnificent insolence, and before his eyes slowly crunched a luscious berry between her white teeth. Then she turned and walked slowly to the fence with a swaying, conscious motion, such as a duchess might make use of in leading a promenade. There she turned again and grilled Dry Valley Johnson once more in the dark flame of her audacious eyes, laughed a trifle school-girlishly, and twisted herself with pantherish quickness between the pickets to the O'Brien side of the wild gourd vine.

Dry Valley picked up his whip and went into his house. He stumbled as he went up the two wooden steps. The old Mexican woman who cooked his meals and swept his house called him to supper as he went through the rooms. Dry Valley went on, stumbled down the front steps, out the gate and down the road into a mesquite thicket at the edge of town. He sat down in the grass and laboriously plucked the spines from a prickly pear, one by one. This was his attitude of thought, acquired in the days when his problems were only those of wind and wool and water.

A thing had happened to the man—a thing that, if you are eligible, you must pray may pass you by. He had become enveloped in the Indian Summer of the Soul.

Dry Valley had had no youth. Even his childhood had been one of dignity and seriousness. At six he had viewed the frivolous gambols of the lambs on his father's ranch with silent disapproval. His life as a young man had been wasted. The divine fires and impulses, the glorious exaltations and despairs, the glow and enchantment of youth had passed above his head. Never a thrill of Romeo had he known; he was but a melancholy Jaques of the forest with a ruder philosophy, lacking the bitter-sweet flavour of experience that tempered the veteran years of the rugged ranger of Arden. And now in his sere and yellow leaf one scornful look from the eyes of Panchita O'Brien had flooded the autumnal landscape with a tardy and delusive summer heat.

But a sheepman is a hardy animal. Dry Valley Johnson had weathered too many northers to turn his back on a late summer, spiritual or real. Old? He would show them.

By the next mail went an order to San Antonio for an outfit of the latest clothes, colours and styles and prices no object. The next day went the recipe for the hair restorer clipped from a newspaper; for Dry Valley's sunburned auburn hair was beginning to turn silvery above his ears.

Dry Valley kept indoors closely for a week except for frequent sallies after youthful strawberry snatchers. Then, a few days later, he suddenly emerged brilliantly radiant in the hectic glow of his belated midsummer madness.

A jay-bird-blue tennis suit covered him outwardly, almost as far as his wrists and ankles. His shirt was ox-blood; his collar winged and tall; his necktie a floating oriflamme; his shoes a venomous bright tan, pointed and shaped on penitential lasts. A little flat straw hat with a striped band desecrated his weather-beaten head. Lemon-coloured kid gloves protected his oak-tough hands from the benignant May sunshine. This sad and optic-smiting creature teetered out of its den, smiling foolishly and smoothing its gloves for men and angels to see. To such a pass had Dry Valley Johnson been brought by Cupid, who always shoots game that is out of season with an arrow from the quiver of Momus. Reconstructing mythology, he had risen, a prismatic macaw, from the ashes of the grey-brown phoenix that had folded its tired wings to roost under the trees of Santa Rosa.

Dry Valley paused in the street to allow Santa Rosans within sight of him to be stunned; and then deliberately and slowly, as his shoes required, entered Mrs. O'Brien's gate.

Not until the eleven months' drought did Santa Rosa cease talking about Dry Valley Johnson's courtship of Panchita O'Brien. It was an unclassifiable procedure; something like a combination of cake-walking, deaf-and-dumb oratory, postage stamp flirtation and parlour charades. It lasted two weeks and then came to a sudden end.

Of course Mrs. O'Brien favoured the match as soon as Dry Valley's intentions were disclosed. Being the mother of a woman child, and therefore a charter member of the Ancient Order of the Rat-trap, she joyfully decked out Panchita for the sacrifice. The girl was temporarily dazzled by having her dresses lengthened and her hair piled up on her head, and came near forgetting that she was only a slice of cheese. It was nice, too, to have as good a match as Mr. Johnson paying you attentions and to see the other girls fluttering the curtains at their windows to see you go by with him.

Dry Valley bought a buggy with yellow wheels and a fine trotter in San Antonio. Every day he drove out with Panchita. He was never seen to speak to her when they were walking or driving. The consciousness of his clothes kept his mind busy; the knowledge that he could say nothing of interest kept him dumb; the feeling that Panchita was there kept him happy.

He took her to parties and dances, and to church. He tried—oh, no man ever tried so hard to be young as Dry Valley did. He could not dance; but he invented a smile which he wore on these joyous occasions, a smile that, in him, was as great a concession to mirth and gaiety as turning hand-springs would be in another. He began to seek the company of the young men in the town—even of the boys. They accepted him as a decided damper, for his attempts at sportiveness were so forced that they might as well have essayed their games in a cathedral. Neither he nor any other could estimate what progress he had made with Panchita.

The end came suddenly in one day, as often disappears the false afterglow before a November sky and wind.

Dry Valley was to call for the girl one afternoon at six for a walk. An afternoon walk in Santa Rosa was a feature of social life that called for the pink of one's wardrobe. So Dry Valley began gorgeously to array himself; and so early that he finished early, and went over to the O'Brien cottage. As he neared the porch on the crooked walk from the gate he heard sounds of revelry within. He stopped and looked through the honeysuckle vines in the open door.

Panchita was amusing her younger brothers and sisters. She wore a man's clothes—no doubt those of the late Mr. O'Brien. On her head was the smallest brother's straw hat decorated with an ink-striped paper band. On her hands were flapping yellow cloth gloves, roughly cut out and sewn for the masquerade. The same material covered her shoes, giving them the semblance of tan leather. High collar and flowing necktie were not omitted.

Panchita was an actress. Dry Valley saw his affectedly youthful gait, his limp where the right shoe hurt him, his forced smile, his awkward simulation of a gallant air, all reproduced with startling fidelity. For the first time a mirror had been held up to him. The corroboration of one of the youngsters calling, "Mamma, come and see Pancha do like Mr. Johnson," was not needed.

As softly as the caricatured tans would permit, Dry Valley tiptoed back to the gate and home again.

Twenty minutes after the time appointed for the walk Panchita tripped demurely out of her gate in a thin, trim white lawn and sailor hat. She strolled up the sidewalk and slowed her steps at Dry Valley's gate, her manner expressing wonder at his unusual delinquency.

Then out of his door and down the walk strode—not the polychromatic victim of a lost summertime, but the sheepman, rehabilitated. He wore his old grey woolen shirt, open at the throat, his brown duck trousers stuffed into his run-over boots, and his white felt sombrero on the back of his head. Twenty years or fifty he might look; Dry Valley cared not. His light blue eyes met Panchita's dark ones with a cold flash in them. He came as far as the gate. He pointed with his long arm to her house.

"Go home," said Dry Valley. "Go home to your mother. I wonder lightnin' don't strike a fool like me. Go home and play in the sand. What business have you got cavortin' around with grown men? I reckon I was locoed to be makin' a he poll-parrot out of myself for a kid like you. Go home and don't let me see you no more. Why I done it, will somebody tell me? Go home, and let me try and forget it."

Panchita obeyed and walked slowly toward her home, saying nothing. For some distance she kept her head turned and her large eyes fixed intrepidly upon Dry Valley's. At her gate she stood for a moment looking back at him, then ran suddenly and swiftly into the house.

Old Antonia was building a fire in the kitchen stove. Dry Valley stopped at the door and laughed harshly.

"I'm a pretty looking old rhinoceros to be gettin' stuck on a kid, ain't I, 'Tonia?" said he.

"Not verree good thing," agreed Antonia, sagely, "for too much old man to likee *muchacha*."

"You bet it ain't," said Dry Valley, grimly. "It's dum foolishness; and, besides, it hurts."

He brought at one armful the regalia of his aberration—the blue tennis suit, shoes, hat, gloves and all, and threw them in a pile at Antonia's feet.

"Give them to your old man," said he, "to hunt antelope in."

Just as the first star presided palely over the twilight Dry Valley got his biggest strawberry book and sat on the back steps to catch the last of the reading light. He thought he saw the figure of someone in his strawberry patch. He laid aside the book, got his whip and hurried forth to see.

It was Panchita. She had slipped through the picket fence and was half-way across the patch. She stopped when she saw him and looked at him without wavering.

A sudden rage—a humiliating flush of unreasoning wrath—came over Dry Valley. For this child he had made himself a motley to the view. He had tried to bribe Time to turn backward for himself; he had—been made a fool of. At last he had seen his folly. There was a gulf between him and youth over which he could not build a bridge even with yellow gloves to protect his hands. And the sight of his torment coming to pester him with her elfin pranks—coming to plunder his strawberry vines like a mischievous schoolboy—roused all his anger.

"I told you to keep away from here," said Dry Valley. "Go back to your home."

Panchita moved slowly toward him.

Dry Valley cracked his whip.

"Go back home," said Dry Valley, savagely, "and play theatricals some more. You'd make a fine man. You've made a fine one of me."

She came a step nearer, silent, and with that strange, defiant, steady shine in her eyes that had always puzzled him. Now it stirred his wrath.

His whiplash whistled through the air. He saw a red streak suddenly come out through her white dress above her knee where it had struck.

Without flinching and with the same unchanging dark glow in her eyes, Panchita came steadily toward him through the strawberry vines. Dry Valley's trembling hand released his whip handle. When within a yard of him Panchita stretched out her arms.

"God, kid!" stammered Dry Valley, "do you mean—?"

But the seasons are versatile; and it may have been Springtime, after all, instead of Indian Summer, that struck Dry Valley Johnson.

XVII

CHRISTMAS BY INJUNCTION

C herokee was the civic father of Yellowhammer. Yellowhammer was a new mining town constructed mainly of canvas and undressed pine. Cherokee was a prospector. One day while his burro was eating quartz and pine burrs Cherokee turned up with his pick a nugget, weighing thirty ounces. He staked his claim and then, being a man of breadth and hospitality, sent out invitations to his friends in three States to drop in and share his luck.

Not one of the invited guests sent regrets. They rolled in from the Gila country, from Salt River, from the Pecos, from Albuquerque and Phoenix and Santa Fe, and from the camps intervening.

When a thousand citizens had arrived and taken up claims they named the town Yellowhammer, appointed a vigilance committee, and presented Cherokee with a watch-chain made of nuggets.

Three hours after the presentation ceremonies Cherokee's claim played out. He had located a pocket instead of a vein. He abandoned it and staked others one by one. Luck had kissed her hand to him. Never afterward did he turn up enough dust in Yellowhammer to pay his bar bill. But his thousand invited guests were mostly prospering, and Cherokee smiled and congratulated them.

Yellowhammer was made up of men who took off their hats to a smiling loser; so they invited Cherokee to say what he wanted.

"Me?" said Cherokee, "oh, grubstakes will be about the thing. I reckon I'll prospect along up in the Mariposas. If I strike it up there I will most certainly let you all know about the facts. I never was any hand to hold out cards on my friends."

In May Cherokee packed his burro and turned its thoughtful, mouse-coloured forehead to the north. Many citizens escorted him to the undefined limits of Yellowhammer and bestowed upon him shouts of commendation and farewells. Five pocket flasks without an air bubble between contents and cork were forced upon him; and he was bidden to consider Yellowhammer in perpetual commission for his bed, bacon and eggs, and hot water for shaving in the event that luck did not see fit to warm her hands by his campfire in the Mariposas.

The name of the father of Yellowhammer was given him by the gold hunters in accordance with their popular system of nomenclature. It was not necessary for a citizen to exhibit his baptismal certificate in order to acquire a cognomen. A man's name was his personal property. For convenience in calling him up to the bar and in designating him among other blue-shirted bipeds, a temporary appellation, title, or epithet was conferred upon him by the public. Personal peculiarities formed the source of the majority of such informal baptisms. Many were easily dubbed geographically from the regions from which they confessed to have hailed. Some announced themselves to be "Thompsons," and "Adamses," and the like, with a brazenness and loudness that cast a cloud upon their titles. A few vaingloriously and shamelessly uncovered their proper and indisputable names. This was held to be unduly arrogant, and did not win popularity. One man who said he was Chesterton L. C. Belmont, and proved it by letters, was given till sundown to leave the town. Such names as "Shorty," "Bow-legs," "Texas," "Lazy Bill," "Thirsty Rogers," "Limping Riley," "The Judge," and "California Ed" were in favour. Cherokee derived his title from the fact that he claimed to have lived for a time with that tribe in the Indian Nation.

On the twentieth day of December Baldy, the mail rider, brought Yellowhammer a piece of news.

"What do I see in Albuquerque," said Baldy, to the patrons of the bar, "but Cherokee all embellished and festooned up like the Czar of Turkey, and lavishin' money in bulk. Him and me seen the elephant and the owl, and we had specimens of this seidlitz powder wine; and Cherokee he audits all the bills, C.O.D. His pockets looked like a pool table's after a fifteen-ball run.

"Cherokee must have struck pay ore," remarked California Ed. "Well, he's white. I'm much obliged to him for his success."

"Seems like Cherokee would ramble down to Yellowhammer and see his friends," said another, slightly aggrieved. "But that's the way. Prosperity is the finest cure there is for lost forgetfulness."

"You wait," said Baldy; "I'm comin' to that. Cherokee strikes a three-foot vein up in the Mariposas that assays a trip to Europe to the ton, and he closes it out to a syndicate outfit for a hundred thousand hasty dollars in cash. Then he buys himself a baby sealskin overcoat and a red sleigh, and what do you think he takes it in his head to do next?"

"Chuck-a-luck," said Texas, whose ideas of recreation were the gamester's.

"Come and Kiss Me, Ma Honey," sang Shorty, who carried tintypes in his pocket and wore a red necktie while working on his claim.

"Bought a saloon?" suggested Thirsty Rogers.

"Cherokee took me to a room," continued Baldy, "and showed me. He's got that room full of drums and dolls and skates and bags of candy and jumping-jacks and toy lambs and whistles and such infantile truck. And what do you think he's goin' to do with them inefficacious knick-knacks? Don't surmise none—Cherokee told me. He's goin' to lead 'em up in his red sleigh and—wait a minute, don't order no drinks yet—he's goin' to drive down here to Yellowhammer and give the kids—the kids of this here town—the biggest Christmas tree and the biggest cryin' doll and Little Giant Boys' Tool Chest blowout that was ever seen west of the Cape Hatteras."

Two minutes of absolute silence ticked away in the wake of Baldy's words. It was broken by the House, who, happily conceiving the moment to be ripe for extending hospitality, sent a dozen whisky glasses spinning down the bar, with the slower travelling bottle bringing up the rear.

"Didn't you tell him?" asked the miner called Trinidad.

"Well, no," answered Baldy, pensively; "I never exactly seen my way to.

"You see, Cherokee had this Christmas mess already bought and paid for; and he was all flattered up with self-esteem over his idea; and we had in a way flew the flume with that fizzy wine I speak of; so I never let on."

"I cannot refrain from a certain amount of surprise," said the Judge, as he hung his ivory-handled cane on the bar, "that our friend Cherokee should possess such an erroneous conception of—ah—his, as it were, own town."

"Oh, it ain't the eighth wonder of the terrestrial world," said Baldy. "Cherokee's been gone from Yellowhammer over seven months. Lots of things could happen in that time. How's he to know that there ain't a single kid in this town, and so far as emigration is concerned, none expected?"

"Come to think of it," remarked California Ed, "it's funny some ain't drifted in. Town ain't settled enough yet for to bring in the rubber-ring brigade, I reckon."

"To top off this Christmas-tree splurge of Cherokee's," went on Baldy, "he's goin' to give an imitation of Santa Claus. He's got a white wig and whiskers that disfigure him up exactly like the pictures of this William Cullen Longfellow in the books, and a red suit of fur-trimmed outside underwear, and eight-ounce gloves, and a stand-up, lay-down croshayed red cap. Ain't it a shame that a outfit like that can't get a chance to connect with a Annie and Willie's prayer layout?"

"When does Cherokee allow to come over with his truck?" inquired Trinidad.

"Mornin' before Christmas," said Baldy. "And he wants you folks to have a room fixed up and a tree hauled and ready. And such ladies to assist as can stop breathin' long enough to let it be a surprise for the kids."

The unblessed condition of Yellowhammer had been truly described. The voice of childhood had never gladdened its flimsy structures; the patter of restless little feet had never consecrated the one rugged highway between the two rows of tents and rough buildings. Later they would come. But now Yellowhammer was but a mountain camp, and nowhere in it were the roguish, expectant eyes, opening wide at dawn of the enchanting day; the eager, small hands to reach for Santa's bewildering hoard; the elated, childish voicings of the season's joy, such as the coming good things of the warm-hearted Cherokee deserved.

Of women there were five in Yellowhammer. The assayer's wife, the proprietress of the Lucky Strike Hotel, and a laundress whose washtub panned out an ounce of dust a day. These were the permanent feminines; the remaining two were the Spangler Sisters, Misses Fanchon and Erma, of the Transcontinental Comedy Company, then playing in repertoire at the (improvised) Empire Theatre. But of children there were none. Sometimes Miss Fanchon enacted with spirit and address the part of robustious childhood; but between her delineation and the visions of adolescence that the fancy offered as eligible recipients of Cherokee's holiday stores there seemed to be fixed a gulf.

Christmas would come on Thursday. On Tuesday morning Trinidad, instead of going to work, sought the Judge at the Lucky Strike Hotel.

"It'll be a disgrace to Yellowhammer," said Trinidad, "if it throws Cherokee down on his Christmas tree blowout. You might say that that man made this town. For one, I'm goin' to see what can be done to give Santa Claus a square deal."

"My co-operation," said the Judge, "would be gladly forthcoming. I am indebted to Cherokee for past favours. But, I do not see—I have heretofore regarded the absence of children rather as a luxury—but in this instance—still, I do not see—"

"Look at me," said Trinidad, "and you'll see old Ways and Means with the fur on. I'm goin' to hitch up a team and rustle a load of kids for Cherokee's Santa Claus act, if I have to rob an orphan asylum."

"Eureka!" cried the Judge, enthusiastically.

"No, you didn't," said Trinidad, decidedly. "I found it myself. I learned about that Latin word at school."

"I will accompany you," declared the Judge, waving his cane. "Perhaps such eloquence and gift of language as I possess will be of benefit in persuading our young friends to lend themselves to our project."

Within an hour Yellowhammer was acquainted with the scheme of Trinidad and the Judge, and approved it. Citizens who knew of families with offspring within a forty-mile radius of Yellowhammer came forward and contributed their information. Trinidad made careful notes of all such, and then hastened to secure a vehicle and team.

The first stop scheduled was at a double log-house fifteen miles out from Yellowhammer. A man opened the door at Trinidad's hail, and then came down and leaned upon the rickety gate. The doorway was filled with a close mass of youngsters, some ragged, all full of curiosity and health.

"It's this way," explained Trinidad. "We're from Yellowhammer, and we come kidnappin' in a gentle kind of a way. One of our leading citizens is stung with the Santa Claus affliction, and he's due in town to-morrow with half the folderols that's painted red and made in Germany. The youngest kid we got in Yellowhammer packs a forty-five and a safety razor. Consequently we're mighty shy on anybody to say 'Oh' and 'Ah' when we light the candles on the Christmas tree. Now, partner, if you'll loan us a few kids we guarantee to return 'em safe and sound on Christmas Day. And they'll come back loaded down with a good time and Swiss Family Robinsons and cornucopias and red drums and similar testimonials. What do you say?"

"In other words," said the Judge, "we have discovered for the first time in our embryonic but progressive little city the inconveniences of the absence of adolescence. The season of the year having approximately arrived during which it is a custom to bestow frivolous but often appreciated gifts upon the young and tender—"

"I understand," said the parent, packing his pipe with a forefinger. "I guess I needn't detain you gentlemen. Me and the old woman have got seven kids, so to speak; and, runnin' my mind over the bunch, I don't appear to hit upon none that we could spare for you to take over to your doin's. The old woman has got some popcorn candy and rag dolls hid in the clothes chest, and we allow to give Christmas a little whirl of our own in a insignificant sort of style. No, I couldn't, with any degree of avidity, seem to fall in with the idea of lettin' none of 'em go. Thank you kindly, gentlemen."

Down the slope they drove and up another foothill to the ranch-house of Wiley Wilson. Trinidad recited his appeal and the Judge boomed out his ponderous antiphony. Mrs. Wiley gathered her two rosy-cheeked youngsters close to her skirts and did not smile until she had seen Wiley laugh and shake his head. Again a refusal.

Trinidad and the Judge vainly exhausted more than half their list before twilight set in among the hills. They spent the night at a stage road hostelry, and set out again early the next morning. The wagon had not acquired a single passenger.

"It's creepin' upon my faculties," remarked Trinidad, "that borrowin' kids at Christmas is somethin' like tryin' to steal butter from a man that's got hot pancakes a-comin'."

"It is undoubtedly an indisputable fact," said the Judge, "that the—ah—family ties seem to be more coherent and assertive at that period of the year."

On the day before Christmas they drove thirty miles, making four fruitless halts and appeals. Everywhere they found "kids" at a premium.

The sun was low when the wife of a section boss on a lonely railroad huddled her unavailable progeny behind her and said:

"There's a woman that's just took charge of the railroad eatin' house down at Granite Junction. I hear she's got a little boy. Maybe she might let him go."

Trinidad pulled up his mules at Granite Junction at five o'clock in the afternoon. The train had just departed with its load of fed and appeased passengers.

On the steps of the eating house they found a thin and glowering boy of ten smoking a cigarette. The dining-room had been left in chaos by the peripatetic appetites. A youngish woman reclined, exhausted, in a chair. Her face wore sharp lines of worry. She had once possessed a certain style of beauty that would never wholly leave her and would never wholly return. Trinidad set forth his mission.

"I'd count it a mercy if you'd take Bobby for a while," she said, wearily. "I'm on the go from morning till night, and I don't have time to 'tend to him. He's learning bad habits from the men. It'll be the only chance he'll have to get any Christmas."

The men went outside and conferred with Bobby. Trinidad pictured the glories of the Christmas tree and presents in lively colours.

"And, moreover, my young friend," added the Judge, "Santa Claus himself will personally distribute the offerings that will typify the gifts conveyed by the shepherds of Bethlehem to—"

"Aw, come off," said the boy, squinting his small eyes. "I ain't no kid. There ain't any Santa Claus. It's your folks that buys toys and sneaks 'em in when you're asleep. And they make marks in the soot in the chimney with the tongs to look like Santa's sleigh tracks."

"That might be so," argued Trinidad, "but Christmas trees ain't no fairy tale. This one's goin' to look like the ten-cent store in Albuquerque, all strung up in a redwood. There's tops and drums and Noah's arks and—"

"Oh, rats!" said Bobby, wearily. "I cut them out long ago. I'd like to have a rifle—not a target one—a real one, to shoot wildcats with; but I guess you won't have any of them on your old tree."

"Well, I can't say for sure," said Trinidad diplomatically; "it might be. You go along with us and see."

The hope thus held out, though faint, won the boy's hesitating consent to go. With this solitary beneficiary for Cherokee's holiday bounty, the canvassers spun along the homeward road.

In Yellowhammer the empty storeroom had been transformed into what might have passed as the bower of an Arizona fairy. The ladies had done their work well. A tall Christmas tree, covered to the topmost branch with candles, spangles, and toys sufficient for more than a score of children, stood in the centre of the floor. Near sunset anxious eyes had begun to scan the street for the returning team of the child-providers. At noon that day Cherokee had dashed into town with his new sleigh piled high with bundles and boxes and bales of all sizes and shapes. So intent was he upon the arrangements for his altruistic plans that the dearth of children did not receive his notice. No one gave away the humiliating state of Yellowhammer, for the efforts of Trinidad and the Judge were expected to supply the deficiency.

When the sun went down Cherokee, with many wings and arch grins on his seasoned face, went into retirement with the bundle containing the Santa Claus raiment and a pack containing special and undisclosed gifts.

"When the kids are rounded up," he instructed the volunteer arrangement committee, "light up the candles on the tree and set 'em to playin' 'Pussy Wants a Corner' and 'King William.' When they get good and at it, why—old Santa'll slide in the door. I reckon there'll be plenty of gifts to go 'round."

The ladies were flitting about the tree, giving it final touches that were never final. The Spangled Sisters were there in costume as Lady Violet de Vere and Marie, the maid, in their new drama, "The Miner's Bride." The theatre did not open until nine, and they were welcome assistants of the Christmas tree committee. Every minute heads would pop out the door to look and listen for the approach of Trinidad's team. And now this became an anxious function, for night had fallen and it would soon be necessary to light the candles on the tree, and Cherokee was apt to make an irruption at any time in his Kriss Kringle garb.

At length the wagon of the child "rustlers" rattled down the street to the door. The ladies, with little screams of excitement, flew to the lighting of the candles. The men of Yellowhammer passed in and out restlessly or stood about the room in embarrassed groups.

Trinidad and the Judge, bearing the marks of protracted travel, entered, conducting between them a single impish boy, who stared with sullen, pessimistic eyes at the gaudy tree.

"Where are the other children?" asked the assayer's wife, the acknowledged leader of all social functions.

"Ma'am," said Trinidad with a sigh, "prospectin' for kids at Christmas time is like huntin' in a limestone for silver. This parental business is one that I haven't no chance to comprehend. It seems that fathers and mothers are willin' for their offsprings to be drownded, stole, fed on poison oak, and et by catamounts 364 days in the year; but on Christmas Day they insists on enjoyin' the exclusive mortification of their company. This here young biped, ma'am, is all that washes out of our two days' manoeuvres."

"Oh, the sweet little boy!" cooed Miss Erma, trailing her De Vere robes to centre of stage.

"Aw, shut up," said Bobby, with a scowl. "Who's a kid? You ain't, you bet."

"Fresh brat!" breathed Miss Erma, beneath her enamelled smile.

"We done the best we could," said Trinidad. "It's tough on Cherokee, but it can't be helped."

Then the door opened and Cherokee entered in the conventional dress of Saint Nick. A white rippling beard and flowing hair covered his face almost to his dark and shining eyes. Over his shoulder he carried a pack.

No one stirred as he came in. Even the Spangler Sisters ceased their coquettish poses and stared curiously at the tall figure. Bobby stood with his hands in his pockets gazing gloomily at the effeminate and childish tree. Cherokee put down his pack and looked wonderingly about the room. Perhaps he fancied that a bevy of eager children were being herded somewhere, to be loosed upon his entrance. He went up to Bobby and extended his red-mittened hand.

"Merry Christmas, little boy," said Cherokee. "Anything on the tree you want they'll get it down for you. Won't you shake hands with Santa Claus?"

"There ain't any Santa Claus," whined the boy. "You've got old false billy goat's whiskers on your face. I ain't no kid. What do I want with dolls and tin horses? The driver said you'd have a rifle, and you haven't. I want to go home."

Trinidad stepped into the breach. He shook Cherokee's hand in warm greeting.

"I'm sorry, Cherokee," he explained. "There never was a kid in Yellowhammer. We tried to rustle a bunch of 'em for your swaree, but this sardine was all we could catch. He's a atheist, and he don't believe in Santa Claus. It's a shame for you to be out all this truck. But me and the Judge was sure we could round up a wagonful of candidates for your gimcracks."

"That's all right," said Cherokee gravely. "The expense don't amount to nothin' worth mentionin'. We can dump the stuff down a shaft or throw it away. I don't know what I was thinkin' about; but it never occurred to my cogitations that there wasn't any kids in Yellowhammer."

Meanwhile the company had relaxed into a hollow but praiseworthy imitation of a pleasure gathering.

Bobby had retreated to a distant chair, and was coldly regarding the scene with ennui plastered thick upon him. Cherokee, lingering with his original idea, went over and sat beside him.

"Where do you live, little boy?" he asked respectfully.

"Granite Junction," said Bobby without emphasis.

The room was warm. Cherokee took off his cap, and then removed his beard and wig.

"Say!" exclaimed Bobby, with a show of interest, "I know your mug, all right."

"Did you ever see me before?" asked Cherokee.

"I don't know; but I've seen your picture lots of times."

"Where?"

The boy hesitated. "On the bureau at home," he answered.

"Let's have your name, if you please, buddy."

"Robert Lumsden. The picture belongs to my mother. She puts it under her pillow of nights. And once I saw her kiss it. I wouldn't. But women are that way."

Cherokee rose and beckoned to Trinidad.

"Keep this boy by you till I come back," he said. "I'm goin' to shed these Christmas duds, and hitch up my sleigh. I'm goin' to take this kid home."

"Well, infidel," said Trinidad, taking Cherokee's vacant chair, "and so you are too superannuated and effete to yearn for such mockeries as candy and toys, it seems."

"I don't like you," said Bobby, with acrimony. "You said there would be a rifle. A fellow can't even smoke. I wish I was at home."

Cherokee drove his sleigh to the door, and they lifted Bobby in beside him. The team of fine horses sprang away prancingly over the hard snow. Cherokee had on his $500 overcoat of baby sealskin. The laprobe that he drew about them was as warm as velvet.

Bobby slipped a cigarette from his pocket and was trying to snap a match.

"Throw that cigarette away," said Cherokee, in a quiet but new voice.

Bobby hesitated, and then dropped the cylinder overboard.

"Throw the box, too," commanded the new voice.

More reluctantly the boy obeyed.

"Say," said Bobby, presently, "I like you. I don't know why. Nobody never made me do anything I didn't want to do before."

"Tell me, kid," said Cherokee, not using his new voice, "are you sure your mother kissed that picture that looks like me?"

"Dead sure. I seen her do it."

"Didn't you remark somethin' a while ago about wanting a rifle?"

"You bet I did. Will you get me one?"

"To-morrow—silver-mounted."

Cherokee took out his watch.

"Half-past nine. We'll hit the Junction plumb on time with Christmas Day. Are you cold? Sit closer, son."

XVIII

A Chaparral Prince

Nine o'clock at last, and the drudging toil of the day was ended. Lena climbed to her room in the third half-story of the Quarrymen's Hotel. Since daylight she had slaved, doing the work of a full-grown woman, scrubbing the floors, washing the heavy ironstone plates and cups, making the beds, and supplying the insatiate demands for wood and water in that turbulent and depressing hostelry.

The din of the day's quarrying was over—the blasting and drilling, the creaking of the great cranes, the shouts of the foremen, the backing and shifting of the flat-cars hauling the heavy blocks of limestone. Down in the hotel office three or four of the labourers were growling and swearing over a belated game of checkers. Heavy odours of stewed meat, hot grease, and cheap coffee hung like a depressing fog about the house.

Lena lit the stump of a candle and sat limply upon her wooden chair. She was eleven years old, thin and ill-nourished. Her back and limbs were sore and aching. But the ache in her heart made the biggest trouble. The last straw had been added to the burden upon her small shoulders. They had taken away Grimm. Always at night, however tired she might be, she had turned to Grimm for comfort and hope. Each time had Grimm whispered to her that the prince or the fairy would come and deliver her out of the wicked enchantment. Every night she had taken fresh courage and strength from Grimm.

To whatever tale she read she found an analogy in her own condition. The woodcutter's lost child, the unhappy goose girl, the persecuted stepdaughter, the little maiden imprisoned in the witch's hut—all these were but transparent disguises for Lena, the overworked kitchenmaid in the Quarrymen's Hotel. And always when the extremity was direst came the good fairy or the gallant prince to the rescue.

So, here in the ogre's castle, enslaved by a wicked spell, Lena had leaned upon Grimm and waited, longing for the powers of goodness to prevail. But on the day before Mrs. Maloney had found the book in her room and had carried it away, declaring sharply that it would not do for servants to read at night; they lost sleep and did not work briskly the next day. Can one only eleven years old, living away from one's mamma, and never having any time to play, live entirely deprived of Grimm? Just try it once and you will see what a difficult thing it is.

Lena's home was in Texas, away up among the little mountains on the Pedernales River, in a little town called Fredericksburg. They are all German people who live in Fredericksburg. Of evenings they sit at little tables along the sidewalk and drink beer and play pinochle and scat. They are very thrifty people.

Thriftiest among them was Peter Hildesmuller, Lena's father. And that is why Lena was sent to work in the hotel at the quarries, thirty miles away. She earned three dollars every week there, and Peter added her wages to his well-guarded store. Peter had an ambition to become as rich as his neighbour, Hugo Heffelbauer, who smoked a meerschaum pipe three feet long and had wiener schnitzel and hassenpfeffer for dinner every day in the week. And now Lena was quite old enough to work and assist in the accumulation of riches. But conjecture, if you can, what it means to be sentenced at eleven years of age from a home in the pleasant little Rhine village to hard labour in the ogre's castle, where you must fly to serve the ogres, while they devour cattle and sheep, growling fiercely as they stamp white limestone dust from their great shoes for you to sweep and scour with your weak, aching fingers. And then—to have Grimm taken away from you!

Lena raised the lid of an old empty case that had once contained canned corn and got out a sheet of paper and a piece of pencil. She was going to write a letter to her mamma. Tommy Ryan was going to post it for her at Ballinger's. Tommy was seventeen, worked in the quarries, went home to Ballinger's every night, and was now waiting in the shadows under Lena's window for her to throw the letter out to him. That was the only way she could send a letter to Fredericksburg. Mrs. Maloney did not like for her to write letters.

The stump of the candle was burning low, so Lena hastily bit the wood from around the lead of her pencil and began. This is the letter she wrote:

DEAREST MAMMA

I want so much to see you. And Gretel and Claus and Heinrich and little Adolf. I am so tired. I want to see you. To-day I was slapped by Mrs. Maloney and had no supper. I could not bring in enough wood, for my hand hurt. She took my book yesterday. I mean "Grimm's Fairy Tales," which Uncle Leo gave me. It did not hurt any one for me to read the book. I try to work as well as I can, but there is so much to do. I read only a little bit every night. Dear mamma, I shall tell you what I am going to do. Unless you send for me to-morrow to bring me home I shall go to a deep place I know in the river and drown. It is wicked to drown, I suppose, but I wanted to see you, and there is no one else. I am very tired, and Tommy is waiting for the letter. You will excuse me, mamma, if I do it.

Your respectful and loving daughter,
Lena

Tommy was still waiting faithfully when the letter was concluded, and when Lena dropped it out she saw him pick it up and start up the steep hillside. Without undressing she blew out the candle and curled herself upon the mattress on the floor.

At 10:30 o'clock old man Ballinger came out of his house in his stocking feet and leaned over the gate, smoking his pipe. He looked down the big road, white in the moonshine, and rubbed one ankle with the toe of his other foot. It was time for the Fredericksburg mail to come pattering up the road.

Old man Ballinger had waited only a few minutes when he heard the lively hoofbeats of Fritz's team of little black mules, and very soon afterward his covered spring wagon stood in front of the gate. Fritz's big spectacles flashed in the moonlight and his tremendous voice shouted a greeting to the postmaster of Ballinger's. The mail-carrier jumped out and took the bridles from the mules, for he always fed them oats at Ballinger's.

While the mules were eating from their feed bags old man Ballinger brought out the mail sack and threw it into the wagon.

Fritz Bergmann was a man of three sentiments—or to be more accurate—four, the pair of mules deserving to be reckoned individually. Those mules were the chief interest and joy of his existence. Next came the Emperor of Germany and Lena Hildesmuller.

"Tell me," said Fritz, when he was ready to start, "contains the sack a letter to Frau Hildesmuller from the little Lena at the quarries? One came in the last mail to say that she is a little sick, already. Her mamma is very anxious to hear again."

"Yes," said old man Ballinger, "thar's a letter for Mrs. Helterskelter, or some sich name. Tommy Ryan brung it over when he come. Her little gal workin' over thar, you say?"

"In the hotel," shouted Fritz, as he gathered up the lines; "eleven years old and not bigger as a frankfurter. The close-fist of a Peter Hildesmuller!—some day I shall with a big club pound that man's dummkopf—all in and out the town. Perhaps in this letter Lena will say that she is yet feeling better. So, her mamma will be glad. *Auf wiedersehen*, Herr Ballinger—your feets will take cold out in the night air."

"So long, Fritzy," said old man Ballinger. "You got a nice cool night for your drive."

Up the road went the little black mules at their steady trot, while Fritz thundered at them occasional words of endearment and cheer.

These fancies occupied the mind of the mail-carrier until he reached the big post oak forest, eight miles from Ballinger's. Here his ruminations were scattered by the sudden flash and report of pistols and a whooping as if from a whole tribe of Indians. A band of galloping centaurs closed in around the mail wagon. One of them leaned over the front wheel, covered the driver with his revolver, and ordered him to stop. Others caught at the bridles of Donder and Blitzen.

"Donnerwetter!" shouted Fritz, with all his tremendous voice—"wass ist? Release your hands from dose mules. Ve vas der United States mail!"

"Hurry up, Dutch!" drawled a melancholy voice. "Don't you know when you're in a stick-up? Reverse your mules and climb out of the cart."

It is due to the breadth of Hondo Bill's demerit and the largeness of his achievements to state that the holding up of the Fredericksburg mail was not perpetrated by way of an exploit. As the lion while in the pursuit of prey commensurate to his prowess might set a frivolous foot upon a casual rabbit in his path, so Hondo Bill and his gang had swooped sportively upon the pacific transport of Meinherr Fritz.

The real work of their sinister night ride was over. Fritz and his mail bag and his mules came as gentle relaxation, grateful after the arduous duties of their profession. Twenty miles to the southeast stood a train with a killed engine, hysterical passengers and a looted express and mail car. That represented the serious occupation of Hondo Bill and his gang. With a fairly rich prize of currency and silver the robbers were making a wide detour to the west through the less populous country, intending to seek safety in Mexico by means of some fordable spot on the Rio Grande. The booty from the train had melted the desperate bushrangers to jovial and happy skylarkers.

Trembling with outraged dignity and no little personal apprehension, Fritz climbed out to the road after replacing his suddenly removed spectacles. The band had dismounted and were singing, capering, and whooping, thus expressing their satisfied delight in the life of a jolly outlaw. Rattlesnake Rogers, who stood at the heads of the mules, jerked a little too vigorously at the rein of the tender-mouthed Donder, who reared and emitted a loud, protesting snort of pain. Instantly Fritz, with a scream of anger, flew at the bulky Rogers and began to assiduously pummel that surprised freebooter with his fists.

"Villain!" shouted Fritz, "dog, bigstiff! Dot mule he has a soreness by his mouth. I vill knock off your shoulders mit your head—robbermans!"

"Yi-yi!" howled Rattlesnake, roaring with laughter and ducking his head, "somebody git this here sour-krout off'n me!"

One of the band yanked Fritz back by the coat-tail, and the woods rang with Rattlesnake's vociferous comments.

"The dog-goned little wienerwurst," he yelled, amiably. "He's not so much of a skunk, for a Dutchman. Took up for his animile plum quick, didn't he? I like to see a man like his hoss, even if it is a mule. The dad-blamed little Limburger he went for me, didn't he! Whoa, now, muley—I ain't a-goin' to hurt your mouth agin any more."

Perhaps the mail would not have been tampered with had not Ben Moody, the lieutenant, possessed certain wisdom that seemed to promise more spoils.

"Say, Cap," he said, addressing Hondo Bill, "there's likely to be good pickings in these mail sacks. I've done some hoss tradin' with these Dutchmen around Fredericksburg, and I know the style of the varmints. There's big money goes through the mails to that town. Them Dutch risk a thousand dollars sent wrapped in a piece of paper before they'd pay the banks to handle the money."

Hondo Bill, six feet two, gentle of voice and impulsive in action, was dragging the sacks from the rear of the wagon before Moody had finished his speech. A knife shone in his hand, and they heard the ripping sound as it bit through the tough canvas. The outlaws crowded around and began tearing open letters and packages, enlivening their labours by swearing affably at the writers, who seemed to have conspired to confute the prediction of Ben Moody. Not a dollar was found in the Fredericksburg mail.

"You ought to be ashamed of yourself," said Hondo Bill to the mail-carrier in solemn tones, "to be packing around such a lot of old, trashy paper as this. What d'you mean by it, anyhow? Where do you Dutchers keep your money at?"

The Ballinger mail sack opened like a cocoon under Hondo's knife. It contained but a handful of mail. Fritz had been fuming with terror and excitement until this sack was reached. He now remembered Lena's letter. He addressed the leader of the band, asking that that particular missive be spared.

"Much obliged, Dutch," he said to the disturbed carrier. "I guess that's the letter we want. Got spondulicks in it, ain't it? Here she is. Make a light, boys."

Hondo found and tore open the letter to Mrs. Hildesmuller. The others stood about, lighting twisted up letters one from another. Hondo gazed with mute disapproval at the single sheet of paper covered with the angular German script.

"Whatever is this you've humbugged us with, Dutchy? You call this here a valuable letter? That's a mighty low-down trick to play on your friends what come along to help you distribute your mail."

"That's Chiny writin'," said Sandy Grundy, peering over Hondo's shoulder.

"You're off your kazip," declared another of the gang, an effective youth, covered with silk handkerchiefs and nickel plating. "That's shorthand. I see 'em do it once in court."

"Ach, no, no, no—dot is German," said Fritz. "It is no more as a little girl writing a letter to her mamma. One poor little girl, sick and vorking hard avay from home. Ach! it is a shame. Good Mr. Robberman, you vill please let me have dot letter?"

"What the devil do you take us for, old Pretzels?" said Hondo with sudden and surprising severity. "You ain't presumin' to insinuate that we gents ain't possessed of sufficient politeness for to take an interest in the miss's health, are you? Now, you go on, and you read that scratchin' out loud and in plain United States language to this here company of educated society."

Hondo twirled his six-shooter by its trigger guard and stood towering above the little German, who at once began to read the letter, translating the simple words into English. The gang of rovers stood in absolute silence, listening intently.

"How old is that kid?" asked Hondo when the letter was done.

"Eleven," said Fritz.

"And where is she at?"

"At dose rock quarries—working. Ach, mein Gott—little Lena, she speak of drowning. I do not know if she vill do it, but if she shall I schwear I vill dot Peter Hildesmuller shoot mit a gun."

"You Dutchers," said Hondo Bill, his voice swelling with fine contempt, "make me plenty tired. Hirin' out your kids to work when they ought to be playin' dolls in the sand. You're a hell of a sect of people. I reckon we'll fix your clock for a while just to show what we think of your old cheesy nation. Here, boys!"

Hondo Bill parleyed aside briefly with his band, and then they seized Fritz and conveyed him off the road to one side. Here they bound him fast to a tree with a couple of lariats. His team they tied to another tree near by.

"We ain't going to hurt you bad," said Hondo reassuringly. "'Twon't hurt you to be tied up for a while. We will now pass you the time of day, as it is up to us to depart. Ausgespielt—nixcumrous, Dutchy. Don't get any more impatience."

Fritz heard a great squeaking of saddles as the men mounted their horses. Then a loud yell and a great clatter of hoofs as they galloped pell-mell back along the Fredericksburg road.

For more than two hours Fritz sat against his tree, tightly but not painfully bound. Then from the reaction after his exciting adventure he sank into slumber. How long he slept he knew not, but he was at last awakened by a rough shake. Hands were untying his ropes. He was lifted to his feet, dazed, confused in mind, and weary of body. Rubbing his eyes, he looked and saw that he was again in the midst of the same band of terrible bandits. They shoved him up to the seat of his wagon and placed the lines in his hands.

"Hit it out for home, Dutch," said Hondo Bill's voice commandingly. "You've given us lots of trouble and we're pleased to see the back of your neck. Spiel! Zwei bier! Vamoose!"

Hondo reached out and gave Blitzen a smart cut with his quirt.

The little mules sprang ahead, glad to be moving again. Fritz urged them along, himself dizzy and muddled over his fearful adventure.

According to schedule time, he should have reached Fredericksburg at daylight. As it was, he drove down the long street of the town at eleven o'clock A.M. He had to pass Peter Hildesmuller's house on his way to the post-office. He stopped his team at the gate and called. But

Frau Hildesmuller was watching for him. Out rushed the whole family of Hildesmullers.

Frau Hildesmuller, fat and flushed, inquired if he had a letter from Lena, and then Fritz raised his voice and told the tale of his adventure. He told the contents of that letter that the robber had made him read, and then Frau Hildesmuller broke into wild weeping. Her little Lena drown herself! Why had they sent her from home? What could be done? Perhaps it would be too late by the time they could send for her now. Peter Hildesmuller dropped his meerschaum on the walk and it shivered into pieces.

"Woman!" he roared at his wife, "why did you let that child go away? It is your fault if she comes home to us no more."

Every one knew that it was Peter Hildesmuller's fault, so they paid no attention to his words.

A moment afterward a strange, faint voice was heard to call: "Mamma!" Frau Hildesmuller at first thought it was Lena's spirit calling, and then she rushed to the rear of Fritz's covered wagon, and, with a loud shriek of joy, caught up Lena herself, covering her pale little face with kisses and smothering her with hugs. Lena's eyes were heavy with the deep slumber of exhaustion, but she smiled and lay close to the one she had longed to see. There among the mail sacks, covered in a nest of strange blankets and comforters, she had lain asleep until wakened by the voices around her.

Fritz stared at her with eyes that bulged behind his spectacles.

"Gott in Himmel!" he shouted. "How did you get in that wagon? Am I going crazy as well as to be murdered and hanged by robbers this day?"

"You brought her to us, Fritz," cried Frau Hildesmuller. "How can we ever thank you enough?"

"Tell mamma how you came in Fritz's wagon," said Frau Hildesmuller.

"I don't know," said Lena. "But I know how I got away from the hotel. The Prince brought me."

"By the Emperor's crown!" shouted Fritz, "we are all going crazy."

"I always knew he would come," said Lena, sitting down on her bundle of bedclothes on the sidewalk. "Last night he came with his armed knights and captured the ogre's castle. They broke the dishes and kicked down the doors. They pitched Mr. Maloney into a barrel of rain water and threw flour all over Mrs. Maloney. The workmen in the hotel jumped out of the windows and ran into the woods when the knights began firing their guns. They wakened me up and I peeped down the stair. And then the Prince came up and wrapped me in the bedclothes and carried me out. He was so tall and strong and fine. His face was as rough as a scrubbing brush, and he talked soft and kind and smelled of schnapps. He took me on his horse before him and we rode away among the knights. He held me close and I went to sleep that way, and didn't wake up till I got home."

"Rubbish!" cried Fritz Bergmann. "Fairy tales! How did you come from the quarries to my wagon?"

"The Prince brought me," said Lena, confidently.

And to this day the good people of Fredericksburg haven't been able to make her give any other explanation.

XIX

The Reformation of Calliope

Calliope Catesby was in his humours again. Ennui was upon him. This goodly promontory, the earth—particularly that portion of it known as Quicksand—was to him no more than a pestilent congregation of vapours. Overtaken by the megrims, the philosopher may seek relief in soliloquy; my lady find solace in tears; the flaccid Easterner scold at the millinery bills of his women folk. Such recourse was insufficient to the denizens of Quicksand. Calliope, especially, was wont to express his ennui according to his lights.

Over night Calliope had hung out signals of approaching low spirits. He had kicked his own dog on the porch of the Occidental Hotel, and refused to apologise. He had become capricious and fault-finding in conversation. While strolling about he reached often for twigs of mesquite and chewed the leaves fiercely. That was always an ominous act. Another symptom alarming to those who were familiar with the different stages of his doldrums was his increasing politeness and a tendency to use formal phrases. A husky softness succeeded the usual penetrating drawl in his tones. A dangerous courtesy marked his manners. Later, his smile became crooked, the left side of his mouth slanting upward, and Quicksand got ready to stand from under.

At this stage Calliope generally began to drink. Finally, about midnight, he was seen going homeward, saluting those whom he met with exaggerated but inoffensive courtesy. Not yet was Calliope's melancholy at the danger point. He would seat himself at the window of the room he occupied over Silvester's tonsorial parlours and there chant lugubrious and tuneless ballads until morning, accompanying the noises by appropriate maltreatment of a jangling guitar. More magnanimous than Nero, he would thus give musical warning of the forthcoming municipal upheaval that Quicksand was scheduled to endure.

A quiet, amiable man was Calliope Catesby at other times—quiet to indolence, and amiable to worthlessness. At best he was a loafer and a nuisance; at worst he was the Terror of Quicksand. His ostensible occupation was something subordinate in the real estate line; he drove the beguiled Easterner in buckboards out to look over lots and ranch property. Originally he came from one of the Gulf States, his lank six feet, slurring rhythm of speech, and sectional idioms giving evidence of his birthplace.

And yet, after taking on Western adjustments, this languid pine-box whittler, cracker barrel hugger, shady corner lounger of the cotton fields and sumac hills of the South became famed as a bad man among men who had made a life-long study of the art of truculence.

At nine the next morning Calliope was fit. Inspired by his own barbarous melodies and the contents of his jug, he was ready primed to gather fresh laurels from the diffident brow of Quicksand. Encircled and criss-crossed with cartridge belts, abundantly garnished with revolvers, and copiously drunk, he poured forth into Quicksand's main street. Too chivalrous to surprise and capture a town by silent sortie, he paused at the nearest corner and emitted his slogan—that fearful, brassy yell, so reminiscent of the steam piano, that had gained for him the classic appellation that had superseded his own baptismal name. Following close upon his vociferation came three shots from his forty-five by way of limbering up the guns and testing his aim. A yellow dog, the personal property of Colonel Swazey, the proprietor of the Occidental, fell feet upward in the dust with one farewell yelp. A Mexican who was crossing the street from the Blue Front grocery carrying in his hand a bottle of kerosene, was stimulated to a sudden and admirable burst of speed, still grasping the neck of the shattered bottle. The new gilt weather-cock on Judge Riley's lemon and ultramarine two-story residence shivered, flapped, and hung by a splinter, the sport of the wanton breezes.

The artillery was in trim. Calliope's hand was steady. The high, calm ecstasy of habitual battle was upon him, though slightly embittered by the sadness of Alexander in that his conquests were limited to the small world of Quicksand.

Down the street went Calliope, shooting right and left. Glass fell like hail; dogs vamosed; chickens flew, squawking; feminine voices shrieked concernedly to youngsters at large. The din was perforated at intervals by the *staccato* of the Terror's guns, and was drowned periodically by the brazen screech that Quicksand knew so well. The occasions of Calliope's low spirits were legal holidays in Quicksand. All along the main street in advance of his coming clerks were putting up shutters and closing doors. Business would languish for a space. The right of way was Calliope's, and as he advanced, observing the dearth of opposition and the few opportunities for distraction, his ennui perceptibly increased.

O. HENRY

But some four squares farther down lively preparations were being made to minister to Mr. Catesby's love for interchange of compliments and repartee. On the previous night numerous messengers had hastened to advise Buck Patterson, the city marshal, of Calliope's impending eruption. The patience of that official, often strained in extending leniency toward the disturber's misdeeds, had been overtaxed. In Quicksand some indulgence was accorded the natural ebullition of human nature. Providing that the lives of the more useful citizens were not recklessly squandered, or too much property needlessly laid waste, the community sentiment was against a too strict enforcement of the law. But Calliope had raised the limit. His outbursts had been too frequent and too violent to come within the classification of a normal and sanitary relaxation of spirit.

Buck Patterson had been expecting and awaiting in his little ten-by-twelve frame office that preliminary yell announcing that Calliope was feeling blue. When the signal came the city marshal rose to his feet and buckled on his guns. Two deputy sheriffs and three citizens who had proven the edible qualities of fire also stood up, ready to bandy with Calliope's leaden jocularities.

"Gather that fellow in," said Buck Patterson, setting forth the lines of the campaign. "Don't have no talk, but shoot as soon as you can get a show. Keep behind cover and bring him down. He's a nogood 'un. It's up to Calliope to turn up his toes this time, I reckon. Go to him all spraddled out, boys. And don't git too reckless, for what Calliope shoots at he hits."

Buck Patterson, tall, muscular, and solemn-faced, with his bright "City Marshal" badge shining on the breast of his blue flannel shirt, gave his posse directions for the onslaught upon Calliope. The plan was to accomplish the downfall of the Quicksand Terror without loss to the attacking party, if possible.

The splenetic Calliope, unconscious of retributive plots, was steaming down the channel, cannonading on either side, when he suddenly became aware of breakers ahead. The city marshal and one of the deputies rose up behind some dry-goods boxes half a square to the front and opened fire. At the same time the rest of the posse, divided, shelled him from two side streets up which they were cautiously manoeuvring from a well-executed detour.

The first volley broke the lock of one of Calliope's guns, cut a neat underbit in his right ear, and exploded a cartridge in his crossbelt, scorching his ribs as it burst. Feeling braced up by this unexpected tonic to his spiritual depression, Calliope executed a fortissimo note from his upper register, and returned the fire like an echo. The upholders of the law dodged at his flash, but a trifle too late to save one of the deputies a bullet just above the elbow, and the marshal a bleeding cheek from a splinter that a ball tore from the box he had ducked behind.

And now Calliope met the enemy's tactics in kind. Choosing with a rapid eye the street from which the weakest and least accurate fire had come, he invaded it at a double-quick, abandoning the unprotected middle of the street. With rare cunning the opposing force in that direction—one of the deputies and two of the valorous volunteers—waited, concealed by beer barrels, until Calliope had passed their retreat, and then peppered him from the rear. In another moment they were reinforced by the marshal and his other men, and then Calliope felt that in order to successfully prolong the delights of the controversy he must find some means of reducing the great odds against him. His eye fell upon a structure that seemed to hold out this promise, providing he could reach it.

Not far away was the little railroad station, its building a strong box house, ten by twenty feet, resting upon a platform four feet above ground. Windows were in each of its walls. Something like a fort it might become to a man thus sorely pressed by superior numbers.

Calliope made a bold and rapid spurt for it, the marshal's crowd "smoking" him as he ran. He reached the haven in safety, the station agent leaving the building by a window, like a flying squirrel, as the garrison entered the door.

Patterson and his supporters halted under protection of a pile of lumber and held consultations. In the station was an unterrified desperado who was an excellent shot and carried an abundance of ammunition. For thirty yards on either side of the besieged was a stretch of bare, open ground. It was a sure thing that the man who attempted to enter that unprotected area would be stopped by one of Calliope's bullets.

The city marshal was resolved. He had decided that Calliope Catesby should no more wake the echoes of Quicksand with his strident whoop. He had so announced. Officially and personally he felt imperatively bound to put the soft pedal on that instrument of discord. It played bad tunes.

Standing near was a hand truck used in the manipulation of small freight. It stood by a shed full of sacked wool, a consignment from one of the sheep ranches. On this truck the marshal and his men piled three heavy sacks of wool. Stooping low, Buck Patterson started for Calliope's fort, slowly pushing this loaded truck before him for protection. The posse, scattering broadly, stood ready to nip the besieged in case he should show himself in an effort to repel the juggernaut of justice that was creeping upon him. Only once did Calliope make demonstration. He fired from a window, and some tufts of wool spurted from the marshal's trustworthy bulwark. The return shots from the posse pattered against the window frame of the fort. No loss resulted on either side.

The marshal was too deeply engrossed in steering his protected battleship to be aware of the approach of the morning train until he was within a few feet of the platform. The train was coming up on the other side of it. It stopped only one minute at Quicksand. What an opportunity it would offer to Calliope! He had only to step out the other door, mount the train, and away.

Abandoning his breastwork, Buck, with his gun ready, dashed up the steps and into the room, driving upon the closed door with one heave of his weighty shoulder. The members of the posse heard one shot fired inside, and then there was silence.

AT LENGTH THE WOUNDED MAN opened his eyes. After a blank space he again could see and hear and feel and think. Turning his eyes about, he found himself lying on a wooden bench. A tall man with a perplexed countenance, wearing a big badge with "City Marshal" engraved upon it, stood over him. A little old woman in black, with a wrinkled face and sparkling black eyes, was holding a wet handkerchief against one of his temples. He was trying to get these facts fixed in his mind and connected with past events, when the old woman began to talk.

"There now, great, big, strong man! That bullet never tetched ye! Jest skeeted along the side of your head and sort of paralysed ye for a spell. I've heerd of sech things afore; cun-cussion is what they names it. Abel Wadkins used to kill squirrels that way—barkin' 'em, Abe called it. You jest been barked, sir, and you'll be all right in a little bit. Feel lots better already, don't ye! You just lay still a while longer and let me bathe your head. You don't know me, I reckon, and 'tain't surprisin' that you shouldn't. I come in on that train from Alabama to see my son. Big son, ain't he? Lands! you wouldn't hardly think he'd ever been a baby, would ye? This is my son, sir."

Half turning, the old woman looked up at the standing man, her worn face lighting with a proud and wonderful smile. She reached out one veined and calloused hand and took one of her son's. Then smiling cheerily down at the prostrate man, she continued to dip the handkerchief, in the waiting-room tin washbasin and gently apply it to his temple. She had the benevolent garrulity of old age.

"I ain't seen my son before," she continued, "in eight years. One of my nephews, Elkanah Price, he's a conductor on one of them railroads and he got me a pass to come out here. I can stay a whole week on it, and then it'll take me back again. Jest think, now, that little boy of mine has got to be a officer—a city marshal of a whole town! That's somethin' like a constable, ain't it? I never knowed he was a officer; he didn't say nothin' about it in his letters. I reckon he thought his old mother'd be skeered about the danger he was in. But, laws! I never was much of a hand to git skeered. 'Tain't no use. I heard them guns a-shootin' while I was gettin' off them cars, and I see smoke a-comin' out of the depot, but I jest walked right along. Then I see son's face lookin' out through the window. I knowed him at oncet. He met me at the door, and squeezes me 'most to death. And there you was, sir, a-lyin' there jest like you was dead, and I 'lowed we'd see what might be done to help sot you up."

"I think I'll sit up now," said the concussion patient. "I'm feeling pretty fair by this time."

He sat, somewhat weakly yet, leaning against the wall. He was a rugged man, big-boned and straight. His eyes, steady and keen, seemed to linger upon the face of the man standing so still above him. His look wandered often from the face he studied to the marshal's badge upon the other's breast.

"Yes, yes, you'll be all right," said the old woman, patting his arm, "if you don't get to cuttin' up agin, and havin' folks shooting at you. Son told me about you, sir, while you was layin' senseless on the floor. Don't you take it as meddlesome fer an old woman with a son as big as you to talk about it. And you mustn't hold no grudge ag'in' my son for havin' to shoot at ye. A officer has got to take up for the law—it's his duty—and them that acts bad and lives wrong has to suffer. Don't blame my son any, sir—'tain't his fault. He's always been a good boy—good when he was growin' up, and kind and 'bedient and well-behaved. Won't you let me advise you, sir, not to do so no more? Be a good man, and leave liquor alone and live peaceably and goodly. Keep away from bad company and work honest and sleep sweet."

The black-mitted hand of the old pleader gently touched the breast of the man she addressed. Very earnest and candid her old, worn face looked. In her rusty black dress and antique bonnet she sat, near the close of a long life, and epitomised the experience of the world. Still the man to whom she spoke gazed above her head, contemplating the silent son of the old mother.

"What does the marshal say?" he asked. "Does he believe the advice is good? Suppose the marshal speaks up and says if the talk's all right?"

The tall man moved uneasily. He fingered the badge on his breast for a moment, and then he put an arm around the old woman and drew her close to him. She smiled the unchanging mother smile of three-score years, and patted his big brown hand with her crooked, mittened fingers while her son spake.

"I says this," he said, looking squarely into the eyes of the other man, "that if I was in your place I'd follow it. If I was a drunken, desp'rate character, without shame or hope, I'd follow it. If I was in your place and you was in mine I'd say: 'Marshal, I'm willin' to swear if you'll give me the chance I'll quit the racket. I'll drop the tanglefoot and the gun play, and won't play hoss no more. I'll be a good citizen and go to work and quit my foolishness. So help me God!' That's what I'd say to you if you was marshal and I was in your place."

"Hear my son talkin'," said the old woman softly. "Hear him, sir. You promise to be good and he won't do you no harm. Forty-one year ago his heart first beat ag'in' mine, and it's beat true ever since."

The other man rose to his feet, trying his limbs and stretching his muscles.

"Then," said he, "if you was in my place and said that, and I was marshal, I'd say: 'Go free, and do your best to keep your promise.'"

"Lawsy!" exclaimed the old woman, in a sudden flutter, "ef I didn't clear forget that trunk of mine! I see a man settin' it on the platform jest as I seen son's face in the window, and it went plum out of my head. There's eight jars of home-made quince jam in that trunk that I made myself. I wouldn't have nothin' happen to them jars for a red apple."

Away to the door she trotted, spry and anxious, and then Calliope Catesby spoke out to Buck Patterson:

"I just couldn't help it, Buck. I seen her through the window a-comin' in. She never had heard a word 'bout my tough ways. I didn't have the nerve to let her know I was a worthless cuss bein' hunted down by the community. There you was lyin' where my shot laid you, like you was dead. The idea struck me sudden, and I just took your badge off and fastened it onto myself, and I fastened my reputation onto you. I told her I was the marshal and you was a holy terror. You can take your badge back now, Buck."

With shaking fingers Calliope began to unfasten the disc of metal from his shirt.

"Easy there!" said Buck Patterson. "You keep that badge right where it is, Calliope Catesby. Don't you dare to take it off till the day your mother leaves this town. You'll be city marshal of Quicksand as long as she's here to know it. After I stir around town a bit and put 'em on I'll guarantee that nobody won't give the thing away to her. And say, you leather-headed, rip-roarin', low-down son of a locoed cyclone, you follow that advice she give me! I'm goin' to take some of it myself, too."

"Buck," said Calliope feelingly, "ef I don't I hope I may—"

"Shut up," said Buck. "She's a-comin' back."

A Note About the Author

O. Henry (1862–1910), born William Sidney Porter, was a prolific American short story writer. He was raised in North Carolina and educated by his aunt, a local schoolteacher. Despite an early inclination towards literature, Henry earned a pharmacist license, while working at his uncle's drug store. He later moved to Texas then New York, two locations that would influence his future storytelling. Henry became a contributor to *New York World Sunday Magazine* and published his first book *Cabbages and Kings* in 1904 followed by *The Four Million* (1906), which features his most famous work, "The Gift of the Magi."

A Note from the Publisher

Spanning many genres, from non-fiction essays to literature classics to children's books and lyric poetry, Mint Edition books showcase the master works of our time in a modern new package. The text is freshly typeset, is clean and easy to read, and features a new note about the author in each volume. Many books also include exclusive new introductory material. Every book boasts a striking new cover, which makes it as appropriate for collecting as it is for gift giving. Mint Edition books are only printed when a reader orders them, so natural resources are not wasted. We're proud that our books are never manufactured in excess and exist only in the exact quantity they need to be read and enjoyed.

bookfinity™

Discover more of your favorite classics with Bookfinity™.

- Track your reading with custom book lists.
- Get great book recommendations for your personalized Reader Type.
- Add reviews for your favorite books.
- AND MUCH MORE!

Visit **bookfinity.com** and take the fun Reader Type quiz to get started.

Enjoy our classic and modern companion pairings!